354
50

Guy Davenport was born in South Carolina in 1927, and was educated at Duke University, Merton College, Oxford, and at Harvard University. He is the author of several books including a collection of translations and a book of essays, entitled *The Geography of the Imagination,* which also appears in Picador. He is now Professor of English at the University of Kentucky.

Also by Guy Davenport in Picador
The Geography of the Imagination

EIGHT STORIES BY GUY DAVENPORT

ECLOGUES

The Trees at Lystra The Death of Picasso The Daimon of Sokrates Christ Preaching at the Henley Regatta Mesoroposthonippidon Lo Splendore della Luce a Bologna Idyll On Some Lines of Virgil The Trees at Lystra The Death of Picasso The Daimon of Sokrates Christ Preaching at the Henley Regatta Mesoroposthonippidon Lo Splendore della Luce a Bologna Idyll On Some Lines of Virgil The Trees at Lystra The Death of Picasso The Daimon of Sokrates Christ Preaching at the Henley Regatta Mesoro

 **PICADOR** published by Pan Books

First published in Great Britain 1984 by Pan Books Ltd,
Cavaye Place, London SW10 9PG
9 8 7 6 5 4 3 2 1
© Guy Davenport 1981
Collages © Roy R. Behrens 1981
ISBN 0 330 28417 7
Printed and bound in Great Britain by
Cox & Wyman Ltd, Reading

FOR BONNIE JEAN

ACKNOWLEDGMENTS

Four of these stories have been published before in magazines and are re-printed here with the kind permission of their editors, "The Death of Picasso" in *The Kenyon Review*, "Christ Preaching at the Henley Regatta" in *The North American Review*, "Lo Splendore della Luce a Bologna" in *Glitch*, and "Idyll" in *Sands*.

"The Daimon of Sokrates" is a kind of translation of Plutarch's *Perí toû Sokrátous Daimoníou*; the flatness of its text is meant to imitate Plutarch's starkness and narrative simplicity. I have added embellishments from the fragments that survive of his lost life of Epameinondas, his life of Pelopidas, and from other sources, when I could add a detail of manners or an object which Plutarch took for granted. "Idyll" derives from Theokritos' *Carmen V*, "The Trees at Lystra" from Acts XIV:6–20. I am indebted also to Stanley Spencer's unfinished "Christ Preaching at the Cookham Regatta," Montaigne's *Sur des Vers de Virgile* (*Essais* III:5), and Diogenes Laertius' *Lives of the Philosophers*.

The Trees at Lystra The Death of Picasso The
Daimon of Sokrates Christ Preaching at the
Henley Regatta Mesoroposthonippidon Lo Sple
ndore della Luce a Bologna Idyll On Some Lines
of Virgil **The Trees at Lystra** The Death of
Picasso The Daimon of Sokrates Christ Preach
ing at the Henley Regatta Mesoroposthonippi
don Lo Splendore della Luce a Bologna Idyll
On Some Lines of Virgil The Trees at Lystra
The Death of Picasso The Daimon of Sokrates
Christ Preaching at the Henley Regatta Mesoro
posthonippidon Lo Splendore della Luce a Bol
ogna Idyll On Some Lines of Virgil The Trees
at Lystra The Death of Picasso The Daimon of
Sokrates Christ Preaching at the Henley Rega
tta Mesoroposthonippidon Lo Splendore della

Hermes laid back his jackrabbit ears and looked around at me with his girlish eyes as much as to say that, yes, as long as my playing took us to the patch of nettles and thistles out by the Consular Road I could ride. There, with the evening cool coming on, we could all have a munch, flounce our tails, and bray at the corners of the world. He'd had his sheelings, and wanted a stretch and a hamp of weeds to chew. Those of us with a posthidion no bigger than a puppy's must do as we would.

He answered the bounce of my heels with a slew of his butt, and off we went, Hermes happy to be shut of his baskets and muzzle. A spadger on his back was of no matter. We were old friends. He knew that my hair's not good to eat, as he once imagined, and I knew how to knuckle his noggin and make him laugh.

Ahead, along our way between two fields of barley higher than our heads, larks and crickets babbling deep in the dark of the green, ran the Consular Road to Isauria. Here you could see barbarian couriers on long and lean Italian horses. With a leather wallet and a horn on a shoulder strap, a short sword, and a tumpline, they go at a gallop and pass like the wind, Roman riders with their faces shaven by a razor.

A nettle here, a stinkweed there, Hermes has his due, and I egg him on toward the road in between the juicier clumps. Half the road is neatly paved. No one may step here. It is for the Roman administrators alone. On the other half of the road come the caravans and wayfarers on foot. We are in time for the late afternoon rider. You can hear him two stadia away.

Hermes backs, I wave, the courier gives me a salute, a stiff arm straight out to the right. I pull the air, which in the language of their army means to make haste. Some smile, some give the fig, some glance and ride on with no sign. If one were to stop, I was to skidaddle, Hermes and I, as Pappas says they will make love with you and not even know your name.

My reputation in those days was for eating prodigious amounts of grape-hull barley cakes, shooting a strict toy, walking on my hands, dancing the Artemis Free Frolic, imitating a partridge so well I could bring them out of the brake, singing the Linden and the Oak, making a Gongyla face that never failed to frighten Grandmama and make her put her apron over her head, doing everything wrong, on purpose, in the opinion of Nossis my sister, worrying the pee out of my brother Philodemos, and riding Hermes when he was not at his work.

— One is as big a muggins as the other, Pappas says. By the gods, I can scarcely tell them apart. The one with all the ears and the handsome face is the donkey, I do believe. The one with the rusty knees must be our Damis, is that your opinion?

Whereupon Nossis holds her nose and the hem of her peplon in two fingers. So I make horns at her, she squeals, and Hermes brays.

We reached our favorite thistle patch just as the trees were going blue and the day's light lay level and sweet on the world. We heard the rider down the road. The Emperor of Rome, Pappas says, must hear day by day from all the cities he taxes, whatever news there is to tell him. He knows the weather, the fishing, the hunting, the crops, the breaking of his law, and where his ships are on the sea. All this the riders bring him along roads the Romans have paved from countries in the far north where there are bears and wolves and snow the year round, to deserts in the south of nothing but sand and more sand and never a tree.

But before the rider passed, Romeward bound, Hermes and I saw two men on the unpaved side of the road, merchants as they seemed, coming our way. They walked bravely, with long steps, as if they were walking across the world and meant to make a thorough job of it. I would get a good squinny at them as they trod past, though I hoped they would not ask directions, because if you're waiting for something, as I for the Roman courier, it is always when you're seeing what you came to see that a pest arrives and bodgers your pleasure of it.

In the Underworld, Pappas says, he hopes there is a judgment of Uninvited Guests all interrupting each other interrupting each other for all eternity.

A shaft of sparrows from a hedge zipped between me and the strangers, bad luck for them, as they bore down on us, and I gave them no heed until the courier passed. His saddlebags were biggish, lots of reports for the Emperor of Rome. I waved. He gave the salute. Hermes popped a rispy fart and hitched his ears forward, twirling his tail for the sheer fun of it.

— The grace of God be with you! the strangers greeted me, lifting their walking sticks.

Would this road, they asked, take them to Lystra proper, the market and the inn? It would, I said. No distance at all. They mopped their brows with their sleeves, thanked me, and off they went.

Hermes and I took the road by the old Temple of the Trees, dark in its grove, the oldest thing in the world except perhaps the dragon houses in the hills, and the sacred trees beside it are older than the temple, the linden and the oak of our rites. Somewhere, nobody knows, is the tree that's a wife to the god Hermes. I liked to think my donkey knew when he was near his namesake. That, and the quiet of the road, brought us home this way, through crickets loud as a festival and butterflies and shearmice trotting in circles and midges in swarms and early bats.

SOMETHING HAD HAPPENED. THERE'S A WAY OF WALKING THAT MEANS GOSsip's to be told, and as I rode home I saw women on the trot along every path, news to tell on their faces, elbows out, eyes searching for ears to fill.

I was not one to waste gossip on. I was only an overhearer, so that when I called to Philippos' aunt as she was clearing a stile as nimbly as a girl, all I got was an arm pointed toward town and the word *whoop-dedoo*.

Farther on I found a bunch of fieldhands leaning on their hoes. It was my two strangers they were talking about, some ruckus they'd caused as soon as they'd got to the market.

— Walking, I heard, as good as you and me.

— Born lame, he was. Never took a step ever.

— *Git up,* was all the outlander said, and by Zeus up he got. Walks some, dances some, and is out of his mind wondering over it.

The disturbance, as I pieced it together all the way home, was that the wayfarers were magicians and had healed Polydas the cripple, who was now walking round and round the market for all to see. And I was the first they spoke to. I gave them directions into town. My ears burned, my heart thumped, and Hermes complained because eating weeds had gone clean out of my head.

EVERYBODY WAS HITHER AND YONDER WHEN HERMES AND I GOT HOME. And they were there, at our place, the strangers. Grandmama had sent Papa to get them once she'd heard the wonder they'd done.

— All over again! she said to me. No mistake about the sign. I've had the feeling for days, first in my bones, and then a flutter behind my eyes, like somebody in the room when there was nobody at all. Old Thunderer and the Tree Elf! That's who they are. Who else could they be?

I could see the strangers in the arbor. They'd had their feet washed and were sipping saucers of wine with Papa and Pappas, the housefolk looking on from behind doors and posts.

Grandmama hugged me to her, said she was too scared to face the strangers, and said I was not to venture near them unless called.

She meant that the grand old story of Baukis and Philemon and the strangers at their table was happening again, now.

— It's them, she said. A sign has come to me and I know it's them.

How many times I'd heard the tale. She never told it right off, even when she was in a mind to tell the old tales. There was a whistle wetter beforehand. She told tales while she was shelling peas or stitching or plaiting a basket.

— The way you catch an owl, she'd say, is this. You go into the woods with a little drum, the kind you tap with your fingers, and a whistle with three stops, the kind the goatherds play.

I'd settle in to listen: no better tale teller than her.

— When you come to a likely thicket of tall trees where you think an owl might be, begin the nice little dance children learn for the harvest. Two hops backwards and a curtsey with crossed shins, shuffle to the left and clap your hands. You know the dance, and the tune's *The Partridge Wedding* or *Hen Cluck, Hen Strut, Peck Your Pick of Corn.*

She'd siffle the music, patting her foot, and I'd do enough of the dance to make her cackle.

— An owl, now, hearing and seeing all this, will want to join the dance, and step out lively, grave a fowl as he is, all along his limb, keeping time with his wings, and singing in owl, *hoo hoo, hoo hoo, whoodle wee hoo.* Then all you have to do is nip up and snatch him. Owl stew.

Then she'd get onto the old temple on the hill, which was to Hermes of the Trees. He mates with saplings and his blood is green. His hair is partly leaves, his knees and elbows are bark. His daimon is the woodpecker, who carries his soul around when he is asleep.

— Ah yes indeed, she'd say while spinning or resewing the quails and mulberries on the hem of my sark.

She'd take it right off my nakedness, the sark, and rummage in her basket for lavender wool, or white, or ruddle.

— This child needs his hair dressed, she would grumble. He looks like a marsh sprite. And the girls had better look out: his puppy tail looks to me like it's racing with his hair, which can do the more prominent mischief. Have those knees ever been clean?

And, with a new breath, she'd take on her important voice and begin the grand old story.

— Once the Lord of the World and his handsome son Harmiss, Ziss and Harmiss she always pronounced them and if corrected would allow that people didn't know how to say words proper any more these days. Well, Ziss and Harmiss gave themselves a shake and became, to look at, a distinguished landowner and a tall and fetching boy, but not too distinguished, you understand, a trifle somebody but not anybody special. They didn't want to stand out.

She liked me to give a nod that I was following and was eager to hear the tale again.

— They came across Kappadokia, as if on a journey, each with a staff. They were soon as dusty as all travellers, with dirty feet and sweaty around the neck. They stopped at this well and that, expecting a drink, and like as not they had the dogs set on them. Everywhere they met with impudence, with stinginess. Oh yes, people are like that, out in the world. Now round about here, nigh onto Lystra, where the marsh stands beyond the road, the people were uncommon hateful. Outlanders not welcome around here! People should stay where they belong!

— Now the poorest house in the town was that of two old folk.

— Baukis and Philemon, I'd say.

— That was their names. They had only the roof over their heads, and a watch goose, and a bean patch out back, cabbages too.

They were not stingy or tacky in their manners. When the strangers came there, old Philemon, with his beard down to here, and old Baukis, who was weaving a basket of wicker, they both said, *Do sit for a spell*.

— And, I chimed in, invited them to share their dinner.

— Exactly, Grandmama said. There was cabbage cooked with a hambone, and olives, and cherries preserved in wine, and endive and radishes, whey and white honeycomb, and eggs roasted in the shell, and figs and plums and apples. Something even told her that it would be proper to cook the watch goose, but when she went to catch it, she couldn't, and she had another sign inside her heart, as clear as sunlight on a rock. *We do not want you to kill your watch goose*. And when she was scouring the table with mint and setting out her best beech goblets coated inside with yellow wax, she began to have her suspicions.

— They were gods, I said.

— No sooner had she tipped the gotch to fill their cups than she knew she was eyebitten, rhymed by the glamor of her company. The elder had a kingly eye, like a bull, that found everything familiar, and the younger, so handsome that he took your breath and doubled your heartbeat, had the finest manners in the world and a smile as warm as a summer's day. And the wine changed as it was poured, from their black, vinegary country wine to a musky rich red wine that a goblin had magicked with a pass of his warty hands.

— And the strangers were Ziss and Harmiss. They drowned all the rest of the valley, that's why we have a marsh to this day, and gave old Baukis and Philemon their wish to be together forever, oak and linden side by side. Their little house became a temple sacred to trees and birds and hospitality.

THE MAGICIANS HAD COME TO OUR GATE AFTER PAPA HAD SENT FOR THEM. They were dressed in the colors merchants wear over near the sea, reds and purples and pinks, with too many sashes. The shorter, the one with a beard as black as a crow, was bald when he took off his big round hat. They had stopped at our herm all but hidden under honeysuckle this time of year.

— Are there hounds? The tall one had asked.

The shorter of the two said his name was Shaul Paulus, from Tarsos over in Kilikia where the school is of philosophers. The other was named Yosef Enlightenment Barnabas, a Kyprian from the sacred island of Aphrodita of the Doves.

They were Jews, people who won't eat pork or eels, and follow a book that has their laws and history in it, and cruelly cut off the sleeve of their pizzles. They were so respectful of Zeus Thunder Hurler that they say there are no other gods but him.

— Be you then Judaeans? Pappas asked after they had washed their feet and shaken the dust from their clothes.

— Yes and no, they answered.

— Freemen but not citizens?

— We are walking around the world, the one named Shaul said, with good news to tell all mankind.

He had a nubecula, a little cloud in his eye, that smudged his full jolly gaze.

— What did I tell you? Grandmama said when we listened to their talk, and the Jews explained to Papa and Pappas that the news they had to tell was that their god had taken a man's form and lived in Judaea until he was grown, and taught his lessons there, and had been understood and followed by many, but not by all. He had been wickedly and falsely accused of sedition against the Romans, was crucified, and had come alive again in his tomb, from which he came out and talked in private to several of his followers, giving them instructions. Then he went away, with a promise to return.

— To speak in figure, said the man Shaul, Yeshua the Redeemer sought to have us all die, so to say, to our life of human bondage, to be as dead men to our own selfishness, to lust, gluttony, theft, hatred, anger, jealousy, all the passions that make us blind to our brothers and sisters and to the goodness of the god who made the world.

Grandmama gave me a nudge and a look of glee.

— They are gods themselves, she whispered, pretending to be messengers.

— A change of heart, the man Barnabas put in, is what we teach. A metamorphosis. But there is no magic to it, no miracle. The resolution to die to the claims of the flesh will release the full life inside. God must have an empty pitcher to fill. We use the sign of water, though the cleansing is of the heart.

He was tall and brown, this man Barnabas, brown haired, brown eyed, his face as honest as a dog's, an easy man. When Paulus talked (we were to call him that, he said, not Shaul, which in any case we could hardly say, and without *Kyrie,* as if he were a slave) Barnabas listened more carefully than any of us, as if he wanted to remember every word.

— I am a Roman citizen, yes. But I am no man's overlord. I own no property.

— Why then, said Pappas, you're a philosopher.

— I have studied philosophy. It is all vain.

— Exactly, Pappas said.

— I am, however, one of my Redeemer's faithful, filled with hope, and, God give me grace, a striver after charity.

— Well, Papa said, that's being a philosopher, I would say.

— I was trained to be one, Paulus said, for the law and rhetoric. As with all my people, I also learned a craft, the tailoring of tents. My school of rhetoric goes back in its origins to a Greek named Diogenes, a pagan in the days of Alexander, who had a rough and sturdy virtue I can still admire. Would that I had more of his stalwartness under a shower of rocks, or his indifference to pain. Or his precision in the use of words. He invented the word *cosmopolitan* to counter Athenian pride. *A citizen of the whole world.* That's what Barnabas and I, and others of our witnessing, must learn to be.

The talk was wonderful. Paul said that the divine hand that made the sun and moon and trees and creatures was worthy of worship. Papa and Pappas agreed. They got into an argument about the souls of animals, but did not fall out over their differences.

— The good news we bring, Paulus said, is that there is but one god, not many. When he made the world, long ago, he gave man every blessing. But man in his arrogance and greed threw away the blessing and brought death into the world. But this one god loved mankind still, and became one of us, to show us how to live and how to die.

— You are worshippers of many supposed gods whom you imagine to be pleased by your mysteries and sacrifices of spilt blood and burnt flesh. You worship the created rather than the creator.

He made us sound like foreigners. How had he known about us? Did he know properly about the spirits in the trees and the mountains? About Grandmama's elves behind the oven with their mushroom hats? The daimons that are sometimes owls, sometimes a hill lion?

— But each people, Papa said, have their own gods. I have heard tell that they are indeed the same gods known by different names, tongues being different. Some gods move about everywhere, some stay in particular places. I cannot think our gods here would like the fish and fields and skies of somewhere else.

— There is but one sky, Paulus said with absolute conviction.

— Is there now? Pappas said, and was instantly confused.

— And one god, who made the one world.

Their talk went on, prying, poking, colliding. Pappas said that to us folk the Jews are wonderfully strange, so picky about everything.

— We are freed from all that, Barnabas said. There is now but one law, to love each other as we love ourselves.

— We will eat pork with you, Paulus put in. We will mix flesh and milk. We will do as you do in these matters, out of friendliness, to have that much in common with you, to be that much your brother. The philosophers of the Greeks say that all things are the same substance in many states: that air and water are the same material. It is the creating hand of God that has knit from one thread the grasshopper and the lightning, a horse and a dandelion. To know that should make us shout with joy. To make a grasshopper is one thing, to make it alive is another, to make it a world to live in is another, and to fit it into the community of all living things is yet another. Let us praise forever the maker of living things!

— We do, Pappas said. We always have.

SPOT BARKED, ROVER BARKED, TANGLEFOOT BARKED, SILVERHEELS BARKED, Old Red barked, Sylvia barked, Diana barked, and Hermes tore the air in half with a bray that shook the water in the well and gave the chickens fits.

I added my whistle to the music when I saw what had come into the yard.

A white bull wearing flowers on its horns. The archon in his festival dress. The priest. Altar boys in camlets, their hair braided wet and shiny. A priestess in her Thesmophoriazousa embroideries, with baskets of wheat and cornflowers. Drummers. Pipers. And behind them the town, some climbing our wall. Silverheels was cutting backflips. Sylvia was barking so hard her ears were flat along her neck and her tail was whipping like a willow switch. The bull was dropping flop.

The priest came halfway to our door. He planted his staff. He spread a hand on his chest.

— Come out, Lord Zeus! he shouted. Come out, Lord Hermes! Thy suppliants beg mercy at your knees. We bring a perfect male beast. We bring our adoring hearts.

The travellers Paulus and Barnabas huddled behind Papa and Pappas, wonder on their faces.

No one said a word. Grandmama held me by the shoulders. We backed away from it all together.

Paulus squared his shoulders and taking Barnabas by the elbow boldly walked outside.

— Brothers, he said. What means this pageantry?

The priest and his priestess kneeled.

— O Lord of the World! they had just enough breath to say.

Paulus put his hands to his temples. Barnabas wrung his.

— Brothers! Paulus said. My name is Gaius Julius Paulus, a citizen of Roma, and this is my brother in God, Yosef Enlightenment Barnabas. We are but men, and lowly men at that. We are preachers of the word of the rabbi Yeshua ben Yosef, the very son of God Almighty.

— Jews? the priest asked, rising from his knees.

— Jews, Paulus said, and brothers to all men.

— You are Zeus, O Lord! And him yonder is Hermes. You healed lame Polydas, who had never walked in his life.

— The living God healed him. I had but the faith that He would do it. So might you, if you will believe.

The priest had the strangest look on his face that I had ever seen, as if he were awake in a dream, nothing anywhere that he could trust to be what it seemed.

— These, Papa said to all our surprise, are my guests. I do not know who they are any more than you. Gods or not, they are within my hospitality.

— We are only men, Barnabas said, like you.

I DID NOT SEE THE ROCKS, OR THE STRANGERS RUNNING. GRANDMAMA GATHered me into her apron and took me into the house. I heard the angry words, the shouts, the pleading. I got a glimpse of Papa looking terrible.

Grandmama made me stay with her for the night, claiming she wanted the company of a man. She put together a batch of her favorite drink, grated walnuts and dill and honey in water steaming hot from the kettle. We drank it by the fire and talked about how soon the rains would be coming, and after that, the frost. We did not mention the travellers, who, I learned the next day, had run all the way to the Consular Road, the crowd behind them throwing rocks.

The Trees at Lystra The Death of Picasso The Daimon of Sokrates Christ Preaching at the Henley Regatta Mesoroposthonippidon Lo Sple ndore della Luce a Bologna Idyll On Some Lines of Virgil The Trees at Lystra The Death of Picasso The Daimon of Sokrates Christ Preach ing at the Henley Regatta Mesoroposthonippi don Lo Splendore della Luce a Bologna Idyll On Some Lines of Virgil The Trees at Lystra

The Death of Picasso The Daimon of Sokrates Christ Preaching at the Henley Regatta Mesoro posthonippidon Lo Splendore della Luce a Bol ogna Idyll On Some Lines of Virgil The Trees at Lystra The Death of Picasso The Daimon of Sokrates Christ Preaching at the Henley Rega tta Mesoroposthonippidon Lo Splendore della

Het Erewhonisch Schetsboek:
Germinal, Floréal, Prairial 1973

12 GERMINAL

Anderszins 2 april. Fog until almost noon. Wild glare in lakes over the sea. It has been but a month from putting in the eight-by-threes, treated with creosote and laid a foot and a half apart in the long northernish rectangle of our cabin's base, construction fir let into grey marl on the chine of an island, to the last sheet of shingling on the roof. An island that, as Archilochos said of his Thasos, lies in the sea like the backbone of an ass, Thasos a ridge of primrose marble in the *wijndonker Zee,* our Snegren a hump of old red sandstone in the cold North Sea. Plain as a shoebox, it is little more than a roof, chimney, and windows. The Eiland Commissaris did not bat an eyelash when I registered it under the name Snegren, *grensbewoner* being the allusion he supposed. Sander has already coined *snegrensbewoner,* Erewhonian pioneer. If I had explained that it is *nergens* reversed, he would have made a joke about so remote and *lilliputachtig* an island being precisely that, nowhere.

Parmenides is wrong: the nothing he will not allow to be is time itself. Time is the empty house that being inhabits. It may well be the ghost of something in the beginning, before light became matter. But it went away, so that something could be.

13 GERMINAL

Coffee, journal, a swim with Sander, just enough to count as a bath, the water Arctic. We built the Rietveld tensegrity table, razored labels off windowpanes, squared things away so that for the first time the long room begins to look like home, practised Corelli on our flutes, Telemann and Bach. Baroque progressions, the wind, the waves. Thoreau had a flute at Waldenpoel I think.

14 GERMINAL

Vincent's *Stilleven met uien.* It is the first painting he did after cutting off part of his ear according to the Sint Mattheus Evangelie. In a rage at Gauguin, a blusterer like Tartarin de Tarascon. They had a kind of marriage, those two, a companionship as chaste as that of the apostles Paulus and Barnabas. All their talk was of color and form, of *motif* and theme. But Gauguin would talk of the hot girls upstairs over the café and Vincent would stop his ears, and rage, and pray, and resort to Raspail's camphor treatments to ward off impurity. To talk of the Christus only generated blasphemies in Gauguin. What indulgence in the flesh did to the creative spirit was what syphilis did to the flesh itself; worse, to the mind. And Gauguin only laughed and called him a big Dutch crybaby.

The painting is a resolution, a charting of the waters after almost foundering. A drawing board in a room at Arles. It is as if we have zoomed in on a table top that had hitherto been a detail in all the scenes of Erasmus writing, of Sint Hieronymus with his books. The two things that are not on the board are a bottle of white wine and a jug of olive oil. The board is a bridge from one to the other.

The doctor's diagnosis of Vincent's hot nerves was based on learning that Vincent's diet for some weeks had been white wine and his pipe. Malnutrition! Look, *mon vieux,* anybody who subsists day after day on cheap wine and shag tobacco is going to cut off his ears. Nervous prostration: it is no wonder that you are out of your mind.

And in Raspail's *Annuaire de la santé,* there on the drawing board, the book that broke the doctors' monopoly and placed a knowledge of medicine in every humble home, it explains the nutritiousness of onions and olives, the efficacy of camphor in preventing wet dreams and lascivious thoughts.

The candle is lit: hope. Sealing wax: for letters to Theo. Matches, pipe, wine.

The letter is from Theo. It is addressed *Poste Restante* because Theo knew that Vincent had been turned out of his house. The postman, whose portrait Vincent had done, would know where he was. That is the postman's mark, the numeral 67 in a broken circle. The R in an octagon means that it is a registered letter: it contained a fifty-franc note.

There are two postage stamps on the letter, one green, one blue. The green one is a twenty-centime stamp of the kind issued between 1877 and 1900. The numeral 20 is in red. The only other French stamp with which Vincent's block of color might be identified is a straw-colored twenty-five centime one with the numeral 25 in yellow. Since the other stamp on the letter, however, is definitely the fifteen-centime of the same issue and is the only other blue stamp in use at the time, the post office in Paris would have affixed a forty-centime stamp to the letter rather than a fifteen and a twenty-five. There was no thirty-five centime denomination.

So unless the bureau had run short of the forty-centime denomination and unless petty exactitude is a new thing in French post offices, the stamps are the blue fifteen centimes, and green twenty-centime issues current at the time.

The design on both, which Vincent made no attempt to indicate, was an ornate one: numeral in an upright tablet before a globe to the left on which stood an allegorical female figure with bay in her hair and bearing an olive branch. To the right, Mercurius in winged hat and sandals, and with the caduceus.

A harmony in gold and green.

15 GERMINAL

The Vincent *Onions* is the center of a triptych I think I have discovered. Vincent's chair, with pipe, is the right-hand piece, Gauguin's empty chair, the left-hand.

Sun burned through the fog quite early, and we rowed around the island in a wide loop, Sander stark naked. I had better sense: he was splotched with strawberry stains under the remnant of last year's tan, goose bumps all over. He stuck it out, though, rowing with a will. In a blanket before a fire the rest of the morning.

16 GERMINAL

Warmer, and with an earlier lifting of fog. Even so, Sander turned out in jeans and sweater, sneezing. *Vrijdagheid als kameraadschap maar dubbelzinnig genoeg: men moet een gegeven knaap niet in het hart zien.* Caesar and Pompey look very much alike, especially Pompey. Sint Hieronymus with lion, breath like bee balm. Grocery lists, supplies. Reading Simenon: the perfect page for the fireside. Maigret is comfortable in a constant discomfort, wrapped in his coat, cosseted by food and his pipe.

In the post that old Hans had for us: Manfredo's *Progetto e Utopia,* with a note to say it will for the most play into my hands but has vulnerabilities (he means Marxist rhetoric) that I will go for with, as he says, my Dutch housekeeping mind. And Michel's *Cosmologie de Giordano Bruno.* Sander remarks that Italian looks like Latin respelled by an English tourist. Letters from Petrus and Sylvie, wondrous dull. Clerical humor, but it's worth knowing that Bergson went around calling the American pragmatist William Jones.

17 GERMINAL

Schubert's second quartet on the radio, fine against the mewing of gulls and the somber wash of the sea. A Soviet trawler in the channel.

Worked all day, off and on, at the iconographica. Neumann on Greek gesture, Marcel Jousse, Birdwhistell. Painter feels the body of the sitter as he works, two mimeses. Open hand in David, beauty of legs in Goya. Watch contours and see what else they bound other than the image we see: thus Freud found the scavenger bird. Philosophical rigor of moralists: Goya, Daumier, van Gogh. It has taken a century for drama to catch up with the painters. A line through Molière, Callot, Jarry, Ionesco. Themes refine, become subtle and articulate from age to age: children who will become artists brood in window seats on art they absorb into the deep grain of their sensibilities: Mr. Punch and Pinocchio in the lap of Klee become metaphysical puppets in a series of *caprichos* to Mozart rather than the Spanish guitar.

Sander maps the island with compass and sighting sticks, reinventing geography and surveying.

18 GERMINAL

We hear on the radio that Picasso is dead. He was ninety-two.

19 GERMINAL

Sander in *Padvinder* boondoggle and Bike *skridtbind* rings the island double time. At the outcrop on the promontory he must scuttle up and spring down. The rest of his circumference is shore, shale, pebble, sand, his pace lyric and sweet. *Ah!* he gasps at the end of it, down on elbows and knees, panting like a dog. *Ah* is an undictionaried word implying joy, rich fatigue, accomplishment, fulfillment. How many such words are missing from the lexicon: the gasp after quenched thirst, the moo at finding food good, bleats and drones of sexual delirium, clucks, smacks, whistles, mungencies, whoops, burbles.

I ask why the boondoggle, out of waggish curiosity. I get a gape and

stare and something like a bark. Patches of the young mind remain animal and inarticulate, not to be inspected by sophistication, such as a
grave study of toes, heroic stretches on waking, the choice of clothes, the
pleased mischief, lips pursed, eyebrows raised, of padding about in the
torn and laundry-battered blue shirt only, *tumescens lascive mentula
praeputio demiretracto.*

Een herinnering: Bruno at Sounion. August. Columns of the Posei-
donos Tempel sublime and Ciceronian, purest blue the sky, indigo
charged with lilac the sea, a brightness over all, light as clean as rain,
every texture, stone, cicada, thorn, shards, pebbles, exact and clear. Vile
Germans leaving as we arrived, laughing over some rudeness to a family
of kind Americans. Two ironic French adolescents, boy and girl, playing
at being amused by their own boredom. They shambled away. Another
batch arriving, we could see, at the awful restaurant down the hill, ad-
justing cameras and sunglasses for the climb. Bruno set the reading on
our camera and handed it to me. Pulled his jersey, then, over his head,
schadelijk, bent and unlaced his sneakers, peeled off his socks, stepped
out of his jeans, doffed his briefs, unbuckled his wristwatch. There are
tourists coming, I said. One, he said, arms folded and legs spread. Two: at
easy attention by a pillar. Three: sitting, elbows on knees, a frank and
engaging look into the lens. *Om godswil!* I cried. *O antiek wellustigheid!*
he sang back. Four: profile, hands against a column. *Er vlug mee zijn!*
Golden smile, glans roused and uncupped, left hand toying with pubic
clump, right fist on hip. People, Japanese and British, Toyota executives
and bottlers of marmalade, rounded the corner of the temple. Bruno into
jeans as an eel under a rock, into shirt, buttoning up cool as you please as
the first foreign eyes found him. Into socks and sneakers as they passed.
British lady stared at his briefs lying on brown stone in brilliant light,
their crop dented, convex, feral, male. Reached them over, slapped them
against his thigh, and stuffed them in his pocket. And what in the name
of God was all that? *Grieks,* he said.

20 GERMINAL

His 75 years of meditation on a still life: this is like a sonnet cycle, the
progression of Montaigne's essays, Rembrandt's and Van Gogh's self-
portraits. A natural rhythm, as all the variations of fish and leaf make a
coherent harmony. A fish is a leaf.

Wine, bread, table: his Catholic childhood. Perhaps his Catholic life. Lute, guitar, mandolin: the Spanish ear, which abides life as a terrible dream made tolerable by music.

Spain and Holland. Felipe's expulsion of farmers and bankers, whom he saw with fanatic eyes as Muslims and Jews, shifted the counting houses to Holland. Spain dreamed on in its pageant of men dressed in black and women in shawls, surrounded by agonies they kept as symbols to validate, as ritual, the cruelty they claimed as their piety: the lynching of ecstatics, heretics, and humanists, the slaughtering of bulls, the sending of navies and armies against all other cultures of the Mediterranean.

Silver to the east, pepper to the west, silver and pepper, wool and cloves, gold and wheat, cannon and Titians. And on this theme the old man ended, with a vision of sworded gallants idiotic in the cruelty of their pride, women as a separate species, available by property deeds, a blade through a gut, a trunk of coins, a point of honor precluding reason or forgiveness.

His study of Velazquez parallels the researches of Braudel; his intuition of a deeper past rivals the century's classical studies, the prehistorians, the anthropologists.

21 GERMINAL

Een herinnering: Paris 1947. A glimpse, a mere passing sight of Picasso inside the Deux Magots, before a bottle of Perrier at a table, his hair combed across his bald head in a last desperate coiffure, already grey. But there he was. Bruno has seen Max Ernst walking his poodle on the Avenue Foch.

Sander begins a notebook of our island's natural history, climbs trees to include our neighbor islands in his map, exercises like an acrobat. How smoothly he is beginning to forget I dare not guess.

22 GERMINAL

We row over for newspapers and mail, a cold and blustery voyage, and wet. Water and wind are a havoc of power. We are colonists who can make an excursion back to Europe, shopping list in hand.

A blind old Minotaur pulls his household goods along in a cart, washpot, skillet, quilts, mangle, bust of Lillie Langtry, framed lithograph of Napoleon, rotary eggbeater, bread board, Raspail's *Home Medical Practitioner,* a felt hat from Milan, a map of Corsica, a sack of roasted chicory, the key to a barn, tongs, a reading lamp mounted on a porcelain parrot, bulbs of garlic, a tobacco tin containing fishhooks, brass centimes from the Occupation, buttons, a bullet, a feather from the tail of an owl.

Sander says he discovers that shopping can be fun, and I try to penetrate his meaning. Is it that the ordinary becomes known only as the unusual? It is the convenient we are giving up, what he agreed to, with diffidence, when I offered him the stint on the island.

23 GERMINAL

O well, says Sander, *O well.* He organizes himself at various times of day by turning in circles, batting the air with his hands. An inventory of energies. He glances at the pages of this journal, briefly, as if to register that writing is a thing I do, like reading, walking. I keep thinking that he is a median between Bruno and Itard's Victor, between urban sophistication and benign savagery. He has a penchant for botany and zoology. That is, those subjects caught his fancy. Spells badly. Found all the sociological courses meaningless and history is still so much hash.

24 GERMINAL

Jean Marc Gaspard Itard, *De l'Education d'un homme sauvage, ou des premiers developpemens physiques et moraux du jeune sauvage de l'Aveyron,* Vendémiaire an X.

The pathos is one all teachers feel, all parents. Repeated now by the American psychologists training chimpanzees to sign with deaf-and-dumb hand language. Itard's Victor had had his attention fixed by his own strategies for survival in a forest. So are all attentions fixed. His skills were animal and they were successful. Eat, scutter to safety, hide from enemies, sleep, forage. He was unfamiliar with fire, with warmth, and loved in Paris to roll naked in the snow.

De Gaulle remarked, from under that nose, that we raise our own Vandals. What is the grief I feel when I admit the truth of that? I also deny it.

25 GERMINAL

The feeling again yesterday afternoon that the hour belonged to a previous, perhaps future, time, but was decidedly not *now*. I was looking out of the window, at afternoon light on bushes, in an elation of melancholy, savoring one truth and another without fear or anxiety, at peace with myself. Then this deliciously strange feeling that time is nothing, or is my friend rather than my enemy.

Time, like the sea, is layered into nekton, plankton, and benthos.

Long deep rhythms like the turning of the planets and the drift of the stars, the decay of matter, the old-turtle creep of continents around the globe. Evolution. Over which lie the adagio rhythms of history, the play of fire over burning sticks.

Picasso at the last was gazing at the immediate pressures of Renaissance Spain on the France of Georges Pompidou: moth flicker of individual sensibilities around a flame of money, cherished proprieties, romance, a dreaming life with no notion of what it is to be awake, the sleep of reason. He felt the tension between the Netherlands and Madrid, north and south, prudence and passion. Titian and Rembrandt, and yet his heart was with those foragers who suffered the violence of making sense of these extremes, Van Gogh and Rimbaud, Rousseau le Douanier.

His genius was satisfied with two forms only: still life and tableau. He stepped over the moment of Cézanne, Manet, Courbet like a giant negligently striding over a garden whose order and brilliance were none of his concern. All of his tenderness is like a Minotaur gazing at a cow. There was sweetness in the regard, submerged in a primal animality. He was like a grandee from the Spanish courts trying to behave himself among people with polished manners, books, philosophy, graciousness. He played their game, assumed French liberalism, pledged brotherhood with Marxist babblers, commanded charm enough to make friends with civilized people like Gertrude Stein and Cocteau, Apollinaire and Braque. Barcelona stood him in good stead.

26 GERMINAL

Roads, paths, and rivers in XIXth Century painting. And windows. Corridors was their theme, and corridors for the eye. Picasso sidestepped this brilliant understanding of the world, and returned to the theatrical, the Spanish room that is not properly a room but a cell, a dark place. The

Spanish have no love for or understanding of roads. They are perilous in *Quijote*, bandit-ridden in Spanish history. Suspicious stay-at-homes, the Spanish. A public place is still vulgar, one's dignity can be exposed to the affront of a stare. A morbid pride, which Goya saw as insanity.

How lovely Paris must have seemed to the young Picasso, with its guileless Max Jacob, laughing Apollinaire, rich Americans who were affable, friendly, and intelligent: Miss Stein, Miss Toklas, the sisters Cone, John Quinn, people who knew nothing of the dark anguish of the Spanish mind.

Sander making a list, with characteristics, of our birds. We cannot identify the half of them.

Hò siokómos skaphiókouros orchidionon monózonos.

Corelli sarabandes, good talk by the fire, the wind in a huffle after sunset making a humpenscrump of the waves and trees.

27 GERMINAL
De dageraad met rooskleurige vingeren. Coffee, journal in a seat on the rocks, warm enough for shorts and *visnet jersey.* Fine iodine kelpy green smell of the sea. No fog at all, a sharp sight of all the islands around us. Yachts. *The life!* crowed Sander naked.

Itard failed with Victor (assuming that Victor was not an idiot, which no evidence indicates) because he was trying to teach him manners.

He should have allowed himself to be taught by Victor, as the cat teaches us the rules of a companionship, as Griaule learned from the Dogon.

Teacher as student, an inside-out idea. Useful where applicable.

Art is bad when it is poor in news, dull, and has no rich uncle to boast of. Culture abhors a plenum and has its finest moments hunting on a lean day.

Philosophy is the husband of art: the civility they beget is not a hostage to fortune but our fortune itself.

Nature has no destiny for us: our boat is upon her ocean and in her winds, but she has expended as much ingenuity designing the flea as she has expended on us, and is perfectly indifferent to Hooke's conversation at Garroway's Coffee House. We, however, perish the instant we take our eyes off nature.

28 GERMINAL

One of the things Hooke said at Garroway's was that he suspected insects of being the husbands of flowers. Fourier was capable of believing that as fact.

Schets: Quaggas at noon under mimosa green and gold, graceful and grey like mules by Gaudier-Brzeska, with boughts of silver silk, stripeless zebras, gazelles with heft.

Does Fourier's uncluttered imagination belong to philosophy or art? I see him surviving in the verve and color of Roger de la Fresnaye, Delaunay, Lurçat. Was he a philosopher at all? Braque is the better epistemologist.

Something of a serious talk with Sander. I tell him that he can go back to Amsterdam anytime he wants, but to Dokter Tomas. The terms and happenstance of the custody, which is entirely informal and fortuitous.

I suggest that we are on a voyage, the island our ship, that we are Crusoe and Friday, two characters out of Rousseau living civilizedly as savages.

29 GERMINAL

We learn on the radio that Picasso was painting a picture when he died.

Water and land. When they found the first dinosaur track in America, a three-toed footprint in old red sandstone, the *predikant* (top hat, frock coat, buttoned leggings) said it was the *voetspoor* of Noah's raven. Grey troubled waters everywhere, and the raven's cry the only sound over their tumult.

A red cry. And next the dove, olive sprig, and ground. The rivers went back to their beds, the sky to its blue, a rainbow spanning the shining mud. Out onto which ventured goose and gander, hen and cock, quagga, mastodon, dik-dik, ostrich, tarpan, opossum, elk, baboon.

Sander notes that already we have our *schapewei* around the island, our movements preferring a path. I have not mentioned routine except to insist that beds be made, dishes and cookware washed, the lime turned and renewed in the outhouse, clothes hung up, and so on. Surprised that he likes sweeping a floor.

30 GERMINAL

Vreemheid en tovermiddel! A shore of gulls, quarreling and milling in a clutter of white. *Quark!* they squawk in Joyce, giving physicists a name for a hypothetical particle that has the hypothetical quality charm. Clustered and clinging to the nucleus of an atom, they congregate as hadrons, or if paired with an antiquark, a kaon, which is perhaps a charmed meson, or disintegration of light into matter, a process in which some quarks display strangeness, some display charm, with so ready an affinity that kaons and mesons exchange the one quality for the other as a firefly flicks off and on. It is thought that strange quarks prefer to couple with charmed quarks, electric bees quick for the rich of the nectar.

Tributes to Picasso on the radio: Malraux, Pompidou, Miró, Chagall, some functionary of the Spanish government in exile. He was not, it turns out, painting when he died. He had dined as usual, with Jacqueline and some friends, excused himself to go to his studio, painted a last canvas, presumably one of the courtcard cavaliers or duennas, and went to bed. He died in his sleep. Eighty-five years of drawing, painting, sculpting!

Sander comments that he finds chastity interesting, that word, interesting. *Moedernaakt, waarachtig, met een starende blik op zijn penis.*

I tell him, with coffee after supper on the shingle, the sea changing from its silver and rose of day's end to the flint and gleaming greys of dusk, about Ludwig Hänsel's *Die Jugend und die leibliche Liebe* that Wittgenstein found so strangely moving and Otto Weininger's *Geschlecht und Charakter.* The phrase *sexual purity of boys* got me a sideways glance of comic surmise. Why don't they know, he asks, after all this time? Mentioned Marcuse's perception of tolerance as repression, and bandied ideas about. Thought is enhanced by the tumble of waves, the sound of rain. I remark that so much forbidding sweetened the value of the forbidden. Man has always savored the irony of having to believe an idea and its opposite. All these furry old doctors, Sander says. Even so, I've had it with too much.

Innocence is regenerative, he is teaching me.

I FLOREAL

Window washing, painting the trim outside, a swim, a run in the boat. We become brown.

Through the chryselectric green with goatstep, ramshorns curled, sharp of eye, satyrs. Their musk precedes them, armpit and honeysuckle, quince flower descant upon a rackle of billy pizzle. Tuscan tan and with the visages of Italic gods, their pentathletic torsos flow with bestial grace into dappled haunches. Stag tails frisking up from the holybone wag above the flat of narrow butts.

One munches an apple, one buzzes his lips like a hornet, the third twiddles the radical of his stegocephalic posthon. Their knowledge of the gods is intuitive, fretful, dark. Of Zeus they know but the suddenness of the lightning and the thunder's hackling of its neck, hateful winds, snow, and rain. Artemis they know as the Mother of the Bears. Hera they do not know. Their Lord of the Dance is not Apollo but Pan, whom they call Humper. Asklepios is Snake, Demeter the apple, pear, and plum, Persephatta the poppy and the wren.

Their language is inhuman. They can chatter with the squirrels, using squirrel words among themselves to bound their peripatesis. For time they use the vocabulary of the grey wolf, for elegy and boast the nicker and whinny of the horse, for familiar discourse a patois of birdsong, fox bark, goat bleat, and the siffle and mump of their cousins the deer.

Hesiod first mentions them, *the race of satyrs about which nothing can be done.* In Sicily they are called Tityrs. Silenos the friend of Dionysos was one of them, prophet and drunkard. I see Asia in this detail, a transference onto the leafgod Dushara through whom the dead speak of some shaman whose trance came from wine.

The true satyrs were shy woods creatures whose only boldness was in mounting hamadryads, fauns, maelids, sheep and their snubnosed shepherd, goats and their darkeyed goatherd, country girls out berrying, pious wives at the spring, anything with penetrable *pterygomata* into which their impudent *saunia* might squeeze, poke, slide, prod, or slurp. Neither voluptuaries nor lovers, they never thought to mention in their talk of weather and time with the wolves that the day had seen them chase and hump a nimble wench and her cow, a brace of oreads whom they found in each other's arms, a pastureful of horses, and an hysterical swan.

Coffee and notebook on the hearth. A fire of sticks and fircones feels good in the evening. A domestic animal, fire.

2 FLOREAL

Writing in our seat on the big rock, the day sweet and gentle, Sander beside me just out of the sea, out of wholly unconscious habit, scritched Sander's tummy along the mesial, nudged the lens of water from his navel, and was tracing absentminded patterns when he said with singsong parody that Dokter Tomas had vetted me as gentleman, scholar, and man of letters whose *beschaafde manieren* were supposed to be a model and an inspiration to a teenager with fried nerves and staring at the wall. Three weeks of carpentry had cured that, together with fresh air, the sea, and the company of a philosopher. *Niettegenstande dat,* he said, see the willful nosecone volunteer to join in.

3 FLOREAL

Scumble sienna over bronzen green, the ruddle gold. The wax is vermilion, to pick up the *vert Louis XV* of the bottle on the other end of the diagonal. With a charcoal stub he put in the lines of the drawing board. Two corners would be out of the picture, as in Degas, as Hokusai would want it, as the perspective frame indicated.

He will eat the onions, but first he will eat them with his eyes. He put two of them on the white plate, the third beside the plate. Two quick rectangles with the charcoal: letter and book. A fourth onion on the book, on Raspail. Box of matches.

Bottle in the lower left corner, both in and out of the frame, something for the eye to move over. A jug of olive oil beyond the drawing board, contrast and balance. Shag tobacco in its paper, open. His pipe.

The onion on Raspail's book begins the meaning. Then candle, lit, immediately above. Theo's letter with a burnt match laid against it. *Still-even met uien, tabak, pijp, kaars, een brief.*

The still life is the painter's sonnet, the painter's essay. Did he dare to put in an allusion to Ricord as well? No, for Raspail was Ricord enough.

He had tried to make himself clear about Ricord in a letter to Theo soon after he cut off his ear, was it two weeks ago already? Three? It was in his reply to the letter with the fifty francs that he was putting in the still life. He had been oblique, comparing Raspail and Ricord. If Theo understood, he did not say. Delacroix and after him Seurat had sorted out the colors into their components, like ancient men sorting out the notes of the scale, the Goncourts were sorting out the emotions, and Ricord had distinguished between the two dread diseases caught through the genitals. One never went away, but moved through the system until it reached the spine and the brain. It caused madness. The other was a disease that could be cured, though never with complete certainty. He did not know which he had. But one could hope.

And one could make a vow, with the help of the Christus, to remain chaste and pure. The doctor had seemed to think that his madness was dietary, and that Raspail could bring him around to health, of body and mind, again. How the rich doctors and professors tried to suppress the *Annuaire de la santé*! No country other than France had such a book, a medical guide for the home, with all the science known about disease in clear prose that even the most simple could understand.

And what had he had for, say, an average meal, the good doctor had asked after he had cauterized and bandaged what was left of his ear? Meal, meal? He did not rightly take meals, he was ashamed to say. He lived off white wine and shag tobacco, with the occasional glass of Pernod. The doctor had buried his face in his hands. And blasphemed. We are commanded not to blaspheme, he had said to the doctor.

We are also commanded, by Nature, if you will, Monsieur Vincent, to nourish our bodies with food and not with poison. We are also commanded not to mutilate our ears.

Raspail recommended onions for the poor as the most nourishing of foods for the least sous. And olive oil. He drew onions that were beginning to sprout. Green is the symbol of hope. And the olive jug must be green as well.

4 FLOREAL

Sander delights to sit suddenly and inventory his precocious and wicked past, knowing that mine is nothing like, amazed that he is shocked by it and cheerfully shocked by his amazement. Item, his best girl, as was, before she went off with hippy creeps in a tide of macramé, transcendental meditation, and organic meals that tasted like paper, sand, and whey, well he made it with her little sister one afternoon on the sly, scarcely thirteen, eager as a *poesje* rolling in catnip. Never mind *his* sister, since they were in rompers practically. He was an accomplished smoocher at ten, a rake at eleven, a Ganymed at twelve, a father, probably, at thirteen, outcoming Don Juan at fourteen. It was lovely, *slordig*, messy. Item, every girl in his set, too many out of it (what slobs! what smarm!), somebody's soused mother on a bed at a party, unwashed French sailors in dingy hotels, a divinity student with halitosis and hung like a chihuahua.

Impressive, I said, suggesting it was *kinderspel* and the evidence of a warm heart. A sigh and a dirty look. You don't even think I'm a monster, he said. Dokter Tomas wanted to hold his nose.

5 FLOREAL

That the world is a skin of air around a sphere of rock is so modern an idea that no culture knows it. We mites, the big roaming animals, inhabit this balloon much as microbes swim about in the film of a bubble, which must have its Asias and Alps, just as motes of dust have their moons, seasons, and geology.

The scale of *ubi* and *quando* is, as far as we know, one of the infinitudes so strangely interrelated, so perfectly harmonized, that we shall probably never perceive how time is knit with space, how the pulse of light is also the pulse of time, or how the energy of radiant stars can brake and still itself to become matter.

The stuff of a world, ant, iron, canteloupe, is light ash accumulated over quadrillions of quadrillions of eons. Finished time, said Samuel Alexander, becomes a place. This is an angel's sense of things. Our attention is too frail to focus on it, however awful it is to admit that the nature of being is a boring subject.

6 FLOREAL

Chastity as contempt of the sensual. The word *sensual* troubles Sander, makes him wrinkle his nose. Chastity he may well never have heard of, though he keeps to it with a will.

Value as the judgment of a discerning mind, not as agreeing to the crowd's approval. Sander nods his seeing. Later: that things are what you are capable of making them. No cheating allowed.

7 FLOREAL

Shopping on shore. Our supplies over a choppy sea coming back. Sander took in a movie while I called friends: Keirinckx is doing some topnotch work he wants me to see soon. Bruno and Kaatje splendidly happy (Hans and Saartje crowed over the phone), but didn't believe the USA where they're just back from. Paulus says the summer students are duller than ever before.

Sander's film was a skinflick, French, in which mother and daughter seduce each other's boyfriends: too gooey, his verdict, but with lots of girl on show, some grunty bedwork, make believe in his expert opinion, and lots of neat cars. Had I ever been to Paris? Tried to give him some idea of how beautiful it is, how congenial, how orderly. He said his friends told him it was a cruddy place where you had to beg in the underground. Impulsively said I would take him to see it. When? he replied.

A place is defined anew even when returning to it after a few hours. My island, my cabin, my books, my sea.

See how the book of essays will fit together. What the pastoral does in Picasso, what a still life is, how the erotic, like wild ginger in the Seychelles, thrives domestically in a cultivated ecology. Goya and Theokritos, Jarry and Virgil converge in Picasso's last etchings. Cézanne comes from Virgil. Picasso takes up the Classical just when it was most anaemic, academic, and bleached of its eroticism.

8 FLOREAL

Finish painting the composition-board inner walls. Their white takes the sun beautifully. Pictures up, finally. The Marc Bauhaus calendar, several early Kandinskys thumbtacked up, arrangements of postcards.

Whitecaps, a warmish wind from the east. A storm brewing far out, could move in.

9 FLOREAL

A gale drenching the windows: can scarcely see out. Began in the night. We feel wonderfully isolated. The Island of Snegren, Sander says in a radio voice, completely cut off by North Sea storm from Europe and all the continents. The population of two, Professor van Hovendaal the noted philosopher, and Alexander Brouwer, the *schaamteloos tiener*, asked for a statement by the press, replied that they couldn't care less.

We go out and secure the boat, leaning into the wind and getting drenched. Toweled down, Sander wears a denim jacket only. So dark we need lamps: a comforting and congenial light.

Reading awhile, drawing awhile, Sander's up every five minutes or so to peer out the windows, out the door, getting dashed with rain. As often, he pokes his scrotum, which seems swollen, unsettles his foreskin, and counts the days of his resolute chastity. Something short of two months, he figures out loud, not counting a wet dream a month back.

Thought of Itard's Victor, who needed to escape from time to time to bat the water of the stream and howl at the moon.

Traverse Picasso with two vectors: the long tradition of the still life (eating, manners, ritual, household) and the pastoral (herds, pasturage, horse, cavalier, campsite).

10 FLOREAL

Strangeness and charm. After a convivial meal laid out in front of the fire late yesterday, the dark squall continuing, I had suggested that I read us a ghost story as befitting such a night. Suddenly, a slam of the door, and no Sander. Stood only half surprised, as I assumed he was making a dash for the outhouse. Half an hour, and no Sander. Either he was ill, or had not gone to the outhouse. Or was ending his chaste fast, more than likely. He would return spent and relaxed.

An hour. I dressed for the solid rain and slashing wind. Rapped on the outhouse door: no reply. Inside, no Sander. Called. Walked and called. Back to the cabin to see if he'd returned. No. An uneasy dread. One side of the island under an assault of champing, raging waves, the other awash. Walked and called.

Was sick with anxiety when I found him at the far end, standing braced against a tree, his face streaming in the beam of my flashlight. His eyes were closed, his mouth open. One hand kneaded his testicles, the other was satisfying his body's demand with profligate frenzy. I clicked off the flashlight as soon as I saw. See you when you get back, I said as cheerfully and as normally as I could.

Itard's Victor, I said all the way to the cabin, Itard's Victor, slipped loose into the elements, gone wild. Broke up two crates for the fire, got out a bathrobe and towels. It was another hour before he returned.

Dried him before the fire while he shivered, hair, body, sex, which stood, his streaming eyes, tears as I discovered. His teeth chattered. Wrapped him in the bathrobe and a blanket. Put him in my bed and held him until he was asleep.

13 FLOREAL

Sander still feverish but, I think, in the clear. The gale left our island tangled with detritus, the staves of somebody's dory, shells, limbs, tackle, nameless trash. Sea still high and boisterous, clouds scudding in glare.

14 FLOREAL

Calm. Sander for a walk with me to inspect the island. Though warm, and clearing steadily, insisted on jeans, sneakers, shirt and sweater. Has slept in bed with me since the wild night, sexless and cuddly as a puppy. Temperature normal. Will I tell Dokter Tomas? he asks. What's to tell? I say.

15 FLOREAL

Fine weather again. Sander sets to cleaning up. A storm, he says, is to provide firewood for islanders. I get back to writing. Sander in jeans, as if the nudity he loved so much were ruined.

16 FLOREAL

We study phyllotaxis, diagramming arrangements of leaves on stems, using a string to plot the Fibonacci proportions. Sander's good at this.

Each species of animal lives in its own world. Each being lives in its own world.

In Virgil the shrill cicada's cry is the symbol of appetence. It is the edge of desire that gives the pastoral its identity. The erotic moves along fine gradations and differences, Daphnis and Chloe discovering each other's bodies, the opposition of sheep and goats, sun and shade, summer and winter, grassland and rock, field and wood. Leporello's classification of charms begins in the *Anthology*: I kissed, says Artemon, Erkhedemos twelve, when he was peeping around a door, and then I dreamed that he wore a quiver, was winged, spry, and beautiful, and that he brought me a brace of bantams, awful omen, and smiled at me and frowned. I have walked into bees swarming. Twelve! Thirteen is the age preferred by adepts, fourteen is Eros in full blossom, fifteen sweeter still, none sweeter than. Sixteen is for the gods to love, seventeen, bearding out and well hung, is for Zeus alone. At twenty they go for each other.

17 FLOREAL

Euphoria. Sander's blue disc of eye is again calm, and he has returned to wearing water only. His chest runches out from chinning, heaping niftily where it reefs underarm at the nipples.

We row in great sweeps around the island, brown as Choctaws. Sander refuses a haircut and begins to look like Victor when Itard first saw him.

You know, he says, I've never really looked at things before, or tried to get alongside them in the right way. Selfish pig, he calls himself.

18 FLOREAL

The six essays are beginning to fit together just as I want them to. Find I can work on them all at once. I begin to find everything in Picasso in the Mediterranean past, of which he is the great custodian in our time.

Sander, sprag imp and stinker, turns up glossy with sweat from running, unties his sneakers on the edge of my worktable, and says with bright sincerity, you can have my body if you want it. A scrunch in my scrotum, but I'm speechless. Don't look so hacked, he says. I am the new Sander. I don't take, I give. I've figured it out: give me credit for being smart. I'll stay horny in my head, ready anytime, for whatever.

But I love you just so, *liefje* Sander, charmingly naked and good natured. You keep my imagination alive. You've helped me write my book, you have beguiled all our time here into a kind of ancient ambiance, Damon the old shepherd I, Mopsus the young shepherd you, full of piss and vinegar.

I can always go jump in the sea, he says. You aren't old.

What if I wanted you, what would you want me to want?

Grown people are Martians, he says. They don't know nothing from nothing, but I mean nothing!

20 FLOREAL

Coffee and journal on the rock. Sander brings out second mugs of coffee. *Iets reusachtigs!* he says, adding a whistle and a shake of his ankle. Crouches on my knees and we sip our coffee. We could row over to the mainland and brag, he says, I mean just by walking around and laughing with our eyes.

22 FLOREAL

The dedication, if I dared, of the essays might be *Péoi Aléxandros Pentekaidekaétes*.

30 FLOREAL

Crushed green smell of fir needles, sweetgrass, bee balm in salty hair, tang of creosote at the roots, earwax faintly acrid, sweat licked from the upper lip, axial sweat the odor of hay and urine, olive and soda the pileum, celery and ginger the sac. You, Sander says, giving me look for look, bright as a wolf, smell like billy goat, tobacco, onions, *zaad,* Aqua Velva, licorice, and wet dog. Doesn't all that hair tickle?

1 PRAIRIAL

It was the Englishman John Tyndall who discovered why the sky is blue. What we see is dust suspended in our shell of air, quadrillions of prisms shattering pure sunlight into spectra. Blue is the color that scatters. The moon's sky is black, Mars' is red.

The Trees at Lystra The Death of Picasso The Daimon of Sokrates Christ Preaching at the Henley Regatta Mesoroposthonippidon Lo Splendore della Luce a Bologna Idyll On Some Lines of Virgil The Trees at Lystra The Death of Picasso

The Daimon of Sokrates

Christ Preaching at the Henley Regatta Mesoroposthonippidon Lo Splendore della Luce a Bologna Idyll On Some Lines of Virgil The Trees at Lystra The Death of Picasso The Daimon of Sokrates Christ Preaching at the Henley Regatta Mesoroposthonippidon Lo Splendore della Luce a Bologna Idyll On Some Lines of Virgil The Trees at Lystra The Death of Picasso The Daimon of Sokrates Christ Preaching at the Henley Regatta Mesoroposthonippidon Lo Splendore della

There was snow in the air, the horse troughs were frozen, and our breaths made fists of cloud before our mouths. We hung our brusk wool cloaks on pegs along the wall, as if we were actors in a drama, shy and proud of the double meaning of what we were doing.

We had talked about Simmias' rotten leg on the way, hoping to be overheard by the spies, and carried his *Treiskaieikosi Dialogoi* openly. Nondaki wore his greyest solemn philosophical coat and his round Pythagorean hat.

Arkhias, when he came, arrived by his own distinguished and separate way, staff in hand, preceded by a decent and grave butler and followed by a slave bearing an extra coat, cushions in a sack, pattens in case of a snowfall or siege of sleet, a cordial, onions, assafoetida, a box of *kottaboi*, and books on geometry and government.

The eyes of Lakonia could be assured by his presence that our gathering at Simmias' house was so much *babax* and *kokkysmos*, the local philosophers at their strange talk. If the polemarkh was amused by such company, there were handsome boys enough among us to excuse him in the Spartan mind of having a serious interest in philosophy.

By yet another way Leontiades arrived with his dancing-eyed corporal by the wrist.

Were they there on the day of emblems and knives? I think so, though those leskhenorian afternoons began in the first quiet days after harvest, when the whispers arose, and went on into the white frosts and bladed winds. Kharon called them *the traitors* when they were not there, but Nondaki always reminded him that they were simply men.

Kharon would open and close his hairy fingers at this, lifting his chin, looking at Nondaki out of the sides of his eyes. Kharon was my Damagetos' father, a richly bearded man in a thick willow-dye wool khlamys and deerhide boots, a broad man whose mind was on his crops and livestock. He was a man of sense, but Nondaki was a philosopher. I watched Kharon's blunt fingers, Nondaki's still shoulders.

More than likely we would encounter on our way to Simmias' house a detail of the Spartan guard doubletiming to the gallop of a drum and cadenced chime of a barbitos, their unpainted ash spears as parallel as the palings of a fence, hale raw-boned fellows blond and blue-eyed in their unbleached jerkins and perizomas. Their heavy marching boots beat on the cold stones like hammers on so many anvils.

The mantis Theokritos would usually fall in with us near the Old Market. He and Kharon were good at the show we were obliged to keep up.

— Brighter the day, Cousin Kharon, wintry as it is, for seeing you and your young friends! What takes you, may I ask, to the philosopher's house at the very skirt of a snowstorm?

— O indeed, Kharon would say as loud as a captain on horseback, I have come like you to learn of the mathematics at Sais. Kaphisias here and I are making progress in the Egyptian grammar: your asp is a *phi,* your bucklebee is pronounced *bot,* your calf *baa,* and your cat *meow.* All very foreign and logical, by the knees of Delia.

That was the password, the knees of Delia.

Simmias' house sat back from the Tanagran road under the spread of three monumental oaks, so that out every window we saw tangled branches stubbornly keeping their dead leaves and all stippled with snow and chittering in the saw-toothed winds that whipped down the river gorges from the mountains.

Simmias, who was just back from his journey to Syria and Egypt, was a thin, horse-faced man with tightly bound yellow hair. I have always found it hard to imagine that he had travelled with the Athenian Plato, the dramatist turned philosophical reporter of Sokrates the ironist, a man, they say, as ugly as a toad.

Raised as I had been in a Pythagorean family, getting philosophy with my goat's milk and bran cakes, I grew up thinking that all families are philosophical. Between the piety of my father and the giddy seriousness of my older brother Epameinondas I scarcely needed to be a philosopher myself. Philosophy was in my bones, though, but I had never seen a dry and meticulous philosopher like Simmias. He spoke crisply, which I did not like. He worried about thinking more than he thought.

Was Plato like this, a schoolmaster rather than a man wrestling meaning to the mat? Surely not Sokrates! A visitor once told about Sokrates' feet, and instantly I perked my young ears. Feet I understood. Feet, by Zeus, are character.

Sokrates' feet, we heard, were enormous, bony, unshod, knuckly of hallux, hairy, with oxbone ankles. The man's mind was all there, its strength and endurance.

And Simmias' feet were long and womanish, clad in stockings against the cold and in supple foreign sandals against the rocks of Thebai. One foot was now on a cushion on a stool, the thin leg wrapped like a gift. He had twisted and torn it on the way home. It would not heal. His room reeked of pungent herbs cooked in wine, a splendid odor except that a second aroma of vinegar ruined it all.

— Thy leg, Simmias, can we hear that it is better?

Arkhias taking off two of his cloaks asked the question.

— Alas, no. It drains and drains, and throbs throughout the night.

He should have said it was better, even though it was parting with rot shin from thigh at the knee. The young are without mercy, and I found myself looking at the wide rocky knees of Nondaki, with their suave scoop of hough, their double fist of knit sinew, the silver boss on the brown of the boll.

Arkhias had never learned to take things in, politicians never do. I never saw him scritch Simmias' tortoiseshell cat Hatshepsut, as Simmias and the beast expected, or admire the *ka* on the clothes box, or give any sign that he had looked into Simmias' dialogues.

He understood sickness and asked about the suppurating leg. He had a word for the weather and the wine. Otherwise he thought it sufficient participation to have brought his person among our company.

He brought a tuzzymussy and sniffed it while we talked.

A lamp beside Simmias' head divided his long face into a mask of winter shadow and a nervous face with an intense blue eye, a beard combed until it was silken, a mouth as thin as a string drawn tight.

He spoke of the Egyptian cosmologies, of the awful width of the yellow Nile, the geometric structures of tombs and pylons plated with electrum and written all over standing stark in the absolute flat of a land all sand and summer the year around.

— Egypt is a Theban's subject, he said with a tickle of interest in his bloodless voice. We went downriver to see the Sphinx, so old that its face is gone except for archaic eyes asleep in their stare. She is not our Strangler from the days of Oidipos and Iokaste. She is the soul's house for the god's portion of a king.

Were the Egyptians as weary as our Simmias? Pythagoras when he went down to the cities of the sun came back with sprightlier knowledge. I have always imagined from my father's talk or that of our teacher Lysis that in Egypt everybody moved in a dance, crocodiles and all, the measures of which had been found in the rhythms of the wanderers and the heartbeat of nature herself.

— The interpreters of *The Book of Coming Forth on the Day* are broken into several factions, Simmias droned on, producing strange rolls of writing, pointing to phrases written in grasshoppers, pots and pans, lizards, flowers, and various kinds of poultry.

It was known to us from Phyllidas, who was one of us, that Arkhias was immensely pleased by our gatherings. He could keep an eye on us, he said, and be assured that we were out of mischief. He knew perfectly well that we were all of us friends of Ismenias, whom the Spartans had bound one day in his garden. They took him to Lakedaimon to defend himself before a court martial on a charge of treason.

— I have done what I could for him, Arkhias explained with a sigh, spreading his fingers on his knees.

Ismenias, we knew, had been murdered in Sparta.

But Pelopidas, our Lopi, Nondaki's other self, was safe in Athenai. Pherenikos and we knew not how many others were with him. Occasionally a shepherd would wander down to the market stalls and ask in the broad Plataian drawl if we Thebans had seen the uncommonly long-toothed wolves in the hills. *By the knees of Delia, I think they come from Attika.*

And then one of us would manage to brush against him on the street to the Elektran Gate and have slipped into our hand an ostrakon on which we might read *We have honed our scythes.*

While Simmias talked about Sais and Ugarit, we darted forward from time to time to warm our fingers at the brazier. The dark man Kharon kept going out of the room into the back passageway, where we could see him consulting with old Simmiké, the housekeeper. She made wonderful faces, talking directly into Kharon's ear, drawing her shawl the snugger, pointing downward, upward, outward.

Kharon returned, a man all black beard and rough grey cloak. The hair on the back of his hands was so thick that it curled down between his knuckles. He listened with feigned interest to Simmias.

Arkhias asked questions, scarcely to the point, so that we had to suppress impish smiles. Simmias kept forgetting, I think, that we were acting a play, as if before the gods and an audience that did not know it was an audience.

— What do the Egyptians call your west wind? Arkhias asked in an important voice, and my lovely brother Epameinondas looked at the ceiling as if to find some long-lost object there.

— My dear Arkhias, Simmias said, wincing at having moved his leg unexpectedly.

But Simmiké was in the room, pulling Kharon's shoulder down to whisper in his ear.

Phyllidas tilted his nose to sneeze, a finger under his nostrils to fend the spasm off.

The slightest shift in the eyes of Arkhias' butler, who stood just inside the door, showed me that he was alert to the signal.

— Your Egyptians ride, do they not, Kharon said quickly, on your hippopotamos while worshipping your cat in a pyramid?

Simmias sighed with patience, and while he was lifting his delicate hands to speak, the butler leaned over Arkhias' shoulder and reminded him in a low voice we could all hear that it was time for him to leave for the Kadmeia.

— So soon? Arkhias said. Are you coming too, Leontiades?

Simmias sat forward with an intake of breath. He had moved too fast for the good of his leg.

— Friend Leontiades, he said, you will give me two *khoes* of your time, as you agreed, will you not?

We all rose and took our cloaks and staffs.

— *Spoudaios zen!*

The snowfall was as soft as down, sweetening the icy air. Arkhias, his butler and slave made off up the hill. We shouted farewells to each other, boisterous and silly, but drifted back together under the wall once Arkhias was far enough away.

— That was a certain Pherenikos at the back of the garden, Kharon said with a fold of his snowy cloak across his mouth.

— *Ah!* Theokritos said.

— He wishes us to know that a party of hunters from Athens is on Mount Kithairon, with their hounds. As the snow is thickening, they think they might come down to Thebai this evening.

— *This evening,* Phyllidas repeated. They cannot come to Simmias' house, surely?

Nondaki, who had stood to one side, said nothing. We knew that he did not go along with the plan, and yet was not against it. His silence meant that our house was not being offered.

— I can hide them at my house, Kharon said.

He opened his great black hairy hands to our confused silence.

— *Elevtheria,* he said with eyes closed.

Getaki would see them before I. He would see them slipping around the wall with their long dogs, smiling Pherenikos with his beard salted with snow, handsome Lopi striding like a god, Stratos with a fascicle of spears sharpened to a razor's edge but not for the nape of a boar. Would Damo peep at them around a door with her mouse's bright eye? I could see her coming in with a bowl of hot wine, looking at every board in the floor. *Koré philitaté emou Demoula!* Lopi would cry out and she would slosh the wine and put it down as red as a rose and disappear as neatly as a lizard at the crack of a twig.

When a thing has come for which you have longed there is the surprise of disappointment in it. I felt hollow.

— There are some deaths, Kharon said, which it is a privilege to die. Shall we say my house then? It is agreed?

We moved our heads from side to side, meaning yes.

THE SNOW FELL ALL AFTERNOON, WHITENING THE MARKET, THE SANCTUARY of Kabeiraian Demeter and Koré, the altar of Apollon of the ashes, the golden roofed temples of the Kadmeia.

The quick of our trouble was there, up the snow-daubed rocky sides of the acropolis, a trouble complex and deep. It began, perhaps with the man, my brother, who was eventually to save us. For Epameinondas learned among the Spartans how to fight the Spartans.

Irony is the very wine of the Greek intellect. Pelopidas, as all Boiotia knows, was the counterpart to my brother Epameinondas. His father was rich, ours poor. Both families descend in honor from the time of Kadmos. The young Pelopidas gave away his inherited fortune systematically, until he was as poor as we have always been.

With what laughter did we greet his offer to give us a portion of his wealth!

— At least, he said, I see where I was moving as I impoverished myself.

He went to school to us, wearing plain clothes of flax as we did, eating peas and oaten bread, sleeping on a pallet.

So Pelopidas became one of our brothers, indifferent as he was to philosophy. He was our hunter, our champion at the palaistra. Wrestling was his mathematics, mathematics Epameinondas' wrestling. Otherwise they were inseparable.

Even before they were sent off in our expeditionary force to fight with the Spartans, they had become twin souls. The Thebans got used to seeing the one where the other was.

I remember them coming in from the hunt, bloody hares hanging from their belts. I remember them on their knees and elbows after the stadion dash, their sides pumping like the flanks of a winded doe, crouched and dancing around each other in the gymnasium, closing in for the toss.

When they came back from the Arkadian expedition with the ugly scars that they hid, we had to wait for the tale behind their valor. Father heard it first, from a Spartan infantryman at the market.

Pelopidas, the story went, had been in the hoplite left at the battle of Mantineia. He was wounded when the line broke, and kept fighting in a circle of isolated Spartan and Theban soldiers. In all he had seven wounds before he fainted from pain and the loss of blood.

Epameinondas, hearing that he was dead, fought his way out to the deteriorated left wing. He found the body and the Arkadians found him.

He stuck the two who came to drive him back, and their howls brought in a whole squadron, wild for easy prey. None had budged him from his stand over Pelopidas' body, though he had a gash down his left arm and a hideous tear in his thigh, when Agesipolas the Spartan commander sent over a detachment from the right wing to save him.

And now the irony begins. For Agesipolas had saved the two men in Thebai who loved liberty most, who returned to join Ismenias and Androklides in our democratic party. Their hope was for raising the commonality to the electorate, for giving generous rights and responsibilities to the people. The city, they said, should be a school and all its citizens students of government.

These ambitions seemed dangerous and even preposterous to the oligarchs. Better foreign domination by a sensible people like the Spartans, they argued to themselves, than the elevation of the rabble to positions of responsibility.

So when Phoibidas the Spartan general was on a campaign that would quarter him and his army in Thebai, the aristocrats whispered to him that he was free to claim Thebai for Spartan rule. They would see that his way was clear.

During the great harvest feast of Demeter, the bandy-legged Phoibidas raised the Lion Standard of Herakles in the citadel.

Lion, Dragon, the indifferent Thebans said with sarcasm. They both collect taxes.

Ismenias was taken to Sparta as a traitor, and it was a surprise even to the aristocrats to learn that he had been murdered there. Pelopidas, so recently a Spartan hero, Pherenikos, the one who came that snowy day to the back of Simmias' garden, Androklides, and many another idealist and democrat were declared outside the law, to be killed on sight with impunity.

They went to Athenai.

It was in the Spartan style, laconic. General Phoibidas stood on the Kadmeia, his bony fists on his hips. He looked as if he had been raised on vinegar and crab apples. He spoke with a burr and a wheeze.

— Your city fathers, he said, have asked me to assume the government. I do.

A brassy trumpet brayed a Dorian tizzy, and there we were, subjects of Sparta.

— We have nothing to complain of, yet, our father said at the time. A man will hesitate less to do bad if we think him bad than if we expect good of him. The Spartans are a people of extremely pure morals.

— Our Epameinondas, he went on, has fought beside them, has lived in bivouac with them for months, and their justice is known to the very boundaries of the civilized world.

— And beyond, Epameinondas said with a smile.

He meant Makedonia.

Of Arkhias and Leontiades our father said nothing. He had not been consulted by them about their treacherous and arrogant signing of the polis over to Spartan domination. Nor did he know all of the party of the rich.

— The *rich*! There are the people of Zeus, the people of Apollon, and the people of Demeter. Are we to understand that the order of nature has been revised to include a new kind of people, who are distinct because of their usuries and the number of their slaves?

SO WE STOOD OUTSIDE SIMMIAS' GARDEN IN THE THICKENING SNOW, THE chill sharper in our hearts than in our feet and hands. Like the birds under their eaves, we pulled our necks in and hunched our shoulders.

Kharon nodded farewell and left. It was to his house the exiles would come if they got through the sentries. Darkness would fall early.

There was a fine sifting of snow on the garland of Simmias' Priapos that blessed and mocked its convivial grin, its garden belt, and its impudent gooseneck capped in white.

— That man, dear Kaphisias, Theokritos said to me from the hood of his cloak, knows not a word of philosophy.

I sensed the edge of reproach upon his words.

— Nor has he been schooled by a teacher like the Lysis who came here from Italy and taught you and Epameinondas.

I saw what he was leading up to.

— Yet you see how he grasps the nobility of our cause, how he responds to what it asks of us. He knows the risk he takes, for he loves Thebai, her ancient code, her freedom.

— He is indeed a worthy citizen, I said, and a brave one. What you mean is that Epameinondas is not like him.

I had not suspected their resentment of Nondaki.

— You are right, I said. He is not like Kharon.

— Why? You are his brother.

— Are you asking me if he knows things we don't?

— He doesn't. We have kept certain things from him, not being wholly certain of where he stands.

— With us, I said, a flick of bother in my quick answer. He has tried to persuade us to give all this up because it is not his way of doing things. You remember his analogy: a doctor comes to cure us but offers neither to ply the knife nor to sear, neither to physic nor to say a charm. Of course we urge him to try the efficacy of these things before he recommends an obol for the ferry across the Styx and a pomegranate for Persephatta.

— True, Theokritos agreed.

— Epameinondas feels that we are choosing to lynch rather than try the traitors.

— The law, Theokritos said with an indignant hoot, is in a treasure chest, the key in a rascal's hand.

— Nondaki will fight, I said. But only when he sees the hard necessity for it.

— He will see it.

Not so clearly, Epameinondas had said to me, not so clearly as all that. We had taken javelins out to the hills beyond the stubble of the harvested barley, where we could see that no one could hear us. He began, bouncing the javelin on the heel of his hand in the fine cold air, by saying the name of his other self, *Pelopidas*.

Lopi would certainly be among the exiles coming from Athenai. If they were going to slaughter the polemarkhs and the Spartan officers, he would do it cleanly and without mercy. So would Pherenikos.

But Eumolpidas was with them, who had private enemies to dispatch. At the palaistra he racked up penalties until all the coaches fouled him out, and he then lay for his opponents afterwards and fought them with thumbjabs to the eyes and kicks in the flanks and balls.

And there was Samiadas, coward and bully together. I remember asking when he had pitched the javelin on an incredibly long and level flight if an army fighting for justice would ever be made up entirely of just soldiers.

Such an army, he reminded me with a smile, marched with the Master and brought confusion to the Sybarites. The second javelin thucked into the lower pasture beside the first, not five palms away.

After the third javelin, which was hurled with an elegant wind correction, he took off his sheepskin jerkin and stood naked in a chaff of that splintery gossamer of ice that comes before the snow.

He weighed the next javelin in his open hand, backing on his toes and tossing his hair from his eyes. I could see the pale scars of Arkadian blades in the musculature strapping his ribs and in the long quadriceps of the thigh.

A sudden wind caught the javelin on its pitch and whistled it spinning a good ten cubits wide of its aim.

— Mark the sign! he called. That gust was the rage I see in this whole affair.

Years later, on an Athenian porch, I remembered that bleak afternoon, but by then the memory was blended with that of a blue spring day on the road from Orkhomenos to Tegyrai when in the twinkling of an eye the vanguard of the Sacred Band saw the bronze masks of Spartan infantrymen a half furlong away, the scarlet cloaks from chin to feet, the round Medusa shields, and heard on all sides the cry, *PAI — — on — i!*

The drums began to beat and the salpinx strutted out its notes with the splendor of cockcrow, and threw in a backfall and tril for insult.

And for the first time in the whole history of the world Spartans went down in defeat under Greek swords.

What, an Athenian poet leaned forward and asked when I was telling these things, did I *feel*? In the villas of Italia and icy governor's headquarters of Makedonia men knew of the Sacred Band, every two members of which were joined in the oath of Iolas, and which was commanded by two chaste Pythagoreans as tall as Enyalios and as handsome as Apollon.

I replied that as I ran to take my place with my shield-fellow in the ashlarwork of the line I kept in my mind's eye Nondaki and Papa and I sitting straight on our kitchen bench, our hands flat on our thighs, our feet parallel in a row, ideally, for mine would not reach. And before us there was Lysis our teacher in his linen peplon, his eyes as bright as a mountain lion's. The bones of things, he said, are numbers.

And I remembered teaching numbers to Getaki, and eventually to Damoula, who listened after the manner of girls with her eyes.

WHILE THEOKRITOS AND I WERE THUS TALKING IN THE SNOW, A MAN WALKing down the road from the Kadmeia suddenly crossed over to us. When he greeted us from under the brim of his broad blue hat we saw that it was Galaxidoros.

— His worship Arkhias and the Spartan Lysanoridas are just behind me, he said quickly, quite out of breath. Where else but here would they be coming?

— But he left here just a bit ago, Theokritos said. He came to the gathering, to hear the philosophy, and left when his butler said he was expected on the Kadmeia.

— He left because of a signal, I reminded Theokritos. The pretended sneeze.

And here he was back, with a Spartan in a summer khiton. It was Theokritos he wanted, as he pointed at him with his staff. The Spartan scratched his mustache with his riding crop. He wore a dagger at his left hip.

— Would Theokritos, Arkhias said with a twiddle of fingers, honor him with a word apart?

The Spartan Lysanoridas had walked on, and Arkhias led Theokritos to him by the elbow. The three of them went to a circle of trees at the foot of the steps leading up to the Ampheion. We could see Theokritos leaning his head in attention.

I looked at Galaxidoros with widened eyes, he gave a low whistle, and we drew back deeper into Simmias' garden.

—I do not like this, he said. Not at all.

—But if they knew, wouldn't they have sent guardsmen to frogmarch us all to the Kadmeia?

—It is suspicion, I think. A detail here and a detail there from the spies, and they could easily have put it together. Fear of an uprising must have crossed their minds more than once.

—Someone's coming, I said quietly.

A figure crossed the garden, shaking snow from low branches.

—Ho! the figure said from among the laurel stippled white, and we could see that it was Phyllidas.

—I came for the philosophy, he called, but everyone seems to have gone away. You two not quite, as I see. Ah, Galaxidoros and the wrestler and runner Kaphisias! I saw you the other morning down by the Ismene nipping along as gracefully as a buck. That, said I to myself, is the stripling Hermes or the handsome Kaphisias Polymnides.

And in a voice all but inaudible:

—They're coming?

We answered with nods.

—Today?

—They are coming down from the hills. They hope to look like so many *ephebai* out with hounds.

—The gods are giving their consent, he said. Weeks ago I planned a supper at my house for tonight.

Phyllidas was scribe to the three Polemarkhoi. It was known that they used his jovial household for their more strenuous banquets. We had our gossip of the girls and boys and the kraters drunk of choicest wine.

—Can we, then, Galaxidoros asked, expect to find the lot of them there together?

The thought weakened the knees and wrapped the undertaking in an appalling reality. I had always imagined fighting as I imagined Epameinondas in battle, on a plain wild with rearing horses, the sky stormy, the emblems rippling in the wind.

This insurrection was to happen in a dining room.

—I think not, Phyllidas replied, working something out in his mind, running his finger along his nose. Arkhias has plans for a certain lady of a certain family, which gallantry is to be kept from Leontiades. There will therefore be at least two houses to enter like wolves snuggling into the fold.

I have seen the wolf sidle into the flock from the rear, on tip toes, its noble shoulders bristled, its long tongue out and watering. We crept toward it, Epameinondas and I, glancing at each other in disbelief, for we had never seen the wolf at this business, though it is a figure of speech we had heard all our lives.

The wolf trotted as if it were a sheep, caressing the poor sillies with wifely affection. Then he mounted one, as if to mate with it, but climbed the length of its back and lay there like a sphinx, and the idiot sheep smiling all the while and its fellows too stupid to notice.

A rock from Epameinondas' sling sent it bounding off and Epameinondas's ash spear with the bronze head shot after it, scattering leaves and birds. The sheep ran in a circle bleating, mindless, pitiful.

Like wolves snuggling into the fold.

—If we get there, Galaxidoros said, taking Phyllidas by the arm and pointing to where Arkhias and the Spartan were talking with Theokritos.

—What does that mean? he asked.

He stared, obviously disquieted. He knew what we were thinking.

—Not that, he said. I think they may well be asking him about the signs we have heard of. Yesterday a fish was caught in the river that has a head on both ends. An old woman brought in a goose egg with a lambda and alpha on it. A shepherd has seen a hare hopping backwards.

While he was talking we saw Theokritos raise his staff in farewell, genially enough. We waited for him at the edge of the garden, thoroughly frozen by this time. When he drew nigh he allayed our fears with a smile and suggested that we return to Simmias.

—For the warmth of his mind and of his brazier.

In the antechamber we met Pheidolaos, the Haliartian. He was waiting to see Simmias, who, he informed us, was still conferring with Leontiades, who had stayed behind when we dispersed before.

—About Amphitheus, he said, and we fell silent.

Amphitheus was under guard in the citadel. We had but recently learned that his sentence was death, his crime treason. He had struck the stones in the agora with his thumbstick on market day. How much longer, he cried, are we Thebans to wear the collar and leash of Sparta? A man ran and whispered in his ear, and got a hateful look for his solicitude.

He had obviously memorized his speech, for it had in it rhetorical figures from the classroom, *the flower of our youth, though my beard may be streaked with grey, the torch of freedom,* albeit his tongue's native grit supplied some phrases before the guardsmen came. We whispered around his *bowlegged fodderfed prickmedainties* and *sheepshanks pisspothelmeted bullies* and *stubborn goatwezanded foreigners.*

The severity of his sentence and the secrecy of his trial had added their weight to the intolerable load, and had precipitated the furtive return of the exiles.

Simmias, always more liberal of mind than anyone, felt that the harshness with which Amphitheus was struck down was a symbolic gesture, an example to us rather than an example of justice. A sensible talk with Leontiades would soften the matter: banishment at most. Clemency is always a popular gesture.

We asked Pheidolaos with looks what he thought of Simmias' chances.

— Well, he said, they are still talking. That's something.

He drew his cloak about him and studied the floor.

The ironies fall into place like the first fat drops of a summer rain. Epameinondas the Spartans and the aristocrats thought nothing of. He came from a strange Pythagorean family that practised ritual poverty and was by doctrine pacifist and hermitish. Epameinondas was under a vow of chastity, he spent his time at numbers. What danger could such a fool be to them?

Aie, the Spartans! Their torturous minds fined Phoibidas a hundred thousand drakhmai for presuming to take Thebai without orders from headquarters. They apologized through diplomatic channels for the bad manners of adding us to their colonial system on the most holy feast of Demeter.

But they let the garrison stay, and we learned that we lived under Spartan law. The Spartans could not imagine any city not grateful for the discipline of their government.

Our new leaders learned that a Theban band was being trained in Athens and sent instructions to the Athenians to jail them. The Athenians fed them and armed them instead.

THE SPARTANS TOOK OUR CITY THREE YEARS AGO, ON THE FEAST OF DEMETER.

Not a javelin hissed across the wind, not an arrow jumped from the bow, not a blade drew back red from a thrust around the shield.

Thebai went to the Spartans with a speech. It was not even a speech, all goose gabble and earache, with windy words and sudden silences for the staffs to beat on the stones in applause.

SIMMIAS' WOMAN SIMMIKÉ BROUGHT US CUPS AND WINE, TOGETHER with a plate of cheese, bread, and honey.

We did not ask Theokritos what Arkhias' business with him had been. That he showed no discomposure may have been an act for Pheidolaos, with whom he instantly began a conversation.

— We have all been wanting to know, he said, about the opening of Alkmena's tomb at Haliartos. We know only that the Spartan Agesilaos wanted the tomb opened and the remains removed to Lakonia. Can you tell us?

— I was certainly not present. I did everything I could to keep them from performing such a desecration. Every priest and official whose ear I could reach heard my mind in thoroughly strong terms, I assure you. My shame was deep. What times in which we live!

He told us that no body was found in the grave when they opened it, only a stone, a small bronze bracelet, and two clay urns that seemed to be filled with earth, though their antiquity was such that no one could be sure what substance they had contained.

— The stone confirms history, as you recognize. We are told in the poems that Alkmena's body disappeared at its burial, and that the gods replaced it with a stone. With the other objects in the tomb was a bronze tablet blackened with age. When it was washed it proved to have writing on it which could not even be identified, much less read. The assumption, probably vulgar, was that the writing was Egyptian, as it was partly pictures. Argesilaos accordingly had copies sent to Pharaoh Nektanebis at Sais, requesting a translation.

— That is why I have come to see Simmias, to learn if when he was recently in Egypt he talked with any of their philosophers about this matter.

— Meanwhile our crops at Haliartos have failed and the lake is rising.

The people have no doubt that the opening of the tomb is the cause of our lucklessness.

He sipped his wine, a man impatient and perplexed.

Alkmena's, we knew, had been a holy death, as befitted the mother of Herakles. In Attika our great Oidipos went to the gods in the sacred wood at Kolonos. Some say he dissolved in light, some that the earth opened and he sank down, kingly man that he was, with great majesty. Others, that certain birds not of this creation bore him away. The Kekropians would never be so impious as to look into the tomb of Oidipos.

— You know, of course, Theokritos said to the miserable Pheidolaos, that the Spartans have not escaped the curse you speak of. Just now I have been consulting with Lysanoridas, their satrap magistrate, about the signs and portents they have had. They are indeed quite concerned, so much so that I have suggested that they put the sacred objects back in the tomb, close it reverently, and pour libations to Alkmena and Aleos. This he says he will do. He is particularly disturbed by the rising of your Kopaic lake. Chthonic powers are behind that. The Spartan mind has a firm respect for the netherworld, though Lysanoridas had never heard of Aleos.

— Ah! Pheidolaos said, as if a suspicion had been proved true.

— Once he has placated Alkmena, he intends also to find the tomb of Dirke and pour libations there. Naturally he does not know where it is.

— That is a secret place, is it not, Pheidolaos interrupted, known only to the Theban hipparkhs?

— The outgoing hipparkh takes the incoming to it, by night and with the utmost mystery. They do rites there, involving no fire, and when this ceremony is over, all traces of the visit are obliterated, and the two hipparkhs return by separate ways.

— Nor will the Spartans find Dirke's tomb. And all our hipparkhs are in exile.

We dared not exchange glances.

— All except Gorgidas and Platon. The Spartans might consult them or they might consult the stones of the city wall. The answer they would get would be the same.

— The so-called Boiotarkhoi now on the Kadmeia were handed the spear and signet in utter ignorance of the proper ritual. The hipparkh no more knows where the tomb of Dirke is than my mare the meaning of the epsilon on the omphalos.

Suddenly Simmiké and Leontiades' butler were among us, carrying cloaks and staffs. Leontiades followed, saying farewells and giving us a cursory nod.

Simmiké latched the door, muttering that the object of all this coming and going was to freeze the household. She motioned us into Simmias' sitting room.

He put his hands to his cheeks when we gathered around him. His face was like a tragic mask.

— O Herakleis! he said. They think like wild animals and their minds are barbarian. I kept remembering what Thales said when asked what was strangest among the things he had seen on his travels. *A tyrant who had reached old age.* Even without being touched by their cruel and arbitrary laws, it is brutalizing to live among them. Their rule is an obscenity, is misrule, is the perversion of justice.

He sank back on his pillows. Galaxidoros gave me a look that meant *it has got through to him*.

— Amphitheus is to die? I asked.

— I think so, he said wearily. He tried to convince me of the rightness of it, but said that he would take it up with the hipparkhs. May the gods show their hand.

We sat in silence for awhile, not being able to touch the subject most crucial to us all.

— Tell me, Simmias said to me, who the stranger is who is visiting at your house?

— I don't know, I said. Who said a stranger is at our house?

I feared horribly that it was one of the exiles who was on his own or had misunderstood the plan.

— Leontiades tells me that a most imposing man with a largish following of servants and companions has arrived at your home. Leontiades is of course told everything. His first report of them was last evening, when the stranger set up camp at the tomb of Lysis. This morning the outguards reported rude beds of tamarisk and chaste tree, the trace of a fire, and a bowl of milk left as a libation for the manes of the blessed Lysis. And this morning he was heard asking for the sons of Polymnis.

— Who could he be? He sounds like a man of great importance, and not just anybody.

Simmias guessed my fear that the stranger was one of the exiles, and added that his accent was foreign.

— A distinguished guest indeed, Pheidolaos said, as if to remove the subject from between him and his business.

He drew closer, spreading his hands on his knees.

— Esteemed Simmias, he began, and repeated the story of the desecration of Alkmena's tomb, the blight, the bronze tablet with the curious writing that had been sent to Egypt.

— Of your tablet, Pheidolaos, this is the very first I have heard. But I remember that the Spartan Agetoridas came to Memphis with a rather long document sent by Agesilaos to be translated by the prophet Khonouphis, a man I know well, as Plato and I and, who else, yes, Ellopion of Parethos, have had many philosophical conversations with him.

— I remember that Agetoridas turned up with orders from the Pharaoh that Khonouphis was to translate the document. Khonouphis was three days at dictionaries and ancient books and rendered the pages into Greek. It gave orders and instructions for a contest in honor of the Muses.

— How had an Egyptian document appeared in a Spartan tomb? Well, that's interesting enough, and clear enough. The style of lettering was from the days of Homer's Proteus, or Prouti, very old indeed. We know that Herakles learned to write around that time. Naturally he wrote in the Egyptian syllabary.

— The inscription went on, purporting to have been taken down by divine inspiration. The Greeks, it said, must learn to live in peace and leisure by laying their arms aside and solving all disputes through philosophy.

Theokritos and I savored the irony with glances. But Simmias had spun himself well and the top would take some time to wobble and run down.

— All contentions being a matter of disharmony, he continued after wetting his lips, it is the Muses to whom we should turn. I remember that Plato and I were much moved by this at the time. And we were strikingly reminded of these words when on our return from Egypt we met with a company of Delians in Karia. Plato in those days was best known as a geometer, and they asked him to solve a problem which Apollo had given them at the oracle. *There will be peace between Delos and other Greeks,* the oracle said, *when you double the altar of Delian Apollo.*

— Double the altar? Pheidolaos repeated.

— Ah yes, Simmias went on. Do you see the problem? It looks as if one might be able to double a cube by doubling its dimensions, right? Well, if you do, as the Delians had discovered, you get a figure not twice but eight times the size. If you double the lines of a square, you make it four times as large.

Pheidolaos puzzled at it.

— And how do you double a cube, then?

— That's why the Delians turned to Plato, whose brilliant mind saw into the matter as clearly as if a lantern had been introduced into a dark house. The oracle was chiding the Greeks for their ignorance of learning in general. It was intelligence that brought about peace, and intelligence is trained in the gymnasium, where one can learn how to find *two* mean proportionals. Plato showed them this problem and its solution in Eudoxos of Knidos. It has also been demonstrated by Helikon of Kyzikos. But the god, Plato explained, was not interested in their doubling the cube of the altar but in turning from war to the kind of education by which their energy flowed not into death but into music, geometry, medicine, poetry, and the law. Mathematics, he said, is the harmony of the mind.

— And, Pheidolaos asked rather anxiously, that is also what the bronze tablet in Alkmena's tomb means?

But Simmias had obviously forgotten Alkmena's tomb, and had to marshal his thoughts afresh.

— But how do we know that Khonouphis' document was the one taken from the tomb in Haliartos?

Pheidolaos had slapped his knee preparatory to asking Simmias how many bronze tablets written in Egyptian had been excavated in parts of Greece under Spartan domination that seemed important enough to require the consulting of the Pharaoh of Egypt and his scholars, when the door opened and Simmiké led in my father.

— Polymnis, Simmias said, there is no one more welcome on such a day.

Father did not ask why, to Simmias' disappointment, but greeted us all warmly and said that we were to stay until Epameinondas arrived with the stranger.

— A generous soul! Father said. A magnificent man! He is Italian! He has come on a noble errand from the great Pythagorean colony because he has had dreams, wonderful dreams. Not only dreams, either: appearances as vivid as day. They all said he was to come here, to cold Boiotia in the mountains, to pour holy libations on the grave of our teacher Lysis. And has brought a considerable sum in gold as a payment to Epameinondas for keeping Lysis in his old age. We will not accept it, of course. I laughed, I had a wonderful laugh with him, mind you, for he too saw how illogical it was for a Pythagorean under a vow of poverty to be given a sack of gold by a Pythagorean. Why, when Lysis was alive and with us, I made him see, we were richer than Persians, richer than the Naga of the Hindu.

— But where is he? Simmias asked. Is he himself a philosopher?

— O yes, dear Simmias. The nobility is in his eyes, in his stance, his bearing, his gait. Wait till you hear his voice! Where is he? Epameinondas has taken him to the Hismenios to bathe. He has been on the road for weeks and last night he camped at the tomb of Lysis, waiting for a sign as to whether he should take the remains back with him to Italy or leave them here.

— How hard it is O Herakleis to find a man whose mind is free of fanaticism and superstition!

Galaxidoros broke in thus on my father's enthusiasm, more rudely than he could have intended. Simmias could not hide his surprise nor my father his annoyance.

— There are fanatics, Galaxidoros went on, who embrace their mystical twaddle through ignorance or weakness of intellect. Others are fanatical through sheer pride, hoping to be thought the darling of the gods or people better than anybody else. These are your dreamers and visionaries who have learned to kick common sense out of the way. For politicians at the mercy of a superstitious people, a show of sanctified delirium has its obvious uses. But surely this seeing of spooks, this solemn interpretation of hen cackle and crossed sticks in the road is counter to all philosophy?

I, for one, did not see what he was talking about, and my father looked at him as if he were an example of what he was denouncing.

— Philosophy, Galaxidoros continued, teaches the good and the true, the whole good and all of the truth, insofar as we can know them through reason alone. And yet everywhere we look we see philosophy abandoning the government of right reason to whore after inspiration and drunken enthusiasm. It is strange and disastrous to see philosophy holding reason in contempt, scorning scientific demonstration, practising divination like a peasant woman. A blacksmith can have as many visions as a philosopher who has given his youth to geometry.

— I myself, he said with growing confidence in his discourse, am a follower of Simmias' friend Sokrates, the truest of philosophers. His mind was virile and guileless. Truth was his whole concern. Was there ever a mind so simple and pure?

— What you are saying, Galaxidoros, Theokritos broke in, is curiously out of tune. I am in sympathy with the drift of your sentiments, but you sound awfully like the accuser Meletos at Sokrates' trial, has it been twenty years ago? Meletos, you remember, charged Sokrates with denying all divinity.

— Of course I know that, Galaxidoros said. Sokrates had a firmer sense of things divine than any of his cowardly accusers. I meant that he saved philosophy from the phantom world into which it had drifted after the death of Pythagoras, and that he pulled it down to human level from the cloudy heights to which Empedokles had soared it. With a philosophy of fable and magic one can do nothing practical. You cannot awaken a man to reality, as Sokrates did with a severe and honest scrutiny, by chasing him into an unreal world of dreams. Sokrates taught men to develop a steadfast understanding of the world as it is.

— True, Theokritos replied, true enough, but what do you make of Sokrates' daimon, that sign that came to him from time to time? Was he pulling our leg when he spoke of it? Not even in the life of Pythagoras do we see so intimate a relation to the divine as Sokrates and his guiding spirit. They were like Odysseus and Pallas Athena. Simmias and others who knew Sokrates can give you other instances, but I can testify that when I was in Athens visiting Euthyphron I saw the great Sokrates mounting the stairs at the Symbolon, on his way to Andokides' house. Wait a bit, *you* were present, too, weren't you, Simmias?

— I was, Simmias said, smugly enough.

— Sokrates had put one of his leading questions to Euthyphron, very playfully, as was his manner, making a lively joke of it all. The tingling eyes would crinkle in that incredibly ugly face, the nose would snuffle, and the satyr's grin would spread his beard like a fan.

— And then he stopped cold on the stairs, utterly lost in thought. In such a brown study his face became like an actor's mask hung on a wall, the eyes empty yet gazing inward, all the features immobile. He stood there quite a long while. Then he loosened a bit, turned, and went down the stairs that he had been climbing. He was already half-way down the shady street of the cabinet makers when he remembered that he had been in company. He stopped and called back to us, *My daimon has come to me!* Euthyphron and I held back, as did some others who knew him well, but some of the pretty boys who were always in Sokrates' wake not only followed him, mischievously, but commanded the flute player Kharillos, who was with me, you remember, visiting Kebes, to dance around Sokrates while playing a tune. This he did, to my shame, and to the merriment of the city and the hooting boys, especially as Sokrates turned down the Street of the Herms, that double row of staring Lords of the Ways that leads to the law courts. Here they met a drove of swine squealing from a sidestreet, as muddy a tribe of grunting sows as I've ever seen. The street is narrow, because of the rows of herms, and there were the hecklers all knee-deep in plunging pigs. The pretty boys squealed because of their finery, which was being painted with mud, and the pigs squealed as tripped boys fell into them. Sokrates walked on, as unperturbed as if he were in a meadow by the Ilissos.

—Did Sokrates' daimon, then, Galaxidoros said, have some grip upon his mind, so that its powers went unexamined by Sokrates, that in fact it took his mind into a dark region beyond the reach of reason? Or was it a mere hunch, a whim, a sudden predilection to do this rather than that? It might have been, you know, like the single drachm placed on one side or another of an evenly balanced scales. Nothing in itself, it yet adds weight. A sneeze, an overheard remark, the unexpected clearing of the skies during a rain, any of these can seem, and can act, like the nod of heaven, giving us a signal for which we are grateful.

—Exactly! my father exclaimed. It was a sneeze, this daimon. I was told that by a philosopher of Megara, who had heard it from Terpsion. His, or another's, it made no matter, a sneeze announced the coming of the daimon. But it had to be a sneeze from the right hand, or from before or behind. A sneeze from the left was the daimon in negative, as it were. He desisted from action in that case. And if he had decided on a course and sneezed, the sneeze confirmed the rightness of what he was to do. If, however, he sneezed after he had begun, he quit. I find all of this wonderfully silly. A grown man being guided by something as natural and ordinary as a sneeze. If only he had said he was the philosopher of sneezes, well and good: the world can stand a little of everything. But no! He said the sneeze was *a sign from heaven,* by Herakleis. This was naughty of him, an affectation, no doubt part of the superb irony he commanded perhaps too well for his own good.

—Not for a moment, Father continued, can I believe in this sneezing daimon. We all know that Sokrates acted forthrightly and effectively in all that he did. He was a man awake, and I cannot imagine his being deflected by a sneeze. Look at him. He remained poor all his life, when there were Athenians who would have vied with each other to heap wealth in his lap. He kept faithfully to philosophy when he saw the danger into which it was leading him. And in the end he declined to escape his fate, and accepted his death with perfect bravery and composure. No, his mind was not at the mercy of signs or disembodied voices. He was guided by the transparent reason of his own noble intelligence.

— Which, Father added, by no means rules out the insight of his piercing mind, the profound intuition which he had about men and events. He confided in several friends his premonition that the Athenian expedition against Sikelia would be defeated. And Pryilampes Antiphontos, Plato's stepfather, said when he was taken prisoner by us in the retreat at Delion that he was captured because he had disregarded Sokrates' advice about which road they ought to take to the coast. You have heard this, too, have you not, Simmias?

— Many times, Polymnis, and from many people. The Athenians had many occasions to marvel at Sokrates' daimon.

— Can we, then, Pheidolaos said, let Galaxidoros get away with belittling to sneezes and coincidence what seems to be an authentic and recognizable instance of a divine hand guiding a pious mind?

— I am most willing, dear Pheidolaos, to hear Simmias speak of the daimon, if he has knowledge of it directly from Sokrates, and shall join you in withholding judgment. What you and Polymnis have had to say on the subject is easily made hay of, I'm afraid. To a doctor a trifling rash or racing pulse may be a sign of grave disorder, to a skipper the sight of a gull or a wisp of yellow cloud, things scarcely interesting to a passenger, may mean high seas to come, so it may be that to a mind as deep as Sokrates' an incident seemingly accidental and negligible may be the sign of much greater things.

He paused, thinking.

— The more a man knows, the more everything is of interest to him. What we deem negligible is always ignorant opinion. A barbarian without writing would marvel at the ability of an historian to look at a page of what he would take to be chicken tracks and see there the movement of armies and the collapse of empires. And we would think him simple if he doubted how the historian could see so much in so little. So in seeing

Sokrates' daimon as a negligible part of his mind, let us note that we are being as simple as the barbarian ignorant of writing.

— Let us, he said, turning to my father, take the objections of Polymnis. You are astonished that a man free of superstition and affectation, a man who made philosophy a human study again, you are amazed, as you say, that he had the presumption to call a sneeze a sign from heaven. I myself would be amazed if a master of words like Sokrates had *not* called the sneeze a sign from heaven. We all say that we are wounded by an arrow when we mean by an archer. We say that scales measure weight, when we mean that a man weighed something with a scales. No act is in an instrument, but in the manipulator of the instrument. The sneeze Sokrates interpreted would be the instrument, and some power would be the user of the instrument. But I think we had better listen to Simmias now, as he knows more about the subject than anyone here.

Theokritos had risen and was going to the door.

— Someone is entering, he said, as Simmias' face fell, for he was arranging the cover on his leg and gathering his mind to speak, no doubt at length.

— I see that it is Epameinondas, Theokritos called. He will be bringing Polymnis' guest, I should think.

We rose and faced the door. Epameinondas with snow in his hair came in, followed by three of us in the plot, Hismenodoros, Bakkhyllidas, and Melissos the flute player.

The stranger came last, aristocratic of face, gentle of eye, and handsome of clothes. The colored flax of his khiton, stole, and sleeved cloak, all with richly figured borders, made our Boiotian winter dress look drab.

He took an indicated place beside Simmias, Epameinondas sat beside me, as always when we were together, and the others drew up chests and stools to supplement the couches in a circle around our host.

— What name and title, Epameinondas, are we to know for our honored guest? Simmias asked. From what country has he come?

— Our guest is Theanor, a citizen of Krotona in Italy. He is a philosopher of the school there, and carries on the work of our master Pythagoras. He has made a long journey on a noble errand.

— Which, the stranger Theanor said with a laugh, Epameinondas will not let me do. If it is noble to befriend, it is also noble to be befriended. A pitched ball is to be caught, is it not? And a man with a favor is like an archer before a target. He is not pleased to miss the mark. But let us place our contention before these fair friends, shall we, Epameinondas?

—Do so, to our honor, Simmias said. We were already dividing up into Pythagoreans and Sokratics to when you came along. This is turning into a symposium to be remembered.

He made a sign over his head to Simmiké as Theanor began. His voice was as level and certain as if he were reading from a book.

—After the cruel revolution which broke up and scattered the Pythagorean cities, and after Kylon, our common enemy, had surrounded the last surviving Pythagorean school, the one at Metapontion, and set fire to it, burning our master alive and all his disciples except the striplings Philolaos and Lysis, who boldly leapt through the flames, we were so many exiles and outlaws where but months before we had been counselors and arkhons, teachers and soldiers.

My father leaned forward with grief. He could never quite grasp the horrible thoroughness of the persecution of the Pythagoreans in Italy.

—Burned alive!

—Philolaos, Theanor went on, escaped to Leukania and from there joined us in exile. We began slowly to regain our positions in spite of Kylon. For a long time we had no news of Lysis. Finally Gorgias of Leontini, who had been on an embassy to Greece, was able to tell our new master Aresas that he had seen and talked with Lysis, who was of course here in Thebai. Aresas was so moved by the discovery of the other disciple who was with the Master at the last that he proposed to come to Boiotia himself, but at his age and in poor health he was clearly unequal to it. So he charged us to make the journey and bring Lysis back if alive, his remains if dead.

—Soon after the discovery, you well know, all Italy was a turmoil of wars and insurrections, and to attempt so long a journey across battlefields was certain death. And then the daimon of Lysis appeared to us, a ghost of breathtaking beauty, the naked Patroklos in his fifteenth year or Apollo Ephebe, and said *Lysis and I are now in the asphodel meadows of the moon: we have eaten the ambrosia: the master of the universe has kissed us: the years are sweet.*

—We then had word from travellers that Lysis had lived with a noble family in snowy Boiotia, under the mountain Teumessos, in the city of Kadmos, Oidipos, and the holy Antigone. From another traveller we learned the name Polymnis, and from another the glad news that Lysis had been enrolled among the citizens of Thebai as godfather to two boys of great virtue and prowess, Epameinondas and Kaphisias. It is like a dream that I sit among them now. So it was thought fitting that I, a young man, should come to Thebai with gold donated by our oldest members, a recompense to speak for what is in our hearts.

His style was like his dress: something on the stage. My father was in tears when he finished speaking, his head high in pride of the moment, his cheeks as wet as a child's.

Epameinondas turned to me with a mischievous smile.

— Are we to lose our poverty, Kaphisias, without a word of protest?

I had caught the stranger's style and got off a phrase of Homer:

— Let us protest, I said. *The dear and best nurse of the young* is for you to defend, elder brother.

Which set off Epameinondas' merriment.

— I had but one defense, Father, that our virtue and our poverty are inextricably twined, and I saw but one objection to that, that Kaphisias could use the gold to dress himself in finery to please his growing number of lovers, and spend it as well on food to keep him beautifully muscular for the wrestling floor. But you have heard him refuse the gold, so presumably he is sure of his lovers in plain dress and does not expect to go hungry. How then can we use the gold? Shall we leaf over our swords and gild our shields? Shall we buy you, Father, a Milesian mantle and Mother a tunic of Sidonian purple? Or shall we accept it openly as a burden, like an unbid guest to whom we have to be nice?

— The gods keep us, my son! Father said. I had not hoped to live to see us *rich*. That would be a thievery of our work, our quiet, our certainty that our friends are our friends. There are purses with many friends who are indifferent and hateful to their owners.

— So be it, Epameinondas said. We decline, dear Theanor, to be the recipients of a favor that to us can be no favor.

— We cannot accept the gold, Father said.

— We are all of the same opinion, I said somewhat unnecessarily.

— It will help you, Theanor, Epameinondas said, to know some family history. Just recently, when Iason of Thessaly offered me a great sum of gold, I was, I'm afraid, boorish to him, and in public. I told him that his offer was like the first slap of a quarrel. I also showed him that he was tempting with sheer lust of gold an independent citizen of a free country. But to you, esteemed Theanor, I hope I am not so rude. We are delighted, we are honored by your gift, but it is like medicine offered to a man in good health. We have no reason to take it.

—Poverty, he said, as if reciting a well-memorized speech, is regarded by most people as an enemy. To us she is a divinity, the best-loved member of the family. She is our teacher.

—But, Theanor said with some heat, it is absurd to confuse the deliberate amassing of wealth and the acceptance of a gift.

—It would indeed be an absurd confusion, Epameinondas replied, if our refusal were not rational.

—I hope I will not be answered like the Thessalian if I ask if it is proper to give money, as surely it must be when we give to the poor and friends in need, but not proper to accept it?

—Of course it is proper to give and to receive, Epameinondas said, but not always. Sometimes, as now, a gift handsomely and generously offered is more valuable for not being accepted. Will you follow my argument if I try to present it lucidly?

—Gladly, Theanor said, a kind of stiffness in his voice.

I listened impatiently to the argument, which Lysis had taught me as well as Epameinondas. There are many objects of desire, and therefore many desires. Some are born with us, hunger, yearning, and pride of place, and some are of the foolishness of the world, such as the desire to eat off silver plates. Desire is a wild horse to be tamed. Virtue is habit long continued. The taming of desire is like the training of an athlete. Discipline is not the restraint but the use of energy.

—For training and the reason for training are ultimately the same thing, are they not? Epameinondas asked. The practise of continence is continence itself. Virtue cannot be summoned when needed, it must be permanently in the fabric of the soul. You know the Pythagorean practise of exercising in the palaistra until you have the appetite of a wolf in winter. Then you strigil down, jog to the river though you are tired to dropping, and swim across and back, across and back. You trot home the longest possible way about, and you appear at the table for dinner. Your portion is lamb roasted in herbs, onions heaped white in a barley sauce, dandelions cooked for hours in a chine of pork, bread freshly baked, a slab of goat's cheese, a bowl deep with hot wine. You adhere to the discipline and call in the stableboy to eat your portion while you watch, only afterwards eating instead porridge and cold water. When I forbid myself what I may have, no man is going to tempt me with what is truly forbidden.

I appreciated Epameinondas' translation of the voluptuous temptations into food, a decent enough argument for a noble stranger, who would have blushed at Epameinondas' fiercer struggles with the flesh. When Pelopidas gave away his inheritance out of great love for Epameinondas he was scarcely prepared for his first lessons in discipline, and had his immediate troubles with sloth, which at that time was uppermost in Epameinondas' war against chaos, as he called it. He had given up sleeping even in our hard beds, and was trying to give up sleep itself. He took the dogs for his model, sleeping curled up in the yard for a while at a time. He slept under the table, under bushes in a driving rain. Pelopidas imitated his every gesture, taking the hounds' faithfulness and adoration as his model, as Epameinondas took their stamina for his, their disregard for furniture and their indifference to the weather.

But the dogs were a poor model for chastity, which was the other hard deprivation to which Pelopidas, following Epameinondas, gave his most agonized efforts. They knew every muscle in each other's body from the wrestling floor, and to my young mind each body was but a *korykos* for the other, and a new mystery was disclosed to my delighted eyes one summer afternoon when with a light in his eye and an honest smile he closed his hand around my brother's *didymoi*, as *kolythrophilarpax* as the *gymnastes*. There was mouse scurry in the tortoises of the *madzos*, a playful *gnyx*. *Tetlathi O makrothyme philé,* Epameinondas said. I had the feeling that I was one too many in the back loft where we three boys slept together, even though we were as frank as goats in our randy play.

Pelopidas in his lascivious tantrums would plead with Epameinondas to be friendlier, by Hermas Korophilos, to have some mercy, by Eros and Anteros, by Artemis Philomeirax. Epameinondas was not always willing to go to Father or to Lysis to learn the exact discipline of friendship, and I think he made lots of it up.

Like watching the stableboy eat his meal to teach his stomach that it was not his will, he would stand *myrrhinon* to *myrrhinon* with Pelopidas, *Aiai!* There would be *kheirourgia* in the night until Epameinondas would drop nimbly out our window and trot across the meadows to the river. When we caught up with him he would be swimming upstream, the moonlight picking out for us shoulder and heel.

He would swim to exhaustion while Pelopidas and I sat with the one old khlamys around us, fascinated by this pigheaded stubbornness against a little pleasure. He never shied from an affectionate arm, or stopped Pelopidas when the god Eros butted in his scrotum and burned stars in his eyes.

Years later, when Epameinondas and Pelopidas led the Sacred Theban Band, every infantryman of which was bound to a friend by whom he fought, this chastity remained his peculiar contempt of our mortality.

THE MAN WHO HAS TRAINED HIMSELF TO WANT NOTHING, EPAMEINONDAS was saying, cannot be bribed by friends, kings, or fortune herself.

—Desire is a rebellion against reason. To remain steadfast against all desire and its lures is a discipline that can admit no exceptions. We have none of us achieved that perfection of discipline. Our poverty is but a compromise with necessity, our certainties are beset by doubt. We therefore plead, Kaphisias and I, that this stranger bearing gifts have the grace of understanding to see that all we hold to be excellent, all that we strive for, would be threatened by a bounty of gold which we do not need and do not want and would have to break the discipline of our lives to accept.

Theanor the stranger threw up his hands, as if in surprise that his gift could elicit such a speech.

I had my speech, too, if I had been asked. I wanted to repeat what Father and Lysis had taught me and which I had grown up to find true, for unlike so many of my agemates I had never thought my parents fools. I would have said, as I had said to the cow and the calf, the goats and the chickens in the Areos Pagos of the barnyard, that our poverty meant that the bread in our mouths had been sown in furrows dug with our own hands, and that the wood for the fire that baked it had been carried on our backs. Our clothes were from sheep we had shepherded, the wool shorn, carded, spun, and woven by our mother.

Be your own slave, Father taught us, and you and another man are free. A family, Lysis liked to say, is a city in small. Its members must be many kinds of citizens, from judge to gardener. He himself took delight in a slave's work, sweeping the floors with a besom which he had beautifully and carefully made. All, he explained, is parallel. The hoplites drive the barbarians from the limits with the same care I must take to sweep trash across the floor. Our tasks differ in degree but not in dignity. Should any man be ashamed to do well what must be done?

In the palaistra it was known that when the wrestling was over, Epameinondas, Pelopidas, and I would go away to draw water, split kindling, milk the cow, and pen the goats. Rather more awfully, they had some half-understood knowledge that we would then do mathematics in the ashes by the fire.

SIMMIAS WAS TO HAVE DECIDED WHETHER WE WOULD ACCEPT THE GOLD, BUT he weaseled out with fine sophistry. He praised the nobility and commitment of Theanor's long journey, he praised Father for having raised such splendid sons, and he praised Epameinondas for his devotion to philosophy and its discipline.

—But I must leave this matter to be settled among yourselves. Your understanding of it is deeper than I could pretend to.

And turning to Theanor:

—We are neglecting half the significance of your visit to Thebai. Is it lawful in your religion for us to know whether you shall remove the bones of Lysis to Italy, or whether you shall allow him to be our guest even in death? He will find us good neighbors still when we come to be with him there.

—He is to remain here, Theanor smiled. Epameinondas has seen to that. In Italy we could not know how he had been buried, whether the cock had been paid to Asklepios, the soul sent on its way with the proper rites, or whether he was still in need of certain observances. I sacrificed at the grave when I arrived, and slept beside it. In a dream I heard the words *Touch not, move not,* and I knew that the burial had been right, and that Lysis' soul has already been judged.

—When I found Epameinondas this morning, he continued with a formal bow toward my brother, I learned that the strictest Pythagorean rules had been observed in the burial, and I realized that Lysis had kept his daimon throughout his life, guiding him like a skilled pilot to the end.

Theanor looked at Epameinondas with a frank eye, as if seeing his beauty for the first time, and as if, after all, he had to stand in awe of his character.

—The daimons lead a few men only, he said, but those few men lead the world.

Kharon, I noticed, had returned, and was standing in the corner by the door.

The Daimon of Sokrates 67

— The mundane must intrude, Simmias said apologetically. I see that the doctor has come to change the bandages on my poor leg.

Simmiké with a bowl of hot water and a length of cheese cloth followed the doctor through the room.

— Let us give physician and patient some privacy, Theokritos said, rising, and we followed his example.

Kharon caught my eye and indicated that I was to follow him. Theokritos, too, got the same sign, and we found Phyllidas with a face as white as wool in the courtyard. The snow was sticking to the columns and the summer seats.

— What has happened, Phyllidas?

Theokritos' mouth was open with alarm.

— Nothing I had not expected, he said bitterly.

Then I saw Hippostheneidas behind him looking miserable, like a man who has been told to keep out of the way.

— I warned you about Hippostheneidas here, he said, and anger made his voice go high. I told you he was a coward with the liver of a doe, and I begged you all not to tell him of the plan.

Kharon looked over his shoulder to see that we were alone.

Hippostheneidas doubled his fists. He was a man beset.

— Damn you! he said in his teeth. Will you not understand that I want the exiles to return, that I want our freedom. All I see, though, is idiot brashness and the half-baked intentions of hot heads. You have an uncoordinated bunch of silly idealists waiting for a dozen boys, if that many, and you call this an army of rebellion. The Spartans will laugh as they tie us up for the dungeon.

— How many men do you think are with us?

— I know of about thirty.

— Thirty *men,* Phyllidas said. And you take it upon yourself to thwart, to trip up the plan in which thirty men are to fight, and have no way of knowing that you have with incredible arrogance changed the plan? *Herakleis lakkoskheas!* Theokritos, Kharon, Kaphisias, do you know what he has done? He has sent a mounted rider into the hills to warn the exiles away!

— For today, Hippostheneidas said miserably, for today. I did not say the rebellion was off.

— Today, Phyllidas said, despair in his voice, today is the only day on which we have a dog's chance!

— You hog's prick! Kharon said, his eyes cold as mountain wind. What have you done to us?

— I've done nothing, Hippostheneidas said. If you will quit backing me to the wall and listen to a man as responsible as yourselves, I'll explain what I've done. If you want to be heroes, the day is before you. Straddle your big balls and draw your swords. I'm with you. Let us kill and be killed, but now, while there is enough of the day to do it by. But let us have none of this childish getting of a few old farts drunk and cutting their throats while they are in their cups.

— *What,* his voice pitched and his fists rose to his beard, what are you going to do with the fifteen hundred Spartan infantrymen in Arkhias' bodyguard? They will be stone-cold sober. And why Arkhias? Are you going to kill him simply because by coincidence there was a party planned for him this evening? Lysanoridas has gone to Haliartos, on some idiot business about opening graves, but Herippidas and Arkesos will be at headquarters like two hornet's nests waiting for the slightest prod. Why must we blunder into the fall of their net? Why, I ask you, by the ears of the Lord of Death?

He knotted his fist at his cheeks and narrowed his eyes.

— You have thrown your plans together like children playing Saians and the Border Guard, armed with fishing poles and wearing baskets for helmets. You don't know, do you, by Zeus, that for the last two days the *phalanggai* at Thespia have had orders to doubletime to the Kadmeia in full armor at a moment's notice! Their officers keep the saddles on their horses. The sparks of the whetstones sharpening swords made the barracks street bright as day all of a night.

We looked at each other. Was this rumor? What if it were true? Hippostheneidas popped his hands together. He was getting beside himself.

— What's more, he went on, they are going to kill Aphitheus this afternoon. This very afternoon. They would have done it already but that Arkhias had to see Lysanoridas off to Haliartos. He will watch the execution as soon as he gets back to the Kadmeia. Is this not, I ask you, is this not their way of saying that they know, that they are prepared for our wrestling-school tactics?

None of us spoke.

— An ox sacrificed to Demeter this morning would not burn on the altar. And yesterday, O Kharon, I met your friend from the country Hypatodoros, Erianthes' son. He dreamed, Kharon, that your house was in labor! It heaved and bellowed and burst into flames, which spread from house to house, until all Thebai was on fire, the Kadmeia hidden by a cloud of smoke. Not until I learned awhile ago that the exiles are coming to your house did so crazy a dream make sense. We are walking to our ruin.

—But, Theokritos said, stepping between Kharon and Hippostheneidas, I like that dream! The fire is our rebellion, the smoke of which chokes the evil in the Kadmeia. As for the inauspicious sacrifice, remember that the altar is the state's. The Theban state, do not forget, is under house arrest, and it is somewhere on the slopes of Teumessos making its way toward us with sharpened swords. It is in our hearts.

—Who, I thought to say to Hipposetheneidas, did you send on horseback into the hills?

—You could never catch him, Kaphisiarion. It is Melon's crack charioteer, the best horseman in Thebai. Melon was one of the first of us.

—Khlidon, you mean? I said.

—Khlidon's the man.

—He must indeed be the fastest rider ever. When did you send him?

—Just before coming here to tell you.

—But, I said with a smile, Khlidon has been standing in the courtyard door over there for half the time we've been talking.

He turned like a man slipping on ice.

—Herakleis! he said.

Khlidon walked toward us as slowly as a scolded child.

KHLIDON HAD BEEN WAITING IN AN ECSTASY OF IMPATIENCE, AS HE DID NOT know if Hippostheneidas was among men who were of the revolt.

—What in the name of Zeus has happened?

Khlidon spoke in shame, looking at his feet.

—When you gave me my orders, I went home for my horse. I couldn't find my bridle. My wife and I looked for it everywhere. She was only pretending to look, the slut, as she knew all the time she lent it yesterday to the wife of a neighbor, who is shiftless enough to borrow rather than have anything repaired. I guess I called her some names, and she started in on her hexing, spitting, and making signs in the air. So I popped her around the legs with the whip, more than I ought, I suppose, as the whole buggering street came in. I pushed one old maia into the washtub, and bloodied some noses and kicked some butts before I could get out the door. You'll have to send somebody else.

He was confused by our looks of relief.

— Here are the signs from the gods! Theokritos said with gusto. How does it feel, dear Hippostheneidas, to be an instrument of heaven?

— God help us, he said.

Kharon made haste to go home, as did Phyllidas. Their work was cut out for them.

— Go sharpen your sword, Hippostheneidas, Theokritos said almost gaily. Kaphisias and I must detach Epameinondas from the philosophical orgy going on inside.

Simmias was finishing a speech when we slipped in. His leg lay in a snowy new bandage, and the light of the braziers had been supplemented by odd Egyptian oil lamps. He was saying that he had once asked Sokrates directly about the matter of his daimon, and had received no answer. But he could say that Sokrates thought visionaries for the most part imposters, tending to place credence in people who heard voices.

— The daimons, Simmias said, speak to us all. The large part of us know these messages as dreams, unskilled as we are in interpreting them. Only men who know how to listen heed the voices of the daimons while awake. We are distracted by our petty concerns, our ambitions, our selfishness, our passions. The great end of Sokrates' subduing of the human traffic, so to speak, in his mind, was precisely to be attuned to the voice of the daimon when it came. In that cocked head and frozen stance you could see his rapt attention to the will of heaven.

He spoke of the physics of hearing, of sound waves through the density of air, vibrant eardrums, and got into the immensely difficult explanation of how the soul, an immaterial thing, can cause a finger to crook, a leg to step, an eyelid to bat.

— It is our ignorance of the range of a process, Simmias said, that keeps us from seeing the infinitely fine articulation of the world. Stand a bronze shield on the ground and with your fingertips on its rim you can hear the adze of miners far below. Your teeth on a knife stuck in the earth can hear distant hoofbeats when the ear hears silence only. The air, indeed all of nature, is vibrant. We detect the twang of things when we find the medium that rings in response to, or in sympathy with, a particular quaver. Sokrates was a man who had tuned his soul, as a lyre player tunes the strings of his instrument. I find it wholly plausible and thoroughly scientific, that he could understand voices too subtle for the untuned ear. For we are not to admit, are we, that the gods are dumb, or that they have no interest in men?

— Life would indeed be absurd and futile, Theanor said.

— My other information about daimons belongs to the realm of poetry, or myth, Simmias said, and cannot be offered as evidence in our discussion. It is an account of a vision which Timarkhos of Khaironeia had. I shall someday work it into one of my Pythian dialogues as a curiosity.

— But you must tell it to us! Theokritos cried. You cannot show us the tag on the scroll this way and drop it back into the jar. Who, in any case, is this Timarkhos? If I've heard the name I cannot remember it.

— Timarkhos, Simmias said, settling himself into his cushions, was the devoted companion of Sokrates' son Lamprokles.

— Back to Sokrates! Pheidolaos said, leaning forward to warm his hands at a brazier.

— He is known only for the vision which you have asked to hear about. He has no other distinction.

— We would hear of the vision, Theanor said in a formal voice, as if he were a judge asking for testimony.

— Timarkhos was young and eager, quite a keen and promising student of philosophy. He conceived the idea that nothing less than the arduous demands of the Trophonian Oracle would reveal anything about daimons. He consulted me and Kebes. We saw no harm in his going to Lebadeia to descend into the cave.

— A deep place, I believe, Theokritos said, with the tomb of Trophonios in its depths.

— He found the tomb, Simmias said. In fact he was in the cave for two days and the better part of a third. We became quite anxious about him, and were mightily relieved when he returned. The wonderful thing was the radiance of his face. You know the reputation of the Trophonian Oracle, how it always depresses its supplicants. Not Timarkhos, who was giddy with elation. He bathed and sacrificed to the god. After an extensive meal he told us what he had experienced.

— So dense was the dark when he got to the tomb that he seemed to be awake in sleep, with a different feeling of weight and touch. He expressed this strange feeling as being alive in a way not his own. There was a pressure in his ears, a rich euphoria in his limbs. He lay down and gave himself up to the dark.

— He felt a voluptuous fatigue, that peace which comes with rest and stillness after long work, a melting drowsiness. He was certain that his eyes were open when he saw a dot of light. Had a firefly got into the cave? Then there was another point, another, and another. He remembered smiling with the recognition that the first four fiery specks defined a square, a very familiar square, he knew, as other points appeared to its right and left. It was the constellation Pegasos, with Andromeda above and the Water Bearer below. The Fish with their umbilicus and field appeared, the Bull, the Hunter, the Snake, and the Swan.

— The equatorial ring of the Animals belted him around, and the fire river of the Way arched over him. He found the Wanderers, and saw spirals of purest blue, of poppy red, of heliotrope mingled with green. There were clouds of coral dust that seemed to boil like autumn thunderheads, and wisps of yellow wrack.

— He saw the southern polestar in the great globe of the heavens. Strangest of all, he saw a long cone of black shadow out across space. *That is the Styx,* a voice said. *To you it is the shadow of the earth cast by the Sun, your star. See how this shadow streaming to its vertex lies on the moon for most days of the month. The moon is your earth's dead sister Persephone.*

— *Who are you?* Timarkhos asked. He felt no fear. The familiar kindliness of the voice was like that of a parent.

— *I am a daimon. I can tell you of the four things in your realm, life, motion, birth, death. They are a chain, a unity. Life, the first link, is joined to the second, motion, on the invisible shell of the celestial sphere. The second is joined by mind to the third, birth, in the Sun, and the third to the fourth by nature in the moon.*

— The daimon explained that the dead inhabit the moon, Persephone's antirealm. In the great serene lake which we can see, the souls of the wicked are cleansed by remorse and suffering until they pass through the straits on the awful lunar desert which always faces the earth to the other hemisphere of the moon which forever faces the stars. This unseen portion is named Elysion. From there the dead, who have completed their earthly life with its complement death, return to the earth to speak through the oracles, to hover at rites, to caution the wayward, and to enter the hearts of men sore of spirit in the gore of battle or white with fear on raging seas.

— *You see the daimons without knowing it,* the voice said to Timarkhos. Timarkhos saw only the starry skies. *Know,* the daimon said, *that*

*every soul is rational. When a soul enters a body, partaking of its pas-
sions and hungers, it mixes in varying degrees with the carnal. Some souls
sink deep into flesh, some leave some part above, like the buoy that floats
a fishnet. This free part of the soul is its daimon. The best daimon is one
which is reflected in the flesh like an image in a mirror. Now, Timarkhos,
look among the stars: do you not see many which are dead? Moons, they
seem, and cinders, and great pitted spheres of ashen rock? These are
bodies which have drowned their daimons in matter. In comets and me-
teors you see souls cleansing themselves of their gross element. In the
bright stars you see souls which have the governance of their bodies, for
the flesh is a stallion and the soul is its rider.*

— Thus, as the daimon explained to Timarkhos, the world is one
animal, one vast but unified liveliness in the mind of god. The stars are
pictures of the world below, each star an intelligence which is in a body.
The world is daimon and matter, soul and flesh, seeking a just proportion
the one with the other, seeking the beauty of measured motion.

Simmias ended with his hands open, as if to show that he had no
more to give.

— Is this true? Pheidolaos asked.

— Perhaps, Simmias said. I myself take it as a myth from the imagination of a young man. It was only after Timarkhos' death that Sokrates
heard of this vision, and he regretted that he had not heard it before. He
wished, he said, that he could have heard it from Timarkhos himself.

He turned to Theokritos.

— There, he said, you have the myth you asked for. Has our guest
Theanor of Sikelia heard it with interest? Can he shed light upon it?

The stranger lifted his arm and staff toward Epameinondas.

— We hold the same doctrines, Epameinondas and I. It would give me
pleasure to hear his interpretation of this vision. He is familiar with its
symbols.

An awkward smile was all we got, a word almost spoken, a nervous
clasping and unclasping of a hand on a thigh.

— It is his way, Father said with a generous smile. He really does not
like to talk, do you, Epameinondas? He will listen forever, and read forever, and he *can* talk: you have heard him defend our poverty. When
Spintharos the Tarantine was here, he said that he had never seen a boy
with more learning and fewer words. So, dear Stranger, we will hear your
interpretation after all.

— The myth is sacred, the stranger began. I shall not profane it with an interpretation. I hope that it has been written out on stone or brass and dedicated to the god. Simmias' preliminary remarks will serve as interpretation enough, if I may add a word. I have always found it strange that men readily see the divine in an extraordinary horse, in birds and bulls and mountain lions. And yet we seem to be blind to the divinity in certain men. We know the best of dogs, but not the best of men. In fact, the best of men can usually be found ruled by rascals and scoundrels.

There were furtive glances.

— How quickly we perk up our ears to the king's trumpets! A bonfire on a hill engages the curiosity of a whole city. These are examples, are they not, of men signaling to men? For men are solicitous of men, whether through benevolence or the grandeur of ruling them. The gods are solicitous of men and speak to them with signs and through dreams, and through those skilled souls which have been released from the flesh and washed with fire, the beings whom we are agreeing this afternoon to call daimons.

— The wonder of the daimons is that they are both human and divine. They know our hearts as the undying gods never can. They understand the world as an old athlete understands a young one. And like the old athlete they are only interested to bring their superior skill to a skill already developed, for they cannot interfere in stubbornness and indifference. They are like men on shore who can help a man drowning only when he has come close enough to be reached. They are the teachers of teachers, the philosophers of philosophers, the rulers of rulers.

He ended grandly, with a finger held up in admonition for us all. Father looked about him, to see that we appreciated the nobility of his guest. Simmias nodded gravely.

The room had filled with shadows, and the snow was falling in earnest. The stranger looked more foreign than ever, an actor dressed to impersonate Teiresias in a play, or a poet from Athenai or Korinthos who might ask about our nightingales or the stone chair of Manto.

— What honor you bring us! Epameinondas said.

— What honor I shall be able to take back to Italy, the stranger Theanor said with a courtly bow. For it is better than a military conquest, this outpost of our learning which has taken hold with such health here in Boiotia. It is ever the lucklessness of tyrants that they usually achieve the opposite of their brutal and clumsy designs. Our persecution in Italy sent

Lysis to these mountains. Trampling the garden down merely scattered the seeds.

—Blessed, Father said, be the will of the gods.

—Kaphisias, Epameinondas said, rising, they will be expecting you at the gymnasium. Off with you, or your friends will be desolate and the coach will give you thirty laps around the track.

—*Tauta prattomen,* I said, giving his khlamys a tug.

—I, for one, by the knees of Delia, Theokritos said, must be on my way.

—And I, Galaxidoros said. A word with you outside, if I may, Epameinondas?

We said our farewells while throwing on our cloaks. At the outer door of the peristyle Theokritos, Galaxidoros, and I gathered around Epameinondas.

—We must know, Galaxidoros said quietly.

—Gorgidas and I have friends ready, Epameinondas said. We intend to watch closely. If we see the need, we will be your reserves. My conscience will not allow me to fight at the outset. I see the splendor but not the justice of what you are doing.

—You know your own mind best, Theokritos said.

—There's this also, Nondaki added, that when it comes to choosing a new government, as Zeus grant it will, is it not of some importance to have men in our party who did not fight in the revolt, whose candidacy will be free of the charge that they forced their way into office?

—True, I suppose, Galaxidoros said.

—There are as many tyrants in Boiotia as in Sparta.

Nondaki said this with a smile.

I RAN TO THE GYMNASIUM THROUGH THE SNOW, MY HEAD FULL OF DAIMONS. O daimons of deer and bear, I prayed, be with us. Daimon of Lysis, enter Nondaki.

Lysis! The mules of the stranger from Italy would have come through the rising mists of the gloaming yesterday, on the forest road from Attika. He would already have found people who could tell him where Lysis was buried. He must have made out the stele in the last of the light, the athlete with his hand on the boy's head, the dove in the boy's hands, the crown of wild olive. *Koina ta philon einai kai philían isoteta.*

And Damo was seeing the exiles, she and Getaki. She would watch them without being seen, as when lacing on my sandal at their house I might feel her eyes peering from the doorpost behind me. Fast as I might turn, she would not be there. I have seen those eyes in the leaves of a rosebush, in the handle of a wine jar, in the laurels by our bathing place on the Ismene.

Daimon of Herakleis, stride amongst us! How many times have I remembered as I sprang down the old stairs to the track, starting the lizards from their sunny place on the wall or felt as now the chill tickle of snow across my face, that the young Herakleis had leapt down these same steps, walked in this dust, fitted his long feet into the same stone at the head of the track. He came here as a child with his earthly father Amphitryon an exile from Tiryns the sister city of Mykinai in Argos.

A trumpet sharp as a silver flute in the tricks of its upper register and as resonant in its low tones as the ring of a hammer against a shield of mountain copper suddenly clamored in the cold air. A sergeant's Spartan voice outbrayed it, the elate roll of a drum, and the stamp of boots across crunched snow. It was the Kadmeian detail doubletiming to the change of the guard, a horsy gallop in their drums.

I nipped around them.

With a shiver I realized that Lopi was perhaps already in the city, his cloak across his face. Nondaki must have thought about him all day.

I had my clothes off as I sprinted through the door to the ephebeion, where the coach was pairing off teams. My friend Glaukos tossed me his oil bottle. I had oiled my shoulders and arms by the time the coach noticed me, with a knowing glance at my hair, which was covered with snow.

After the dark room and the solemn talk I needed to wrestle until I was aware again that I had knees and elbows, hands and feet. The old men were on their benches along the wall, and the Spartans had their tolerant looks on their bony faces.

Wrestling was one of the sore places between us and the dour Lakedaimonians, for it was an exercise with rules, three throws and the game is over. Such is the way the judges at Elis have agreed upon for Olympia. But the Spartans do not like a game in which the defeated concedes that he has lost. It seems to them to be giving up, even though there are four more agons. Three bouts out of five, and the game is yours.

So they wrestle grudgingly in our gymnasium, for the exercise, as they say. They really want to break fingers, and stomp on feet, though our coaches will get them by the ear if they do, and march them dancing with pain to the door.

I took on Glaukos and got thrown straightaway.

— Where's your mind? he said.

— Here! I shouted, squaring my shoulders and sucking my belly in like a greyhound.

We circled, eyes twinking, hopping on our toes. I gave him an arm to dive for, hooked him back of the knee, and strongarmed him off balance. Then I dove into him, wriggling him into the dust. He got a shin across my midrift and heaved me up, but I had a shoulder into his guzzle before he knew it, and he was pinned. Face to face, I made with my lips the shape of the word *tonight*.

Then I was paired with a tall Spartan who wore neither a hairband nor a foreskin toggle. He threw me so hard on my back that I had to wait for my breath to sift back down from midair into my open mouth. He looked disgusted.

He let me throw him the next go, just to show me that I couldn't pin him even when I had him down.

— Draw! the coach said. Adding that we were mismatched, anyway, and gave us new agonists.

When we were warmed up, we practised breaking holds, attacks, backward kicks, feints. Aristolaos and I took time about breaking a neckhold. Strung between gravity and my neck in the vise of his elbow, I heard the word *tonight* before I slammed my heels into his kidneys. I winked at him as we lay tumbled in the dust, to indicate that I knew what he meant.

Pinned and with Glaukos holding me down, I heard him whisper, *look*. Two men were walking through the palaistra in elegant shoes and leggings. One was Arkhias, who had been for a rubdown and bath. He was back, then, from seeing Lysanoridas on his way to Haliartos. Surely he was not going to Amphitheos' execution dressed like that!

The other was Philippos, who was in finery enough for a wedding.

Glaukos nipped out to the door and was back before the coach missed him.

— They're going direct to the party, he hissed in my ear while seeming to be wrenching my arm across my back.

— To Phyllidas', I whispered back.

He tightened the hold on my arm.

— No names.

The coach clapped for the end of practise, gave his criticism of things to work on, punched some bellies that he suspected of being less hard than a plank, chucked the chins of his favorites, and sent us to the baths. We strigilled with our usual mischief and din, tried drowning each other in the cold pool, and helped each other with winding our hair back into place.

It was full dark when Glaukos and I came out into a stiff wind and whirling snow.

— Are you scared? Glaukos asked. It was a frank, friendly question.

— There isn't going to be time to be scared, I said.

— Pappas says that only a fool isn't afraid.

— I'm scared, I said.

But I was too foolish to be scared. I was half out of my mind with excitement, simply because something extraordinary was about to happen, something that would dye the whole fabric of our lives.

On my way to Kharon's, where I had the permission of neither my father or Epameinondas to go, I thought mainly of Pelopidas whom we had not seen since the coming of the Spartans. Walking in the deepening snow, I remembered the first time I saw him.

It was a summer's day. Epameinondas had let me come along with him on one of his crazy rambles that he would take as the notion struck him, whether in the shank of night, to hear owls, letting dawn find him far upriver in a larchwood on the mountain, or in the ripe of afternoon, still unwinded from the palaistra. We all learned to spot the mood. He would straddle the hitchpole and look at the grain of the log as if he needed to puzzle out its pattern, or watch an ant struggling through the hairs on the back of his hand.

On this particular ramble, which was just before Pelopidas came to be our honorary brother and to live at our house, we were shindeep in gorse yellow with blossoms and black with bees.

I cannot say for sure that Epameinondas had not agreed to meet Pelopidas. More than likely, it was one of those meetings that happen when two people are just becoming friends. Fate, or the daimons, seem to bring them together with the goldenest luck. However it came about, here was a tall, fair boy I had never seen but whom Epameinondas seemed to know. They met with the smiles of the holy *kouroi,* shaking hands with a kind of grown-up formality. He even shook *my* hand.

We walked all afternoon, as aimlessly as goats, talking about everything in the world. I saw the depth of the friendship when Epameinondas said *O well,* kindly, to Pelopidas' cheerfully admitting that he scarcely knew one number from another. Once we stopped and made a tetrahedron out of straws, using hog plums for the joints. We did theorems in the river sand.

We talked wrestling, horses, javelins, boxing, archery, bridles, stone bruises, sheep, mountains, boils, vintages, hoopoes, physiques, ash spears, ghosts, and green apples.

The next day he brought me a bird's nest with three brown speckled eggs in it, and Father made him take it back and put it in the tree from which he stole it.

Once they were away all night. Pelopidas brought me a baby owl to make it up to me. And the next time they spent the night on the mountain they took me with them.

Rough, old Lysis said of Pelopidas. *But he has met the granite against which he is to be polished.*

Lysis died. Epameinondas and Pelopidas were impressed into the army of the League to fight the Arkadians. The Spartans took our city with a speech.

I was at Kharon's gate.

The house was as dark as the night itself, except for a single rushlamp in a room toward the back.

A man was hidden at the door. With my heart thumping like a hare I said *the knees of Delia.* He said nothing.

— I am Kaphisias, I said. Epameinondas' younger brother.

— Slip in without any noise, he said.

The inside of the house was as tightly packed as an auction at the cattle market. The floors were wet with melted snow. It was difficult to make out faces in the half light, and many of the men wore charcoal smudges down their cheeks. I heard someone say Damokleidas' name, and when I asked if Pelopidas was there I was told that he was.

— Theokritos is consulting the omens, a stranger said to me. We are waiting to know.

Men were still arriving. The parties had broken up into twos at the ford of the Kithairon. Some were elated at seeing lightning in the sky on the right: certain good luck. Someone said that over forty of us were there. A wine jug went around, and long loaves from which men were tearing mouthfuls. The shuffle of booted feet and the clink of bronze were everywhere.

A pounding on the front door startled us all.

—*Herakleis!*

—*Mama ka' Koré!* an old woman moaned as she was pushed toward the door.

We withdrew from the front room as silently as we could, crowding backward. The pounding continued: someone who did not intend to go away.

—*Tis esti?* the old woman shouted as she opened the door, her lamp trembling and dancing her shadow on the wall.

—Business of the Kadmeia, a man said, entering.

Another followed, shaking snow from his shoulders. They were officers of Arkhias' guard.

Kharon came to meet them, a chaplet of leaves on his head, to show that he was at dinner after offering a sacrifice to the household gods.

The first officer saluted, bringing his short spear to attention.

—Sorry to break in on your supper, he said respectfully. I have orders from their lordships Arkhias and Philippos to bring you immediately to the Kadmeia.

—Whatever for? Kharon said as coolly as you please. Has something come up?

There couldn't have been a man there who did not admire his superb acting. We could hear his clear voice over all the house.

—I couldn't say, sir, the officer replied. Will you come with us?

—Let me just get into some street clothes and lay my chaplet aside, he said.

—It's getting quite nippy out, the officer said, as if to make conversation.

Then, wonderfully and miraculously, Kharon said:

—Why don't you go on? I'll be right behind. God knows what gossip there will be if people see me escorted to the citadel by two of the guard!

He even managed an authentic, hearty laugh.

—Fine, sir, the officer replied. As it happens, we have another order to deliver before we can go back.

— Excellent, Kharon called. I'll see you there!

After the door closed the silence was as solid as on a mountain top.

Galaxidoros was the first to speak.

— It is that pig Hippostheneidas! He tried to use Khlidon this afternoon to wreck the revolt, and you notice he is not here!

A general murmur broke out. *Nor is Khlidon here!* Some spoke of marching to the Kadmeia then and there. Swords slid from their scabbards. Men pleaded with others to lower their voices.

— Thebans!

Kharon's loud shout quieted us. He was dressed to go out. And beside him stood Getaki in all the handsomeness of his fifteen years. He had carried the lamb on his shoulders around the city wall that spring, chosen for his beauty from among us in the ephebeia. I had seen Epameinondas as naked as a god with the spring lamb on his shoulders, marching with the athlete's dignity to the sprightly hymn of the new sun, followed by the hooded priestesses with their arms full of first flowers, poppies and daffodils and curled ismenes, and he was surely the most splendid of the *moskhophoroi* but Damagetos with the snowy lamb across his shoulders was the loveliest.

His hair was the color of molten bronze, the tightly ringleted ephebaion as well, his shoulders wide, his hips as narrow as a boarhound's, his eyes bright flaxflower blue, his lips too rich to close fully. *A boy Pindaros ought to have seen,* the Hipparkh said on the day of walking the wall.

— You know my son, Kharon said. I want you to kill him.

No one breathed.

— I want you to kill him if I betray you to the Kadmeia. Show us no mercy whatever. I do not know why I am being called before Arkhias and Philippos. We all suspect that the plot has been found out. If this is my last word to you, I ask you to fight for our freedom to the death.

— Herakleis, Kharon! Theokritos came forward to say. Not a man here suspects you of betraying us. Besides, I have omens of the very best from the gods.

And then I saw Pelopidas. He made his way through the crowd to stand before Kharon and the handsome Damagetos.

— This boy should not even be here, Kharon, he said. Let us take him to safety at a neighbor's house. Let him be our pledge to the next generation if we fail. Let him be the one who is sure to live.

Athenai had not changed Pelopidas.

— No, never, Kharon said with conviction. Here he stays, with us. May he fight as your companion, dear Pelopidas? He is a man, and to-night he will seal his manhood, or be unworthy of it.

There were tears in older eyes, though Kharon seemed unmoved by what he had said, and took as many of our hands as he could reach before he hastened away.

I saw Damagetos admiring the blade of Pelopidas' long sword. I dared not come near, for fear Pelopidas would ask me where Epameinondas was. I did not have the patience to explain.

Meanwhile a newcomer had slipped in the back, Kephisodoros of Diogeiton, and was making a fuss. If Kharon had been called to the Kadmeia, he argued, we should disperse immediately and do what we could before the guard could get into formation.

— Good God! he cried. We are here like a swarm of bees! Ten guardsmen front and back could dispatch us like Olysses picking off the play-party that insulted his wife!

So we armed and disguised. There were men smearing their faces with rouge and purple eyepaint, slipping gaudy dresses over steel corselets and daggers. I had stashed my old infantry short sword there days before. Captains were checking their men. I was to go with the band to Phyllidas' house, where Arkhias was expecting a woman of a good family to join him. She was to arrive with a troup of revellers, in disguise.

— What, I asked Galaxidoros, if the revellers arrive before we do?

— There are no revellers, he said. You forget that Phyllidas thought all this up. The dear lady is at home with her family. She would be very much surprised to know that she is being waited for by a lecherous polemarkh at a private party.

— *Herakleis!* a shout rang out.

We froze.

It was Kharon, back already.

— There is nothing to fear! he said in a firm, glad voice. *They know nothing.*

— I've run all the way here, he gasped. Just let me get my breath.

He brushed snow from his great black beard, and sweat from his forehead.

— The guards took me to the party at Phyllidas'. Arkhias and Philippos are already as limber drunk as Bakkhos. *We have heard,* Arkhias said with his garland slipped down over one eye, *that the exiles have returned and are all at your house.* I somehow got my tongue to say: *What exiles? At my house? Am I to expect them or did they come and find me away? I'm asking you,* he said, *not you me. All I have is the report. You don't seem to know shit about it.*

There was appreciative laughter, whistles of disbelief.

— I said to him in as casual voice as I could command that it sounded like so much gossip. I remarked that when Androkleidas was around, this was the sort of thing you might believe, but not now, I said. The plans for a revolt growing out of the disaffected in Athenai had pretty well died out with the execution of Androkleidas, had they not?

— But, I said, *I will keep my ears open, if you wish me to, and report anything I hear to your lordship.*

— Phyllidas, as calm and interested as you please, said that I was an excellent choice of a spy to poke around and find things out. *There is nothing,* he said, if you can believe it, *there is nothing like knowing what is about to happen before it happens.* Arkhias nodded like a fool, and I was dismissed.

— Let us pray, O comrades! Theokritos said, and then let us fight.

We said the prayer to Demeter in time of trouble, the prayer before battle to Apollon, the prayer for life to Almighty Zeus.

Group by group we slipped out into the snow and the empty, dark streets. The groups assigned to Leontiades and Hypates went off together, Pelopidas, Damokleidas, and Kephisodoros among them.

I was with the party dressed as revellers which went gaily under torches to Phyllidas' house. Kharon and Melon were our leaders. They wore enormous, silly garlands of pine and silver fir. We had four apparent women with us, most whorish of gait, screaming and giggling. The guards we met laughed at us and shouted obscenities. We shouted back, happy drunks all.

It must have been just before this, we discovered next morning, that Arkhias was handed a letter by a special courier from Athenai. The letter, which we were the first to read, said that the exiles were returning and that the government could expect a daring attempt at a revolt. The rest of the letter was a list of forty-eight names. Had we needed it, we could have used it as a roll call before setting out.

Phyllidas told us next day how Arkhias had received the letter and tucked it under his cushion, calling for more drink. *Sir, it is a most urgent letter,* the courier had said. *All the more reason,* Arkhias had said, *not to read it at a party.*

WE WERE EXPECTED, THE SERVANT SAID AT THE DOOR. WOULD WE HANG UP our cloaks and join the party?

— Come in! Come in, dear friends! Phyllidas called to us, and Arkhias shouted his welcome.

The flutes and the tambourines rose in a melodious catch. Dancers in white masks jigged with their hands on their hips, as weightless as butterflies across a hedge.

At about this time Pelopidas was knocking at the door of Leontiades' darkened house. They came from Kallistratos in Athenai, they told the servant, and must see Leontiades immediately. He was not fooled and met them in his bedroom with a dagger. He stabbed Kephisodoros at the door and threw himself upon Pelopidas with fury. They fought at close quarters, slipping in the blood of Kephisodoros, who lay bleeding to death between them. The fighting was awful, as the hallway was dark, no one knew how to come to Pelopidas' help without hurting him. Finally there was a pitiful, hideous scream, and Pelopidas, himself cut deeply on the face and arms, shouted that he had killed Leontiades.

When a light was brought they saw that Kephisodoros was still alive. His eyes were open and he was trying to speak. They lifted away the slit and red body of Leontiades. Pelopidas held Kephisodoros' hand while he died, an anguished and startled look in his eyes.

At the same time another group of us got into Hypates' house with the same ruse. He, too, saw instantly what the callers meant, and climbed onto his roof. One of us was waiting for him on the roof of the next house as he jumped across, sinking a short sword to the hilt in his chest while he squealed like a pig.

I had not realized how swiftly it would all happen. Epameinondas and Gorgidas assembled their faction at the temple of Athena, which they lit brightly with many torches. Galaxidoros walked with authority to the dungeon in the Kadmeia and said that he came from Arkhias and Philippos with orders to release Amphitheos, against whom, he said cheerfully, there are no longer any charges.

— Show me your orders, the corporal of the guard said, and found three bronze spears at his throat.

When we made our way through diners on couches, there was no recognition whatever that we were not drunks and whores. But our business could be that of acting for a few seconds only, and Melon went straight across the room drawing a battle sword as he strode.

Arkhias, toward whom he was walking with such deliberateness, saw what he was about to do, and tried to rise from his cushions.

Kabirikhos, the magistrate appointed by the Spartans, said with perfect stupidity:

— What is Melon doing here? Why does he have his sword out?

Melon hacked downward into Arkhias' neck. A spurt of blood lept up in a splash.

I saw that every night for weeks when I tried to close my eyes to sleep. I did not see Arkhias again. I saw only Melon standing over a mess of bloody pillows swinging his sword down again and again, like a blacksmith beating on an anvil.

Someone gripped my arm, one of us by the gentleness of the hold, and pulled me back. I watched with disbelief while Philippos tried to fight Kharon with two heavy goblets. Kharon was patient with his womanly flailing, and bided his time. Then, as if to get it over quickly, he drove a knife into Philippos' side with a blow that would have staggered an ox.

Philippos fell into flowers and flagons, choking with pain and outrage.

We had got the other guests into another room, penning them in with spears across the door. They were unarmed and of no importance to us.

Kabirikhos, the fool, stood in a corner with the ritual spear, the badge of his office, which goes with him everywhere. It was not even a real spear, merely an ornate signum.

— Just put that down, please! Kharon said, as if to a child. Why do you think we would want to kill a lickspit like you? Live and enjoy the opinion of your fellow citizens.

— Don't come near me! he screamed. I'll kill the first man who comes near me!

Daimon or bravado suddenly in me, I lept over nimbly and grabbed the spear, pushing it up over my head.

— Turn loose, I said. It's tyrants we're ridding Thebai of, not kissers of Spartan butts.

Before I knew what had happened, Theopompos had run a sword through Kabirikhos' stomach, in and out again with the speed of an arrow.

I jumped back, startled, sickened.

Even faster than Theopompos, Theokritos jumped toward me and grabbed the sacred spear, which I was about to drop.

— This, he said, holding it at eye level like a javelineer, is the Theban symbol of justice. It goes with us to the Kadmeia, and Justice goes with us.

The streets were full of people with torches, but strangest of all the streets were full of women, decent family women who had never before been in the streets at night. They were shouting. They were singing.

When we reached the temple of Athena, which was as bright as day, a man was being handed up to the high propylaia, where my brother Epameinondas was already standing. He pulled the man up beside him, and I saw it was Amphitheos, still wearing his chains. The shout that went up must have echoed off the mountains and made the foxes and owls in the snow look toward Thebai, a city fiery with torches and loud with voices and skillets beaten against pans, with the bells of harnesses jingled by boys and old men, who shook them frantically in their hands.

I heard Getaki shouting my name. He was with the bloody Lopi, who hugged me with a shout. He took us forward, striding between us with his hands on our shoulders, to the square before the temple. The corpses of Leontiades and Hypates, we saw, had been thrown there. While we watched, four men heaved the body of Arkhias across them. I felt as if I had swallowed a mouthful of snow.

And then an old woman, a nurse or cook or grandmother, danced out to the heap of the slain, and decorously lifting her skirts and petticoats, began a lively jig. Other ancients joined her, gossips, fishmongers, and midwives in kerchiefs and shawls. Someone brought a lyre and played them a fine loud song to which they danced in a ring around the dead, laughing as if they were girls again.

The Trees at Lystra The Death of Picasso The
Daimon of Sokrates Christ Preaching at the
Henley Regatta Mesoroposthonippidon Lo Sple
ndore della Luce a Bologna Idyll On Some Lines
of Virgil The Trees at Lystra The Death of
Picasso The Daimon of Sokrates Christ Preach
ing at the Henley Regatta Mesoroposthonippi
don Lo Splendore della Luce a Bologna Idyll
On Some Lines of Virgil The Trees at Lystra
The Death of Picasso The Daimon of Sokrates
Christ Preaching at the Henley Regatta Mesoro
posthonippidon Lo Splendore della Luce a Bol
ogna Idyll On Some Lines of Virgil The Trees
at Lystra The Death of Picasso The Daimon of
Sokrates Christ Preaching at the Henley Rega
tta Mesoroposthonippidon Lo Splendore della

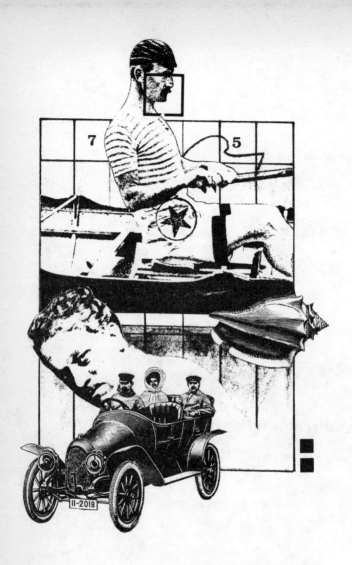

Collages by Roy R. Behrens

Isn't it lovely, the river, with its flags and barges and laughter and music carrying so far over the water? How curiously the tuba, bouncing like the Bessy in a Morris dance, comes through the windwash, while all the other instruments fade in and out of a deafness.

Henley on such a day has touches of Deauville and of Copenhagen, and the Thames through Oxfordshire gleams as if Canaletto, Dufy, and Cézanne had got at it. Flags of Oxford and Cambridge, Sweden and France, Eton and the United States, of Leander and Thames, Harrow and Bordeaux, rill and snap in our skittish English breeze.

Mrs. Damer's sculpted heads of Thames and Isis look from the posts of the High Street Bridge at Scandinavians smiling and gathering to a clapping of hands before the chantry house and at a file of gypsies of the Petulengro clan moved along by the admonitions of a constable.

Above the noise of automobiles and motorcycles there are pipes and drums playing *Leaving Rhu Vaternish* as they swing with Celtic pluck over the bridge. A county fair at Olympia! And English bells above it all, a course of changes joyously in the air.

— *Sex quattuor tris, quinque duo,* Berkshire calls.

— *Duo tris, quattuor, quinque sex,* the answer falls.

— *Twa three fower fif six, six fower, threo fif twa,* reply the bells of Oxfordshire.

Through a window, beyond the geraniums on the sill, you can see a photograph of the Duke of Connaught in a silver frame, wearing a leopard skin, head and all. Its jaws fit the duke's head in a yawning bite. The skin of its forelegs drape his shoulders, its tail hangs between his legs, and its hind feet dangle at the duke's tasseled kilt.

— Commander of a bicycle regiment, says Reggie to Cynthia after they have squeezed each other gazing at the duke's photograph. He was returning a salute while wheeling along in review when he wobbled and crashed, engaging himself so intricately in the ruin of his machine that a boffin from the medics had to come and extricate him, don't you know.

— Reggie old thing! screamed Cynthia. Sausage and mashed!

She was as shy and obvious as a rose, but she could stand on one leg, touch her heel to her butt, flip her scarf and laugh like a gasping halibut.

— Cynthia old darling! Pip pip, what?

Her scarf is in the colors of the London Rowing club. Curls crisp as

leaves flourish around her neat tam. Having laughed, she skips and hums, and chucks Reggie under his chin.

They throw themselves into each other's arms. The interested eyes observing them are those of the painter Raoul Dufy, who has come to sketch the Regatta. He wiggles his fingers and smooths his hand along the air to see English brick, the tricolor against ash and yew, panamas and blazers, the insignia of barges carved in oak argent and d'or, taupe and cinnamon. Not he but Seurat should be here. And Eakins and Whitman. And Rousseau.

> regardez Georges Seurat ces verts
> et ces azurs ces outriggers
> si étroites et si légères
>
> cette rivière plus bleue
> que les yeux saxons
> regardez cet homme si mystérieux

He jumps nimbly, Raoul Dufy, out of the way of a Jaguar XKE nosing toward the bridge and gives it a manual sign of French contempt.

> les coups des avirons les étincelles d'eau
> ces épaules puma ou il y a en marche
> des souris sous le peau
>
> ô filles minces ô garces oiseaux en vol
> mères truitées autruches milords et morses
> ô gigue des parasols
>
> rameurs grands insouciants et blonds
> et delà en maillot rouge
> près de la rive un brave garçon
>
> les mains en conque et florentines
> les joues gonflés et romanesques
> un triton gosse au chapeau mandarine
>
> qui trompete à travers
> la lumière nordique des après-midis immobiles
> un son peut-être imaginaire
>
> que l'oreille soit la preuve
> un air moiré et grec et dur
> et musclé comme la fleuve

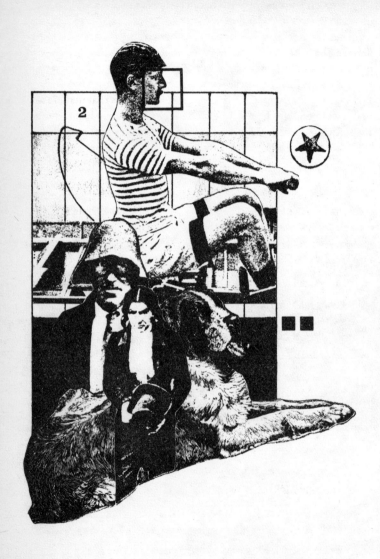

Isambard Kingdom Brunel, spanner of rivers and oceans, pray for us now and at the hour of our death.

A man in an ulster and cloth hat searches the pavements and edges of gardens for the droppings of dogs, which, if the way is clear, he puts in his pockets, for later inspection in his room above the Swan and Maiden. He is, as Raoul Dufy does not know, Stanley Spencer.

A nanny across the street asks herself whatever is that man doing, and her charge, a boy in a sailor suit, reads her eyes and answers.

— Picking up dog shit and squirreling it away on his person.

— God save the poor sod, says the nurse.

— Now he's pulling his pudding.

— Charles Francis!

An old woman in a plaid shawl has caught Stanley Spencer's attention. She wears gaiters and a fisherman's hat. The crop of white whiskers on her chin pleases Spencer. He imagines her as a girl, as a bride, as a woman getting fleshy about the hips, a woman who would cast her eyes upwards when she laughs. If only he could see her feet.

Dancing angels know a fire
makes this river wind and air
seem an iron snarl of wire

The pipe band returns over the bridge, playing *The Hen Scratches in the Midden*. The melody perplexes a poet who has been dreaming with open eyes. Was it the green of the girl's eyes who was talking with British toothiness to a grenadier in mufti, or the gorgeous quiet of the gardens beyond these ancient walls that loosed his mind into revery? Louis Jean Lumière, pray for us now and at the hour of our death.

Girlish, vivacious, and brash afternoon
That lifts with the wine of its wings
From the haunted seasons of yet to be
Summer's blond and Illyrian winters.

Flat light shimmers on the Thames. An airplane drags a streamer through the air, advertising Bovril. A dowager aims her ear trumpet so that a constable can direct her electric wheelchair.

— If Mum will turn left at the pillar box just there at the chemist's and then turn sharp left at the Bird and Baby, you will find yourself right at the royal enclosure. Can't miss it, I shouldn't think.

— Left and left?

Off and away, Spencer's eyes on her Princess Marie Louise hat, she buzzes past tall oarsmen in a row, their fluent sunblenched windblent hair embellished in swirls by limber gusts, Danes in singlets and shorts, with long brown legs and eighteen blue eyes. Louis Jacques Mandé Daguerre, pray for us now and at the hour of our death. Swans ride downstream midriver aloof and alone.

Spencer fixes the old lady and her wheelchair in his memory, the velvet glove at the tiller, the hat that might have been Jacobean, the lace collar spiked out from the back of her neck.

She steers between French oarsmen naked as snakes save for brief white pants and whistles on a string around the neck.

Bugles: a rill and snap of flags. Picnickers look up from their baskets. A couple with loosened clothes behind a hedge look out.

The poet from France adjusts his spectacles.

Launch the antique swan whose silence began
Under Babylon where the wisteria hung,
When he should have sung in the red pavilions
Passacaglia, toccata, and fugue.

He inspected shingles, brick, and windows. Bees stitched along the bells of a file of hollyhocks. *Greatly comforted in God at Westchester,* a voice came through a parasol. And *ever so nice, ame shaw.* And from a clutch of gaitered clergy, *nothing but my duty and my sin.*

There milled and trod and eddied a flock of little girls with the faces of eager mice, a family from Guernsey all in yellow hats, Mr. C. S. Lewis of Belfast in belling, baggy, blown trousers and flexuous flopping jacket, his chins working like a bullfrog's, tars from H.M.S. *Dogfish* with rolling shoulders and saucy eyes, pickpockets, top-hatted Etonians chatting each other in blipped English, a bishop in gaiters regarding with unbelieving mouth a Florentine philosopher peeing against a wall, Mallarmé wrapped in his plaid shawl rapt.

The inward white of radiant space,
Cygnus and Betelgeuse and the Wanderers,
And swam instead but swan, exile and island and
Is now in this utter reality a brilliant ghost,
An archangelical, proud, fat bird,
Ignorant of what the stars intend by Swan.

River light wiggles on the ceiling of the Royal Danish Rowing Club locker room. Oarsmen trig of girth and long of shoulder suit up in the red and white toggery of their *roningteam*. The illapse of a Jute foot into a blue canvas shoe, the junt of hale chests under jerseys, bolled *skridtbinder*, Dorian knees remember, so transparent is time, a tanling foot into a sandal, lynx grace of athletes at The Shining Dog beyond the harness makers, potters, and wine shops on the angled and shady street that crooked from behind the Agora over to the Sacred Way those summers Diogenes made his progress in a wash of curs to the market along the porch.

How foreign and sudden these spare athletes seemed to old men who remembered William Gilbert Grace and Captain Matthew Webb. Longlegged rowers file to their boats, carrying oars like the lances at Breda in Velazquez's painting. Signal flags rise on a mast frivolling. A trumpet, a pistol shot.

By Stanley Spencer tall oarsmen in shorts and singlets bear their boat above their windblent vandal hair. He is preoccupied with another, inward grace.

Wild Sicilian parsley
and wasps upon the pane!

Old Man Cézanne, he tells himself, was all very well for the French temperament, going at things logically, vibrating with a passion for the École Polytechnique, for ratios and microscopes, precisions and a constant polishing of everything with critical sandpaper. He was a Poussin run by electricity. But that woman there shaped like a bottle and her daughter shaped like a churn, they want to be seen by Cimabue, by Polish buttermold carvers, by eyes begot of the happy misalliance of stiff northern barbaric chopped wood sculpture, polychrome embroidery, and beaten gold with autumnal Roman giant stone: roundly ungainly, stubborn as barrels, solid as brick kilns.

A coxswain light as a jockey clacking the knockers swung around his neck whistles with Jacobean trills and sweetenings that some talk of Alexander and some of Hercules, of Hector and Lysander, and such great names as these. To Spencer he is a conceited ass from the continent, the pampered son of a Belgian manufacturer, but he excites the Petulengros who in a fatter time would steal him as merchandise negotiable on the docks.

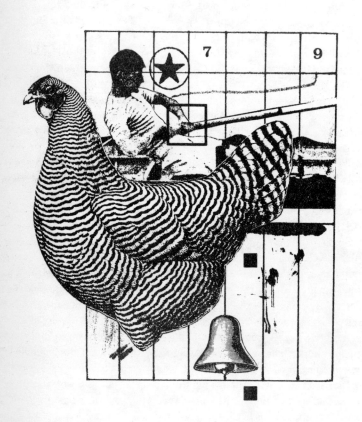

There has not a minute been
in one thousand nine hundred years
twenty months or seventeen

But that one Christian or another
kissed his image in the mirror
standing on his slaughtered brother

A cousin of Vice Admiral Sir Reginald Aylmer Ranfurly Plunkett Ernle Erle Drax snubs a cousin of Commander Sir George Louis Victor Henry Sergius Mountbatten Lord Milford Haven. Lord Peter Wimsey and Bunter bow in passing to Bertie Wooster and Jeeves. The aging Baron James Ensor of Ostend sweeps the horizon with his ear trumpet picking up the piston click of oars, the barking of coxes, and inflorescence of Scandinavian band music, Romany cheek, an indecent proposal in French to a vicar's sister and her reply in the French of Stratford at Bow as to the pellucidity of the day's air, the freshness of all the foreign young folk, and the silvery azure of the Thames.

Stanley Spencer pockets a nice yellow bit of dog shit and lifts off into a revery to the awful knees of Mont Sainte Victoire and the quarries at Bibémus, green wind awash in Cézanne's trees, fiercely mean old man who orders God about, and shakes his mahlstick at Him, *Seigneur, vous m'avez fait puissant et solitaire: laissez-moi m'endormir du sommeil de la terre.* A shaken fist, a plaintive cry. *I have not painted all of this, and until I do I refuse to die.*

It is the *Grande Jatte,* is it not? There is a lady with a whippet on a leash that will stand for the monkey, and clerks from banks, and little girls in tulle and ribbons, and people picnicking and gazing at the river and lolling on the banks. And those fat women over there with parasols from Camberwell, they make a touch of *The Feast of the Sardine,* do they not? The touts in their candy-stripe trousers and panamas, how they contrast with Sir Charles Parsons on the arm of the Very Reverend Dean Inge, with Margaret Jourdain and Ivy Compton-Burnett in such an inexplicable mixture of purples and greys, toques thirty years out of date.

Giacomo Antonio Domenico Michele Secondo Maria Puccini, pray for us now and at the hour of our death.

Stanley Spencer anticipates with relish the droppings in all his pockets, the scorched stink of wheat bunt, the dark odor of blight, mealy mil-

dew, the reek of fomes and juniper conk, of black punk rot, potato scald, bruised galls, and scurf.

What gnathion and gullet to the Finns! They sound like foxes talking, and they laugh with their eyes. The American rowers breathe through their mouths and keep their arms crossed, and walk on the balls of their feet.

Pablo Diego José Francisco de Paula Juan Nepomuceno Maria de los Remedios Cipriano de la Santissima Trinidad Ruiz y Picasso, pray for us now and at the hour of our death.

A roopy laugh and: I can't help it I tell you, Alfie, *whoops! Whoops!* it's the little pants they have on, you can see everything they have as plain as cups under a tea towel, *I'll die!* And: Look it, he's vomited all down his front, the poor sod, gorgonzola and beer it smells like. And: Dear chap, these noonings and intermealiary lunchings in air this electric brace me for excesses unknown at the parsonage. Would you believe that I got to pee next to one of those *matelots* with the pom-poms? His caution was, shall I say, ironic. Democracy is so exciting, wouldn't you say?

Auguste Lumière, pray for us now and at the hour of our death.

Spencer pulled his wool bell hat lower over his thatch, getting now onto fat women's elbows, the wrinkles of the tuck, and the sway of loose biceps rolling. What silly treasure of heart and head I would come and steal, soft as the field mouse's white-foot tread. Like the blind bone in Beethoven's ear, I spoke, she spoke, and the drum spoke that could and could not hear. Under Mrs. Damer's eyes of Cotswold stone the Cherwell marries the Thames.

> *India and Turkey were in her smile,*
> *Madras her breasts, Izmir her hips,*
> *That cross-eyed lady of Carlisle.*

Cambridge, and Bob's your uncle! A boy with a bloody nose stands defiantly by a lamp post, answering *no* to every question a policeman puts to him. A woman stung by a wasp is being helped into a pub by a Jamaican and a Hindu. A member of Parliament who has just exhibited his shrivelled penis to three Girl Guides has sunk to the sidewalk, dead.

The crew of the Club Sporting de Marseilles climbs from its boat, victors gasping, sweating, smiling. Cameras whirr and flash as they toss their coxswain in the river. A toothy official shakes their large hands and

acknowledges their Mediterranean smiles with a rabbity scrunch of his lips.

— Good show! he says.

— Sink you! they reply.

Afternoon's long shadowfall across the grass and the garden walls is like music at the end of a day of self-indulgence.

As the crowds milled to the banks for the last race, which was rowed in late level golden light, a peal of Stedmans rang out from churches round-about.

— *Sex quattuor tris, quinque duo,* Berkshire calls.

— *Duo tris quattuor, quinque sex,* the answer falls.

— *Twa threo fower fif six, six fower, threo fif twa,* reply the bells of Oxfordshire.

The Trees at Lystra The Death of Picasso The
Daimon of Sokrates Christ Preaching at the
Henley Regatta **Mesoroposthonippidon** Lo Sple
ndore della Luce a Bologna Idyll On Some Lines
of Virgil The Trees at Lystra The Death of
Picasso The Daimon of Sokrates Christ Preach
ing at the Henley Regatta Mesoroposthonippi
don Lo Splendore della Luce a Bologna Idyll
On Some Lines of Virgil The Trees at Lystra
The Death of Picasso The Daimon of Sokrates
Christ Preaching at the Henley Regatta Mesoro
posthonippidon Lo Splendore della Luce a Bol
ogna Idyll On Some Lines of Virgil The Trees
at Lystra The Death of Picasso The Daimon of
Sokrates Christ Preaching at the Henley Rega
tta Mesoroposthonippidon Lo Splendore della

Mesoroposthonippidon am I called, a painter of jugs, an owl to Athenai, a straw in the wind, a rat-catching mustard dog of the stables and ordinaries, a narrow-hipped, meter-shanked, wide-teated boy with miscella eyes, an alley tom, an urchin none too nice to sit among the pyes in the shining dirt with that long-shadowed man Diogenes.

My *Eros Astraddle a Goose* has sold well and has been copied in Korinthos. Our pottery got its reputation for its scenes from the Iliad on tableware, I can do an *Akhilleus Bewailing Patroklos* in my sleep, and for larger pieces displayed in corners. We have a profitable sideline in perfume bottles with Demeters and Korés, Peitho with a Dove, and a backroom run of ithyphallika popular with the fast sporting set and the lecturers up at the Akademia.

I also model for the sculptors, am a student of rhetoric and the athletic limb, an adept at the barbitos, and the pillow fellow of the odd-eyed Esperessa. A green eye and a brown she has, and is Aphrodita's very own daughter, sweet as a crush of honey in the comb.

My palaistra is The Shining Dog, Antisthenes' old gymnasion where the tone is several measures racier than at The Wise Owl, The Dioskourides, or The Olympia, and where that grand old man Diogenes is the acknowledged logic dodger.

Diogenes. I have just seen him up to a trick he never tires of pulling. He had talked an admirer of philosophy into buying a large and horrendously ugly fish, one of those monsters with both its eyes on the same side of its head, which he asked the simpleton to carry for him across the Agora.

Diogenes strode ahead like a lord of Asia, his piss-burnt old thirdhand half-cloak all fleas and dog hair flapping about his stork's shins like a tablecloth on a camel-sparrow. The obliging fool trudged behind, lugging the fish.

Eyebrows went up, sleepers came awake to stare, a publican nudged a politician to look, and little boys poured from alleys. Aristocrats left off their silvery chat and gazed with open mouths, the eel seller alerted the chestnut roaster.

Slaves grinned, dogs frisked, and cats loped behind. Whereupon the booby discovered that the subtle Diogenes, with whom he supposed it was all the rage to be seen speaking of the aristocracy of the virtuous, was nowhere about.

And there he was, ruby of cheek and feverish of eye, carrying across the Agora a monster of a fish plain as a baby got on the Gorgon by a Thracian.

— Ha ha! brayed the politician. Ha ha, the publican.

— Feesh! cried the chestnut roaster, fresh feesh an obol the litra!

And the eel seller broke wind loud as a drum thumped with the flat of a hand. Little boys danced in a ring around the toter of the fish. They hummed, they rolled their eyes as at Sybaris, they flicked the tips of their tongues like insolent lizards.

It was when two black-kneed goslings from the Peiriaeus came along with the twin of the fish in their arms that the disciple of Diogenes plopped the monster into a gutter and legged it. I knew what would happen, having seen the trick before. Our outraged enthusiast would catch Diogenes and call him a ninnyhammer, a Boiotian, a mutton head.

— Just think! Diogenes would sigh, all because of a fish.

He would open his honest hands and appeal to the crowd.

— A martyr to friendship! For an obol's worth of fish a friendship is pulped like a platched gnat.

He played the game with Diokles, who found himself abandoned while carrying a huge cheese.

Esperessa painting her eyelids violet, pumicing her heels, and rouging her teats, asked me to go through the whole tale again, please.

— But, Mouse, I say, it is for the laugh he did it. And for the moral.

— If he liked old Mustard and Funny Face, she said, why did he ask them to look silly with a tuna or Cydonian pumpkin or whatever it was in the first place?

— To debase, I said, the coinage.

She stuck out her tongue, purple with berries.

— His old papa Hikesios was ostracized from Sinope, that's in Pontos in Asia, where he was a moneylender and changer, for queering the value of public funds, so Diogenes likes to say that he too is in the family business of debasing the coinage.

— By having a citizen do porters' work!

She leaned over to dab rouge on our akroposthion and missed by a whisker. Then, owing to the passing beneath our window of the mimiambos' barbiteer we danced a frisk heel and toe around the room, wild, a prigger of prancers, talaria ziganka, hoo!

Esperessa was not strictly her name, but Panesperessa was a name as common among companions as Argos among dogs or Kirke among cats. I've decorated a set of plates with her playing the double flute, combing her hair, holding a rabbit, frolicking with a tambourine like a Maenad.

She offered songs on the lyra, walking on her hands, and a supple dance the *igdisma* of which would make the tunic of a Pythagorean stand out and priestesses of the Mysteries raise their hands in scandal. She could also tie her hair back like a boy, nip a *sauridion* and *thylakiskos* and shindy around as Hermaphroditos, one of the sights to see before the ferry ride over Akheron I can tell you, O brother. The rhythm of her hips to a drum!

She was, without her eyelids painted, her cheeks and lips ruddled, her eyebrows plucked and pencilled on in another place, every bit as pretty as a boy. I take my *enausmata* as they fall with the wind, wild oats, Diogenes says, my crop.

A pettos speckled with gold ajiggle with a fremitus from the heart touches me like Athena's hoolet mewing in uncertain dark. So much is nature, whereon we build our particulars fastidious and critical. *Your every arrow O Eros has hit me,* as the song goes. O girls, girls. This arrow is Timo's curls, this is Heliodora's shoes, this the smell of quinces that blows from Demo's door, flowers plaited into Dorothea's hair and ox-eyed Antikleia's smile that is music from the islands, summer's stars.

— Hermes' balls! she says of Diogenes. A boy as handsome as you, to go around with that beanpole of a loon and his dogs, when you could have any admirer you fancy. Has he ever washed his feet? His fleas come home with you and set up house in our bed.

— Why, Diogenes likes to twit me, are spadgers so nice-nasty? Eh! By Hermes Nuktipataiplagios, you have your charming baggage, of whom, mind you, I say nothing acid, and your pal Didymon with well nigh as horsy a pendle as yours, and as if that were not Ossa giddy upon Pelion, you go in for as rammish a *kheirourgon* as one is apt to see outside Lydia, at the turn of every wall, on the way to the gymnasion, on the way back from the gymnasion . . .

— You do it in the Agora!

— That was to show my contempt for desire. You bespatter alleys, tiles, the street, *kynoukhoi,* ceilings, and the inadvertent ankle. And then, by Diana of the Silver Knees, if a silly old paiderastos rotten with piles and gold rolls his eyes at you, jovial as a grandmother, you raise the alarm, and shout that a decent proletarian is being interfered with.

—I'm looking for the trap in logic, I say.

—Even the rats are educated in Athenai, he replies to the rooftops.

—Do you want it? I said, unsheathing in full view of six laughing dogs, the blue sky, an old woman with a basket of olives, two round-eyed little boys, and a portly citizen in a large yellow hat who walked into a donkey laden with six hampers of doves, the bray and ruckus of which brought the entire Hodos Megareus to grin at its doors.

Diogenes bounced a laugh off Hymettos and hooked me in the butt with a kick that lifted me onto my toes.

—Philosopher set upon by a Silenos! he cried.

—Honest apprentice pestered by a philosopher! I hollered louder.

—Decency outraged!

—Virtue assaulted!

Folk approached, to have something to talk about later. The citizen in the yellow hat walked in circles, berated by the owner of the donkey. A slosh of water rode over a wall and splashed brightly at our feet.

—Come, Nippy, Diogenes said with hauteur. Come, dogs.

We left with arms around each other's shoulder, our heads high, in a wash of dogs.

HE LIVED IN A TUB. HE WAS, TO TELL THE TRUTH, THE LEADER OF A PACK of dogs, mongrel strays the lot of them. He wore only a half-cloak all seasons. His sole utensil was a cup until the day he saw an urchin at a trough who drank from his hands, and Diogenes threw away his cup.

Civilization, he said, is weightless. He carried books in his head, and when we sang together he pointed out that he had the voice, I the lyra.

—It is the mice who taught me how to thrive. They live in houses, dine, and breed there. One can live well on the leftovers of a single street. I study dogs, slaves, and the elderly who have perfected their daily round. Monotony is also precision.

He talked best under the trees along the streets behind the Theseion, dark and cool with shade, where you could find conversations to last out a morning and an afternoon.

O the grand old men of Athenai and their lenient eyes! With what patience do they listen to each other along the Porch, sipping hot wine from cups decorated with Eumaios and his swine, Eros and Peitho riding geese, Meleagros and the boar. Here Aristides has just spent the morning talking with Menippos. He meets Heron with a shout of joy and their speckled hands settle on their beards as they ask about wives, sons, grandchildren, and specify arthritic pain as to joint, rage, and interval.

They arrange themselves on the smooth wooden bench under the Aithiopian fig by the weights and measures station. On Heron's bony shoulder Aristides lays his hand. These long days of dry weather are splendid for the wheat.

Three dogs, heralds of Diogenes somewhere about, come to lie in the cool dusk at their feet. A little boy with a skink of a peter rucking the limbus of his shirt, quail and sage in red and bice, listens to them with grave ears, quiddling the fingers of one hand in his hair, winking the other on his chin.

MY DAIMON HAD TOLD ME THAT IF I SLIPPED OUT OF THE COVERS AT first dawn, just when Alektor yodelled his silvery *kokkuba! kokkuba!* in the chicken run below and Hekuba and Koronekuba ruffled from their roosts ruckling, I could get to the Corinthian Road to meet the old Mongrel himself.

— *Teknidion?* Esperessa mumbled. She was sleeping as usual, her knees against her cheeks. With her *stimmi* off, and ochre, and rhodino-porphyry, she looked as unknowing as a milkmaid.

— *Kokkuba!* I crowed, flipping my goose neck toward her while pulling my shirt over my head.

— O for goodness gracious sakes, she said, sticking out her tongue and holding her nose before pulling the covers over her head.

I gave her a kiss on the hair, said I'd be back with fresh bread after seeing a fellow about a dog, and went down the ladder whistling.

The bakers' boys were about, and marketfolk from the country. All was fresh and bright. I leapfrogged a sheep in the Hermes Way, was sworn at, stole a plum from a basket, so good that time of morning that I would not envy the gods their nectar if I could live forever off the tart cold pulpy honey of such plums, bade an early footwoman good day, passed three gossoons comparing peters, showed them mine, shied a pebble into a window, washed my face at a horse trough, ducked into a taverna that was being swept out, took a swallow of the one customer's breakfast wine before he realized what I was about, marathoned out with a shepherd's crook singing in the air over my head, outran a ferocious dog who knew a chase when he saw one, and, wonderfully winded and losing the spring in my knees, I got to the Corinthian Way laughing and hot, just as full day spread white across its dust, already hiphigh around donkeys and peddlars and blithering goats, and, as I saw a hemistadion away, an old philosopher without a staff, swinging his arms as if he loved the world for his own, beard out, barefoot, his half-cloak a disgrace to a rag pile.

— Joy! he cried when he saw me.

And he boomed out, for all to hear on the road, the Shah of Shahs of Persia goes a progress from Susa in the spring, from Babylon in the winter, from Media in the summer, and every year Diogenes walks from Corinth to Athenai! Nippaki me boy, you're as beautiful as Epameinondas.

DIOGENES WAS AROUND TWO HUNDRED YEARS OLD WHEN I TOOK UP WITH his pack. There was this glorious fool Askonides, an autochthonous unwaxed Boiotian from Thebe itself, the kind that arrives in Attika and buys straightway a bottle of moonlight, an aphrodisiac which the seller says he won't in good conscience sell you if you're weak of heart, and an alley cat in a celery hamper, rarest of beasts that the discerning traveller can acquire in Athena's great city, imported from the Hyperborean Islands beyond the Straits of Herakles.

Well. This Askonides, Kratidion to his friends, devised a philosophical mode that no one had seen before. Old Sokrates, before they got him, used to block your path with his staff and wheedle you into a conversation that gathered a crowd, looking at you like a starved man at a roast of lamb, and Antisthenes would slip philosophy into you after throwing you at the palaistra, and Platon invites you to a feed and passes around geometric figures, arithmetic books, and sheet music along with the wine and figs, the prettier you are the more you get. But Askonides would get full of philosophy and nip down the street banging on doors, and where he got in he would exhort the good housewife to give away all her belongings and live in a tub, like Diogenes. He'd shout at sweet old men asleep in their gardens to free their slaves, live on bread and water, and realize the terrible destiny of the soul mired in sloth and estranged from virtue.

TWO TREADERS IN THE CLAY HOLDING EACH OTHER BY THE SHOULDERS SLOWly turn as they knead and squish with rising knees, white-shanked, flesh like young olives spattered hip high. The oven master dollops in water with a dipper.

— Creamier, he says. Thicker and creamier.

The pedals of the wheels thump. I draw an Akhilleus sulking in his tent, a pattern of round shields and spears in slanting stacks. Hounds with curled tails. My brush must drop from neck to shoulder to back to butt to thigh to hough to calf to ankle to sole without being lifted. Then up the groin and back down to the toes again. Then hook in the toes. Sandals, greaves.

Diogenes talks about doing nothing while thinking you are doing something, and calls it the business of Athenai. He means the folk who spend all morning watching the harness makers work, the stonecutters, the potters, the barbers. *The art of doing nothing.*

At The Shining Dog there are the idlers smoothing the dust with their feet. They talk, they fall to arguing. They consult one another about what they have forgotten. Memory takes up awful tasks, as of recalling the name of a Spartan runner two Olympics back, his trainer, his trainer's other runners, who they outran, who carved their statues at what expense.

Here, in a file, arrive Kallixenos, Philippos, and Lysis. Kallixenos walks pigeon-toed, on the balls of his feet, the bounce of his tread tilting his shoulders. He wears a blue shirt, a white Hermes hat, a ribbon on his left ankle, one of the deathless, as Homer says, to see. The hem of his shirt comes down to but not over the knob of his pizzle. Philippos, whose hair was cut under a winebowl, wears his shirt tied around his waist, his aryballos on a thong around his neck, a janus of cocks on a scrotum. Lysis has a gauze bandage around a shoulder, a poultice of figs to bring a boil to a head. They make a show of limbering up, looking at the idlers out of the tails of their eyes.

WE ARE HERE, GENERATED BY LOVERS, TO LOVE, AS MANY THINGS AS WE can perhaps, one thing perhaps which is our care alone. I pitch my conks for the many and the diverse, for when we stand before Persephone and Dis, never again to bounce between frisky thighs, never again to munch fresh bread dipped in wine, we shall have missed tasting and hugging and seeing the things of the world by the height of all the mountains added together.

Reckless Eros hits us all. Our work is a kind of love. And then there are things we love because they are what they are to us, idiomatic loves for which there is no explaining. I know a woman who loves shawls and is on her way to having a hundred of them. With Askonides it is melons, with Esperessa flowers. You can see Diogenes, even, by telling yourself that his maniacal price on simple decency is his human attempt to display his love for the splendid honesty of dogs.

With me, trumpets. Long shining slender silver trumpets. It is for them that I go the theatre, where with the voice of daimons who have fed on white stars and Cnidan roses and the crystal rivers of Arkadia, twenty trumpeters bring the victors at Olympia and the bull to the priests, and the trumpets of Zeus, another twenty, sounding like the sweet fanfares for Demeter at Eleusis, meet the trumpets of Dionysos and bring their long voices together in a harmony.

The trumpets of Zeus begin at his temple, with kettle drums for thunder against which they make a bright dance, joy cherished, rolled around all the forthright colors of their stout voices, tone ringing upon tone, and released to the hills of Attika.

The trumpets of Dionysos come down from the Lykabettos, singing above tambourines and cymbals, frolicsome, pelvic, red.

The trumpeters of Sparta can be heard twenty stadia away. We have abandoned Aphrodita in full melt and pitch, Esperessa and I, to run out along the Sacred Way to hear the trumpets among the harvest fires blessing the fields by moonlight.

AROUND MY NECK BY A LEATHER THONG HUNG AN ARYBALLOS THE SHAPE of a phallos and scrotum full of redolent oil, bee balm and dill, the gift of Didymon, a fine sucking stone from a mountain creek in my mouth, the gift of Esperessa, who filched it from a farmer's son risking his hide by trading her a cheese for a quick wild tup, my shortest skirt, a *skimallos* for the world, for a coltish sweet had clutched my *orchidia* as warm and close as a couple of eggs in the milkmaid's hand, my *stema* nodded as I walked, neither up nor down, and *tò ídíon kybernêsai skáphon* was my philosophy for the day.

Diogenes knee deep in dogs listed from among the green of the fig grove nigh The Shining Hound, coming to cadge our nuts and honey, to twit us and yap at us and enjoy himself to the brim.

— Grace from the gods, I hailed, O dogs and dogherd!

— Nippy you rascal, he shouted. If you've come out so *strabalokomatos* and in so negligible a garment to charm a man, it's deplorable, if for a woman, it's unfair.

—For my friends, I said, batting aside the intimate prod of a dog's cold nose.

—Worse and worse! Reason or a halter!

Didymon, dusty, was at the door, hands on hips, looking at us from under the havoc of his hair. We goosed each other, batted each other's heads, and traded insults that made Diogenes stop his ears. We share a *kynoukhos,* Didymon and I, into which I put my shirt, sandals, and oil jar.

—You have not, Diogenes said, shuffling in among the wrestlers, a game of knucklebones, little boys spinning tops, and the idlers, you have not learned the pleasure of despising pleasure.

I hooted, and Didymon dusted his butt and showed the old carper a saucy big brown eye.

His niggling at the crotch was Diogenes' crankiest twaddle. The warmth of his heart seems never to have spread to his balls.

Match for sweet, philosophers, in plums or hexameters or geometry, in lines bounding colors, or chiseled stone or balanced words, Esperessa's eyes when we can toss a day aside to wallow in each other, a flip for the potters and the hot. You cannot. Nobody can, could, or right minded, would. She whispers, we plot, she slips away from our morning wine to a loving sister in the trade with as congenial a finger and as skilled a friendly tongue, and with as lively lovely nipples, and while I, up and down like a pump handle, square the apprentices for the daylight's work, cadge a cheese, borrow a loaf, come by a handful of olives here and a flask of black wine there, she warms up professionally, wiggling and sighing and trembling for a romp, coming back all slow winks and tongue tip in the corner of her mouth.

We settle in to dally in proven ways that would make them slobber at Sybaris and applaud at Corinth and then begin inventions that redden Aphrodita's cheeks and cause Eros to jump and squeal with glee, and by the time she's taken a hilt holt of the heft of my haft it's still but midday and all the goatish afternoon's before us, and soft evening and randy night. I measure her burrow with a hundred thrusts, each sweeter and slicker than the one before, flood it with twenty more while she drums her heels on my behind and makes vows to Priapos and Hera for wilder spasms, deeper delight. To end with us on such a day is to begin, to glut, to starve, to brim, slosh, and spill but to have our pleasure lay its ears back and feel its oats.

So, spent and shuddered, we begin again, ramming plunges into an improving fit, while the loving goddess' jibbering boy, up, frisked in orchids, tickled teats, licked, kissed, touched, tingled, and cheered us on.

A respite for wine, begrudged but needed, drunk from each other's mouths, olives chewed in her mouth passed into mine, in mine into hers, sweet Peitho with playing finger knocking her heels together between our gaze into each other's eyes, until Eros pulling me, Peitho pushing her, couple us again as we gasp out bleats of craving.

She takes it astride me then, on her toes as agile as a spring, for deepest reach inside, snuggest bore, slickest slide. The morning the almonds bloom and the sun rises in the Ram, figs drowned in honey and melting on the tongue, a drawing with every line just so and every color perfect, a wanton boy as beautiful as a hound, trumpets at the Dionysia, dancing drunk at the Thesmophoria, none matches, none.

By the shank of the afternoon we have milked my didyma spunkless, and hug and roll our tongues together and kiss and joggle her nitch and sip breaths and suck and coddle and whisper soft and silly words until they thrive again.

THE SCULPTOR DOROTHEOS WANTED POSES FOR A HERMES AND I WAS hired for the lion's share, everything except the head, which Kallias, who has a stunning profile and cupidon's mouth, was sitting for, and the feet and posthos, which were to be those of Miltiades. His feet are long and slender, mine large with broad useful toes. His dingus is, as Dorotheos said, modest, with a long akroposthidion. My knockers are satyric, my posthos horsy and as nubby as a cucumber and my foreskin, dressed down, leaves a tetradrachm's worth of acorn bare at the neb. Critics from the Akademe were there to talk art and watch, and Diogenes turned up, with four dogs who had to stand outside the door, looking in. I spoke to them by name, Ratcatcher, Mustard, Polyzelos, and Sniffer, while I shucked my shirt and sandals.

Along with the tap of Dorotheos' mallet and the snick of his chisel the connoisseurs' voices were like a shuffle of leaves. *Good knees, nicely flanched midriff, a certain richness in the nuchal prominence, he is a painter himself, you know, in the Keramika: quite a crack draughtsman, impossibly handsome these artisans' children, and my nephew Theomnestos is as plain as an owl chick.*

— You wear a blush, if nothing else, Diogenes boomed out, and that is as good a clothing as virtue itself!

— Chin down a minim, Dorotheos said.

— Where does he exercise?

— At The Shining Dog.

— Well, as he isn't a citizen.

— Artemis Philomeirax moves her pleated robes where she will.

— And, Diogenes said to us all at large, at The Shining Dog you can hear the noncitizen Diogenes philosophizing with Antisthenes, Athenian of Athenians, and in between *paidarion* and dog, wrestler and slave, you get a fair brand of mathematics and the occasional topnotch epigram.

— Rather a lot of sophists thereabouts, aren't there?

— No more than in the Stoa on marketday.

— You can guddle a spracker spadger there than in any bath in town, Diogenes said in his best, and wickedest imitation of the Athenian dialect, and Dorotheos asked me to wipe the smile off my face.

— *Es kephalèn trápoit' emoi!* Diogenes said.

AS FOR MY BEDDING DOWN WITH ESPERESSA, DIOGENES THREW UP HIS hands altogether. He was not, however, serious in the least. He rather liked experiments and irregularities than not. He once ate a raw squid as a public service, to see if it could be digested. A weasel, too. He recommended neither to the Athenian table.

Civilization, he said, is weightless. The idea came to him when he threw his cup away and thereafter drank from his hands at the horse trough. Hard by the standards bureau.

He carried his books in his head, and when we sang together he pointed out that he had the voice, I the lyra. He learned a great lesson from mice. They live in other people's houses, dine there, thrive there. Stray dogs are fine teachers, too, as are slaves and the old.

— Watch the old, he said. They have perfected all their movements. They have kept things that have gone out of fashion. Only the dispossessed have new things and new ways. Nothing is congenial until it has been around a few centuries. For the congenial and the comfortable, consult the aged.

There are families still on Hymettos so old they are proud of being poor, who look with pity and contempt on the new fashion of the last five-score Olympiads of expecting honor because you have money out on loan. Their children have bigger eyes, their old folk are scandalized by the new officers at Eleusis and the airs of the hierophants in public. Something Persian they say they seem to be. Their figs are bluer, their wasps fatter, their houses cooler. They threw rocks at Sokrates in his day. Diogenes daren't go there at all.

— I must smell of dog, he begins to say.

— You do, I assure him.

— Must smell of dog, he continues, more than anything else, except a dog.

He anticipated me with that last phrase, flicking two fingers on my chine. I danced *ouch* and made a Ker at him with my thumbs in the corners of my mouth.

— And still, he said, their dogs creep at me growling with butchery in their eyes. Dogs are the agents of their owners. If Miltiades' dog bites you, be assured that Miltiades has bitten you.

WHEN DIOGENES FIRST CAME TO ATHENAI IT WAS ANTISTHENES WHO INterested him most among the philosophers, but as luck is a slut, Antisthenes despised students who ask questions. He also disliked the passive, the obedient, the suckers up, the complacent listeners. He disliked students, truth be told, altogether. Students! he would say. They pry, they are obsequious and flattering, and frustrate all exercise of the intellect by agreeing to everything. Fleas of the mind! Ticks! Leeches! Ignorant prigs!

— Even if they have the mesopygion of Ganymedes, the eye of Narkissos, the ankle of Hyakinthos, O cow-eyed Io! they steal your time, your rest, your attention. Be gone, away!

This speech, Diogenes told me, was to him.

— Am I to be pestered into insanity and the grave? I do not want pupils. I hate teaching pupils. They give me diarrhea, fever, hemorrhoids, nausea, despair, fits, toothache, ringing ears, a stiff neck, back pains.

He whacked at Diogenes with his stick.

— What is teaching, the old boy bellowed, but thunder after lightning? With sharper fire than a Scythian arrow, thought splits the dark, crossing a chasm it can never close. The rent it tears in the placidity of opinion, in the weft of custom, closes itself along a crack of vacuum from cloud to oak, with a report and rumble, until of the fierce white clarity only a rumor is left, only a memory of light, a red afterglow.

That was Antisthenes' specialty, making a sight of himself.

— Athenai, her olives, her owls, her mathematicians, carvers of marble, painters, and conversationalists, does not open her lap to every suppliant. Oidipos the blind arkhon from Thebai is buried outside the city wall.

I can remember seeing old Antisthenes out my window making his way with thumbstick and gorgeous beard to The Shining Dog. It had been washed and combed and trimmed, that philosophical beard, into a long fluffy lambswool roundness. And with him walked beardless gymnasts and horsy young men with a thin smudge of beard coming along on their flat cheeks. He could still wrestle with the best of them. Potbellied as he was, when he threw out his grizzled chest like a Persian bantam and squared his shoulders, there was a lot of little boy left in the back of his legs and tilt of his butt.

His old teats on their humps of muscle were pink and hale, his eyes were as fine as a cat's. His poise was soldierly, his step deliberate and wonderfully vain. *His* teacher had been Sokrates.

I had come to Athenai as a half-green tad, not off the islands with the wild boys who run like rats from the fishing boats and coasters up from the Peiraieus, but along the road from Eleusis with bright eyes and dusty knees.

— Me, said Diogenes over a melon I had caught in midair when it was falling from a cart with a little help from a stick, I came here from Sinope. I chose Antisthenes for a teacher partly because he tried my mettle by chasing me away, partly because his mother was a hill woman from Thrakia, partly because he was a foreigner too, partly because I knew that he had had to prove himself, at Tanagra, where he is said to have fought harder than any Athenian there. I liked his style, you see. This business of the Athenians being autochthonous: Antisthenes said that it was a distinction they shared with grasshoppers and snails.

Diogenes had in time made his name with Antisthenian methods. Walking around with a lamp in the daytime, looking for, as he said, a real man, that was in his teacher's style.

And then, after Platon over at the Akademia said man is a two-legged featherless creature, Diogenes carried around a plucked chicken.

—Behold Platonic Man, he said of it, and laughed himself silly when Platon added *having flat fingernails* to his definition.

THE SAYINGS, THE SAYINGS. THEY HAVE BECOME AS MUCH A PART OF ATHENAI as the owls, the little wine shops on every narrow street, the booksellers.

A politician is a slave owned by everybody. A politician is a blowfly, a loaf of horse flop.

There are women who see with their hands, boys who see with their feet.

A woman shelling peas is an education for the fingers.

We walk more gracefully after dancing, speak with firmer measure after an ode.

Put the beat of music into everything.

Celery is the cucumber's wife.

Knowledge is marrying outside the family, intelligence is what the family already knows.

Imagination is private, wit public.

It is an advantage not to fear the dark.

Let us get used to the world as soon as we can.

Everything is made conspicuous for being hidden.

Better to be a Megarian's ram than his son.

Living is good, but a worthless life is evil.

Enemies are better than friends for keeping you virtuous.

Where can you spit in the rich man's house but in his face?

I WAS FINISHING A KYLIX OF BLACKWARE WITH A RUDDLE EROS RIDING his goose, legs spraddled, his heels shoving into the wind, when the oven master came in from the street and said that he had heard that Diogenes was dead at Korinthos.

—He was an admirer of yours, was he not, Nippy?

—No, I said, I was an admirer of him.

Carefully, as best I could see, I rounded out my drawing and left. There was work still to do.

I found Esperessa at some disgraceful place. We borrowed white clothes from here and there, and set out for Korinthos, a walk that would take the rest of the day, all night, and part of the next. He was buried under the pines beside the road into the city. We could not know then how terribly the dogs would howl.

he Trees at Lystra The Death of Picasso The
Daimon of Sokrates Christ Preaching at the
Henley Regatta Mesoroposthonippidon Lo Sple
dore della Luce a Bologna Idyll On Some Lines
f Virgil The Trees at Lystra The Death of
icasso The Daimon of Sokrates Christ Preach
g at the Henley Regatta Mesoroposthonippi
on **Lo Splendore della Luce a Bologna** Idyll
On Some Lines of Virgil The Trees at Lystra
he Death of Picasso The Daimon of Sokrates
hrist Preaching at the Henley Regatta Mesoro
osthonippidon Lo Splendore della Luce a Bol
gna Idyll On Some Lines of Virgil The Trees
t Lystra The Death of Picasso The Daimon of
okrates Christ Preaching at the Henley Rega
a Mesoroposthonippidon Lo Splendore della

Collages by Roy R. Behrens

I

The locomotive bringing a trainload of philosophers to Bologna hissed and ground to a standstill in the long Apennine dusk to have its head-lamps lit and to be dressed in the standards of the city and the university. On both sides of the smokestack and at the four corners of the tender the red flag of the Partito bravely rode.

With dying drivers and rolling bell, victorious whistle and a glory of steam, they slid into the march from *Aida* played by the Filarmonica Municipale deployed along the platform in front of the guard of the Podestà who saluted the philosophers with swords at port arms in the first rank, with gonfalone in the second.

— *Viva la filosofia!* cried the crowd.
— *Portabagagli!*
— *La bandiera rossa trionferà!*
— *È vergine la mia sorella!*
— *Benvenuto, stregoni!*
— *A chi piace una banana?*
— *Alle barricate!*
— *Siempre Marconi!*
— *Carrozze!*
— *Viva la filosofia!*

Kissed on both cheeks by a sashed, whiskered, top-hatted academic as he descended from the train, Mr. Hulme took his seat in a carriage with Henri Bergson, Murray of the London Aristotelian Society, and F. C. S. Schiller the Oxford pragmatist, and rode down the Via Aemilia in a torch-light procession.

II

In the morning, sipping coffee, Mr. Hulme could find no proportion in the arcades, the buildings, the windows, the campanile, the duomi, the typography of the newspaper, that was not perfect. The children and the old people made him sad. All ideas rise like music from the physical.

III

Tomatoes, baroque and crimson. A hobnail-booted priest taking snuff. A cricket on a freckled pear. The way these Bolognese women pick up figs

at the greengrocer's, discuss them, judge them, praise them, is not English. Kensington housewives would say *figs!* and *ever so dear*. How they sort through them here, nibble them, twirl them, choose a clutch, and gabble a minor oration about them.

IV

Cinders and ashes, the world, except where we have made a garden, a kitchen, a shrine, a wine press. In all his life there would be but three moments when the tough opacity of the world became transparent so that he could see the fingers of God at work: on the prairies of western Canada, in the splendor of the light at Bologna, in the trenches of Belgium.

V

Gypsies with black teeth. Boys leapfrogging down the arcades. A nun with two flasks of wine. Punchinello strutting to a drum. Polizia in leather hats with cockades. Caricature, he knew, began here: Annibale Carracci. Two boys peed in a gutter. Bells clanged, chimed, charmed. Bologna smelled of horses, garlic, wine, a sweet rot as of hay, apples, or onions in ferment.

Drum roll and trumpets: the philosophers are going to the convocation.

VI

In 1603, at Monte Paderno, outside Bologna, an alchemist (by day a cobbler) named Vicenzo Cascariolo discovered the Philosopher's Stone, catalyst in the transformation of base metals into gold, focus of the imagination, talisman for abstruse thought. Silver in some lights, white in others, it glowed blue in darkness, awesome to behold.

VII

At the Fourth International Congress of Philosophy, convened in Bologna the first week of April 1911, Mr. T. E. Hulme, registered through scribal error as F. E. Hulme, delegate from the Aristotelian Society of

London, La Gran Bretagna, undertook to exercise the dictum that Henri Bergson passed on to him from the man he called William Jones, namely that one look at a philosopher is enough to convince you that there you need trouble no further.

Did he believe with Aristotle, Lavater, and Lombroso that the supposed rattiness, horsiness, or other animality of a face designated a ferality of the soul? *Bergson?* Surely he meant something else, something quite else.

William Jones, assuming him to be, as we safely may, the same as William James, had died the preceding August in the mountains of New Hampshire, surrounded by his wife, his children, and his brother Henry. He was to have read a paper on *Naturphilosophie* at the Congress.

—A loss, Ernst Mach said, a distinct deprivation. He went up the Amazons with the great Agassiz, you know, and at Harward he was successively professor of medicine, psychology, and philosophy. At my table in Vienna he was a brilliant talker, in good German, on any subject, mechanics, disease, bicycles, madness, religion, politics, fashion, Puccini, frogs, engineering. *Ach,* he would put the tablecloth around his throat without the least diminishment of his dignity and give an imitation of the creole philosopher Georg Santajana, an Epicurus among the Jansenists at the Collegium Harward.

Hulme tried to imagine Aristotle doing Plato, fluttering his hand, pushing his fingers through his beard.

—All my children laugh, they could not but, and even my dear wife, helplessly, permit herself the giggle, it was entirely appropriate. And then this marvellous Herr Professor James would be talking about disjunct personalities in the madhouse, people with two or more different identities, and about his visit to Paris to see the spastic writer Fräulein Stein who was a student of his at Harward, and how in England he climbed a ladder and looked over his brother Henry's garden wall to see some writer of the English who lived next door, H. G. Wells I think it was, or perhaps Jerome Jerome, and how his brother, who has become more correct than the English, was scandalized, and so were we, but vastly amused, you understand. It is a mark of a sensibility enlarged by imagination to have the overpowering curiosity, like a child not yet fully disciplined, to climb a ladder and look over a garden wall. It is something Goethe would have done, in Italy.

—And here we are, in Italy ourselves, Mr. Hulme replied in his best German.

— *Ganz recht!* exclaimed Herr Mach, rolling his wine in his glass. And over whose garden wall should we gaze? Ha ha.

VIII

Images will sharpen, dialectic will assert itself, sculpture will become abstract, painting will return to clear color and geometric line, manners will grow natural and frank, life will be convenient, healthy, sweet. But the morbid, the frenetic, the humbug must go away. Romanticism must die, or daydreaming will drown us all in a great muck.

Against the caress of the smooth put the abrasion of the rough.

Trace every shadow back to the light that caused it. Cherish the light, respect the shadow.

The Bolognese women seemed to be out of the Bible, shawled, competent, chaste, and severe, or out of Goya, trivial, vain, and with a duchess complex.

IX

Samuel Alexander looked like God. Bergson was an elegant cat, privy to the mind of Montaigne. Hüsserl, a chemist who played in a string quartet. A philosopher might well study the human face, like Rembrandt or da Vinci, so long as he kept taxonomy and statistics at bay. Each man is a species and cannot be further classified.

X

Cone, sphere, cube.

XI

A boy leading a horse, an old woman who looked like Pestalozzi drinking a wine as black as ink, an adagio of nuns on a bridge, partridges flecked with blood hanging outside a *trattoria*, melons golden in a basket, an orange and blue poster of an aeroplane pasted beside a board that gave in baroque and gilt lettering the times of the masses at San Procolo, goats with eyes of the Devil wearing long bronze bells that banged as a bass to their bleats, their herdsman talking socialist theory with a tall girl out of the Book of Ruth who was carrying a lute, a baby, a jug, and a parasol with a scarlet fimbria.

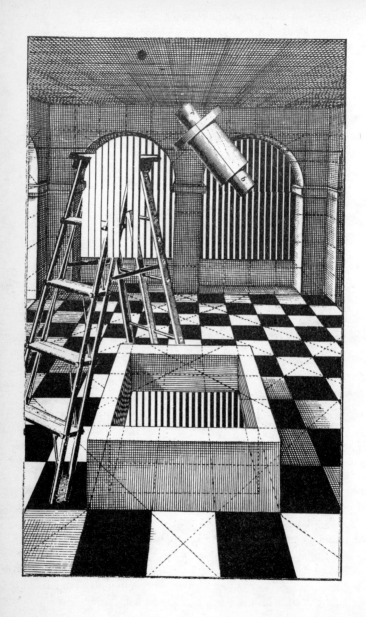

When there shall be no more the slot of oxen in the road past the cathedral, nor ring of sparrows gleaning with the poultry at the mill, nor shoal of sheep by the doors of merchants, then will civilization find itself more a mistake than an advantage.

XII

A discussion over whiskey and figs at the Caffé Garibaldi. Whether phenomenology be idealistic or pragmatic, whether psychoanalysis might contribute to the solution of the problem of other minds.

A troop of cavalry cantered by jingling, red-coated, white-gloved, Mexican of moustache, Greek of eye, rout step, talking of women.

Philosophy in England?

— O, replied Mr. Hulme, it is a little circle of physicists around a New Zealander at Manchester named Rutherford, some mathematicians at Cambridge, a Jew from America, one Epstein, and a young Frenchman, Henri Gaudier, both sculptors, and three Americans, Percy Lewis, a painter, Tom Eliot, and Ezra Pound, poets.

Was Signore Ulmo of a seriousness, or did he, in the idiom, draw the leg?

— Never the leg! roared Hulme. Never the leg.

XIII

Across a stage in Paris, impersonating the puppet Petrushka, Vaslav Fomich Nijinsky hopped on his toes, jiggled his eyes, bounced like a jumping jack, went limp like a doll, sprang up as if shot from a bow, heel circling heel, the silliest of bumpkin's smiles on his carnival face. Hulme and Gaudier would see him in a few months as a faun with a leopard's balance dreaming in a liquid trance.

XIV

To realize, with precision, a feeling in all its fullness. With accuracy of tone. To be in the world is fate, to be aware of the world is, if our minds are analytical, philosophy, if our minds are synthetic, art.

What, it was asked of Monsieur Eulme, would be the philosophy of the twentieth century be, in his opinion, *en effet*.

—Great learning accompanied by squalid ignorance, sophistication vitiated by simplemindedness. Romanticism just might, if the worst happened, amplify fanaticism into hysteria. Classicism, that is, the rational life, had some chance of a renaissance: in the passion of the Mediterranean peoples, in the cold clarities of the French, in the formal intelligence of the Chinese.

—But it is not likely.

—*Perchè non?*

—Original sin. Rascals in power. The triviality of city life. Machines and turbines. Vulgarity.

XV

In the yellow and brown geometry of Bologna stood a figure, a man in a bowler hat. Perspective, with citizen. Hulme approached him with jolly English strides, perfuming the air with his pipe. He had thought, from a distance, that the man was Bergson, but as he drew nearer he saw that he wasn't. One of those Spanish blokes, was he? They fancied dark clothes, too, and were apt to wander off into the streets by themselves, to be shouted at by Italian voices inside dark rooms, from balconies, from behind walls. Or the voices would caution children not to look at the philosophers, who were sure to have the evil eye.

—I say, said Hulme, by way of greeting. *Buon giorno,* don't you know, what?

It surprised him that he spoke at all, but he was on the blighter before he knew it. Italy made one expansive, outgoing, decidedly un-British.

Something, no doubt, to do with the light. The splendid light.

—Hulme, he said. Here for the philosophical conference.

—*É successo qualche cosa? Smarrito?*

—Quite! beamed Hulme.

—*Non ci spadroneggiate!*

—The light! Don't you know, what?

—*Andatevene, feccia inglese, per i fatti vostri.*

—Astoundingly jolly, said Hulme indicating red roofs, long arcades, mellow light on walls. The continuity of it all.

XVI

On the third day of the conference the philosophers were taken by train to Ravenna where there was a reception for them given by the king.

At Galla Placidia Hulme stared at Byzantine mosaics, golden apostles on a ground of blue.

Christ the Shepherd bore a lamb. Christ Pantocrator blessed the world with his hands.

Sant' Apollinare in Classe Fuori stood in its pine grove, cylinder and rhomb, silo and barn, symbol and function inseparable. Stone and pine, gold and marble. The mosaics gleamed in moving glosses as he moved, a sheen of fire running from big eyes to the flow of beards and long calm hands clasping croziers and books.

The infinite moves both ways, inward, as here, outward, as on the Canadian prairies, radiant without bounds, focussed in a design of sharp lines, concavities, surfaces.

XVII
The full moon rose over the pines like the red face of a jolly farmer above a hedge.

The Trees at Lystra The Death of Picasso The Daimon of Sokrates Christ Preaching at the Henley Regatta Mesoroposthonippidon Lo Splendore della Luce a Bologna **Idyll** On Some Lines of Virgil The Trees at Lystra The Death of Picasso The Daimon of Sokrates Christ Preaching at the Henley Regatta Mesoroposthonippidon Lo Splendore della Luce a Bologna Idyll On Some Lines of Virgil The Trees at Lystra The Death of Picasso The Daimon of Sokrates Christ Preaching at the Henley Regatta Mesoroposthonippidon Lo Splendore della Luce a Bologna Idyll On Some Lines of Virgil The Trees at Lystra The Death of Picasso The Daimon of Sokrates Christ Preaching at the Henley Regatta Mesoroposthonippidon Lo Splendore della

The goatherd Komatas came down from the cool of the pines in the stink of his nannies, billies, and kids to find the spring where they were all to water surrounded by long-nosed, stick-shanked silly sheep.

And with them, leaning on his crook, legs crossed and with his free hand on his hip, stood Lakon, studiously unconcerned.

— Whoa, goats! Komatas said loud enough for Lakon to hear. The simples are down there trying to remember what you do to get a drink.

Pappas Posthidion, who smelled like asafetida, armpit, and ammonia, stuttered a bleat and backed behind three of his wives, who looked to Komatas with anxious oblong yellow eyes.

— Patience, he said. Hold it, Amaryllis. Doris, halt. Ninnies enough around here without you showing that the wind can blow through your ears. That's the thief from Sybaris down there who stole my coat.

Lakon bounced a truckle of curl from the bridge of his nose.

— Come on, sheep, he said. Drink up. What you smell is goats and Komatas, who stole my flute the other day, remember. That's why you haven't heard it.

— Happy sheep!

— Go do it with your nannies. They wouldn't notice.

— Fife? Komatas said. You ever had a fife? I've only heard tell of you hanging around with Korydon and toodling on a cane whistle. Other things, too, but not on a fife. Eh, Pappas?

Pappas coughed, peed a little, and stank furiously. Panesperessa stood her forelegs on Doris' flat back. The kids crowded in, nuzzling and wagging their tails.

— Lykon gave it to me, Lakon said with a measure of deference. I had a fife all right, until somebody took it. I'm slave and you're free: But by Hermes I don't steal.

Komatas scratched his testicles, saying nothing.

— What kind of coat?

— Hide. Needlework around the hem. Just your size. And mine.

— Even your master Eumaras doesn't have a hide coat. Nor a hide blanket, for that matter.

— You don't know. It's a coat Krokylos gave me, dyed blue, honor to the nymphs. You took it out of jealousy, didn't you? I see it in your eyes.

— Pan be my witness: I've never even seen your jacket. I swear it, and I swear it by the woods god, it is not Lakon son of Kalaithis who's got your wrap, your cloak, your anything. May I be struck crazy if I'm a liar, climb that rock yonder, and jump upside down into the Krathis.

— And I swear by the water girls who live in this spring (think well of me, ladies!) that I didn't sneak away any fife.

They stared at each other. A thousand cicadas rasped, the goats gargled, the sheep babbled.

— I believe you, Lakon said. Now I have nothing to stake in the match with Daphnis.

He scratched a sheep's withers with his crook. Komatas sat, and a kid walked onto his lap, nattering.

— Tell you what, Lakonidion: put up a kid, and I'll win it off you.

— A hog, as they say, once challenged Athena. You're on! You'll put up a fat lamb?

— Foxy, foxy! You call that fair? You can't shear a goat, and as for milk, I'd as soon pull the teats of a dog with hydrophobia as one of your nannies.

Komatas grinned. He saw the kind of match Lakon meant. Insults.

— You come on like a wasp at a cricket. I'll stake Pappas Posthidion.

Lakon's mouth dropped open.

— Who's set fire to your shirt? Easy, easy boy. Come over here under the olive.

The water's as clear as light.
The shade's green, the grass cool,
The quiet thick with cricket song.

— I wonder at you, Komatas said, knuckling a kid on the knobs. I taught you to sing, I've befriended you since you were waist high. If you were ever to win a singing match, it would be because I've spent whole afternoons keeping you in key, making you chime up and down the scales until singing was as natural as speech, making you learn the old songs. And this is what I get! *This!* Raise a wolf cub, as they say, and it will grow up to bite you. Look me in the eye!

Lakon looked, handsome as Hyakinthos, bright as butter.

— The wonder is, he smiled, how I've learned anything fitten from such a jealous sorehead as you.

— I remember how you squealed when I tupped you, like the nannies getting humped by the billies.

— Let's hope, Crosspatch, that when your time comes you get buried

deeper than you rammed me. Save your grumps until I've bested you.
Come on over, come on over and get beat.

— Not me, puppy.

These are my oaks, ragstone, and galingale,
My fat hives and singing bees, my silver spring,
My leaves alive with birds. Come sing here,
On this sweet crush of pinestraw, in the cool.

— What it comes down to is sheep or goats, by the tresses of Artemis.
Over here it's sheep, soft as a bed, billows of wool, breaths like violets.
Over there, O knackers of Herakles, it's a stink as solid as a plank, and
goats as bony as a rick of firewood and rough as field rocks.

Komatas tickled a kid and yawned.

— *Ah, oh, eh,* he sang, tuning up.

On easy ferns and pennyroyal we lie here,
Goats and herdsmen together, fellows all.
Sleek and smooth, a nanny's flank, nicer
By far than the wadded crump of a sheep.

Eight pails of milk, eight jugs of honeycomb
To honor Pan, lord of goats and the greenwood.

— So stay put, crookback!

So sing your country songs from the oaks.

— And what we need, Goat Boy, is a judge to say who's won. I wonder if we can find Lykopas?

— The cowherd? Not that bumpkin, Lakon, not him, never him. On
the hill yonder I can see Morson cutting briarwood.

— Holler for him. He's fine by me.

— Call him yourself. You're the challenger in this unseemly match.

Lakon ran to the rill and shouted through his hands. Morson, blue-
smocked, long of chin, an ax over his shoulder, strode within hearing distance.

— We're having a match, Lakon called, song against song, a sheep
against a goat. Come be the judge!

Morson arrived with a grin for the honor and the rest.

— No favors, Komatas said. Be fair.

—I know I'm prettier than him, Lakon said. Put that aside and judge the songs alone.

—Whose flocks? Morson asked.

—The sheep are Sibyrtas', of Thurii; the goats are Eumaras', of Sybaris. But for the purpose of the match, they're ours, you may understand.

Morson, dubious, circled his hand in the air and pulled his chin.

—We told you the truth, didn't we? Komatas said. All we're asking is that you decide the match. If you don't want to judge, you can go back to chopping wood. No harm done.

—Komatas is trying to oil out! Lakon complained.

—I'm not! You might even like to know that I made a solemn sacrifice to the Muses just two days ago, and that the priest read in his signs that I have a better voice than Daphnis the cantor of Apollon: wet your whistle with that, puppy pizzle.

—All well and good, stinky, but I dedicated that big ram to Apollon not a week ago, to be presented at the Karneia.

—Except two, all my nannies are giving milk, and all have borne twins, and a certain girl who is not unmindful of my existence has said, by way of broad hint, that she thinks I ought to have someone to help me at the pail and with the cheese.

—Ha! sang Lakon, *and stuff.*

Lakon the shepherd as handsome as Hermes
Has laid by this season twenty slats of cheese
And lain by a beardless boy in a flower bed.
He . . .

But Komatas broke in.

Klearista tosses apples to a goatherd
As he passes with his flock, whistles
And looks sideways with a friendly glance.

Then Lakon:

Kratidas, he of the smooth flat cheeks,
The shepherd, follows me about, and oh!
I am senseless with longing. His bright hair
Curls tight against his stout brown neck.

Komatas:

Neither sweetbriar nor anemone can compare
With the border rose that grows along a wall.

Lakon:

Nor acorns with musk robin pears, bitter
With sweet, oak rough with honey smooth.

Komatas:

I have a dove to give my girl that I caught
In a juniper tree, gentle gentle are those two.

Lakon:

When I've a black lamb shorn, the soft wool
I'll give to Kratidas, to make a fine soft coat.

Komatas:

Sitta, goats! Away from that olive, now.
Come browse this slope, under the tamaracks.

Lakon:

Well away from those oaks, Konaros, Kynaitha,
Come pasture here, beside the ram Phalaros.

Komatas:

I have a carved bowl of cypress wood, the work
Of the sculptor Praxiteles, to give my love.

Lakon:

I have a shepherd dog that throttles wolves
To give my love, to drive away marauders.

Komatas:

Grasshoppers crossing my vineyards, take care:
The grapes are darkening red in the sun.

Lakon:

Watch, crickets, how I annoy this goatherd,
Go, do the same to his harvesters, quick, quick.

Komatas:

I hate a bushy tailed fox roaming at night
To glean and savage Mikon's vines.

Lakon:

I hate the Junebugs who gnaw Philondas' figs
And fly away, creatures as light as the wind.

Komatas:

Have you forgotten the day I buggered you,
When with gritted teeth you hugged that oak
And wiggled your behind in four-four time?

Lakon:

I do not remember it, I do remember, well,
When Eumaras pinioned you right over there,
And drubbed you properly, within the rules.

—Aye, Morson, has either of us drawn blood? Komatas asked. Go gather squills from an old woman's grave for poor Lakon when he's fallen.

—Can't you see that I've defeated him, Morson? Fetch cyclamen from Hales' beds. It's the judge's duty to see to the fallen.

—Fallen? said Komatas.

When the Himera runs with milk and the Krathis
Is a river of wine, and its skirrets bear fruit.

—And I, said Lakon.

When the Sybaritis wells with honey, and girls
Carry pitchers of it away on their heads.

Komatas:

My goats nibble laburnum and havergrass,
They walk daintily on mastic, sleep in arbors.

Lakon:

My lambs bounce in melissa and the rock rose
Makes them a garden, a profusion of salads.

Komatas:

How can I love Alkippa still? She took the dove
But not me by the ears to kiss me thanks.

Lakon:

But I love Eumedes with a great love.
When I gave him my fife, he gave me
A long lovely lingering enormous kiss.

Komatas:

It is forbidden, Lakon, for magpies
To fight with nightingales, hoopoes
With swans: and as for your loves,
All you really like to do is quarrel.

— By the lord Herakles! Morson cried. I beg you to have done. Lakon, you lose. Komatas, you win the lamb. If you give it to the nymphs, remember me in the invitations.

— By Pan, Morson, I shall indeed. Get lost, Lakon! Come, goats, let's all have a bath. We stink. Come, Doris, Leukos, Pappas, Penelope, Artemis, Athena, Esperessa, all.

— Wash Morson's ears while you're at it, Lakon said.

— Come wash off your own blushes, Lakon, Komatas said from the pool. Let me duck your face in and hear the water sizzle.

— Get in there with those goats! Lakon said, holding his nose.

Komatas waved his pizzle back at him and got a gorgon's face in return.

— Freeze that way!

Pappas came gingerly into the water, looking at all his wives as if they might melt.

— Lakon! Komatas called. Come back. The water's delicious. I don't want your lamb.

— You don't?

— I couldn't take your lamb. You'd get your butt beat for it, anyway.

— You want to duck me.

— Wouldn't think of it!

— By Pan?

— By Pan.

Lakon dropped his wrap and ran high kneed and splashing into the pool, backing goats in all directions, where Komatas caught him and ducked him.

They ran to dry themselves and sat, winded, in the last of the sun, gossiping, plaiting grass, laughing.

— There's milk, cool from the spring, back yonder.

— Some loaf's in my kit.

The sky had turned violet in the west and a single star stood above the red peak of the range. The air was now chill, became damp, and quickened into breezes.

— I guess I fell asleep.

— Not long.

— I put your wool blanket over you. You was scrooged like you was cold.

— I *am* cold. And I stink.

— Old Grizzle will be around to change the dressing, never fret.

— He's a good man, is Old Grizzle. No whiskey and no hymns, but if he really can keep that hacksaw-happy major away from my leg, he's my friend for life. And if ever I git back to Ohio, I'm going to ast if them parts of the Bible he reads us are *in* the Bible.

Down by the wagons someone was playing *Poor Kitty Popcorn* on a banjo. It was the blue Susquehanna and riverboats and September rusting into October, sweet smoke from the ricks, and cornshucking and Polly and the round moon red as an Indian pudding over the chinquapin grove.

— I do hate me the Army.

— Anybody liked it would be a fool pure and simple.

— I see the lantern. Next we'll hear old Tolly squeal when the major pokes around in his back again to see did they find all the pieces of that ball. Thar! What did I say!

— Sounds like an old cow lost her calf.

— Next you'll hear that Methodist chaplain hoot off one for Jesus.

— I think he'd pray for a reb fore he knew what he was doing.

— Shit I reckon.

— Boys! Boys!

Old Grizzle came through the flaps whistling along with the banjo. He smiled with his sharp grey eyes rather than his mouth, which was a line of tight resolution in his beard. He laid out a canvas kit, cheesecloth, scissors, needle and thread.

He lifted away the blanket and folded it as he stared at the bandage on which some luxuriant jungle fungus had spread to the size of a plate, a smut or gall. Deftly, with scissors and tongs, he sliced it and peeled it away. He sloshed a mixture reeking of pine tar onto a cotton wad and began a businesslike swabbing of the ugly wound.

— You can have one strong manly example of profanity for the sting of this, he said as he worked.

But all he got was a choked grunt.

— Brave, brave.

— That sheep dip smells considerable better than the overripe possum we been breathing. Here comes the major.

A sergeant with a lantern preceded a weary officer in an apron stained with blood. There was a spatter of some nameless effluvium on the right lens of his spectacles.

— Does that leg smell of gangrene, Whitman? he asked Old Grizzle in a low voice, almost without concern.

— I wonder, Sir. I do indeed wonder.

— Fever in the groin?

— Some. No more than with any other wound, though. The sepsis is under control. I've seen nastier suppurations than this heal over neatly. We cauterized it in time.

Outside, at a distance, a bugle called, and was answered by a spirited *O dear! What can the matter be! The matter be!* on the orderly's cornet.

— God in heaven, the major said. More wagons.

— We heard this afternoon about skirmishes all morning twenty or so miles out from Fredericksburg, sir.

— Are you finished here?

— I won't be long, sir.

— They never learn how to do the tourniquets, the major said, ducking out. A hamper of splints, Whitman, hear? This bitching war, this bitching war!

— Spares us the chaplain: it's a shitten wind don't blow somebody good.

The bugles were pitching high their rallies. They could hear shouts, and the wagons. Grizzle had bound the wound in clean cheesecloth and stitched it fast.

— Orderlies! the cry went up outside. Nurses! On the double, on the double!

Grizzle gave them each a pecking kiss on the forehead, rolled his kit, and left on the run.

In the night there were more wagons, and at least two outfits, they guessed from the artillery and the kitchens, moving south, the lash and clang of their caisson chains ringing above the screams, and toward morning the wind brought the thin sound of a band playing *The Girl I Left Behind Me,* which meant that they were digging in the fieldpieces and dressing on the corporals' guidons across some forsaken field of Virginia where they could see, like a team at the far end of a furrow, three boys in grey, one with a drum, one with a fife, and one with that damned flag, advancing at a slow but intrepid pace.

The Trees at Lystra The Death of Picasso The Daimon of Sokrates Christ Preaching at the Henley Regatta Mesoroposthonippidon Lo Splendore della Luce a Bologna Idyll On Some Lines of Virgil The Trees at Lystra The Death of Picasso The Daimon of Sokrates Christ Preaching at the Henley Regatta Mesoroposthonippidon Lo Splendore della Luce a Bologna Idyll On Some Lines of Virgil The Trees at Lystra The Death of Picasso The Daimon of Sokrates Christ Preaching at the Henley Regatta Mesoroposthonippidon Lo Splendore della Luce a Bologna Idyll **On Some Lines of Virgil** The Trees at Lystra The Death of Picasso The Daimon of Sokrates Christ Preaching at the Henley Regatta Mesoroposthonippidon Lo Splendore della

I

Around the old Hôtel Sassard on the rue Roquelaure in the Quartier Mé-
riadeck of Bordeaux there runs a wall, a high and impressively substan-
tial wall of good grey French stone, and in it for some years there lived
a man, my Uncle Jacques, my mother's brother.

Except from above, where you can see that a walk continues all along the
top, like a battlement, or as I fancied, like the Great Wall of China, you
do not suspect that the wall is so broad. Yet inside, all the way around, it
is uniformly the width of a door.

Some architect from the time when it was usual to live on bridges, over
city gates, and to connect houses to the city wall must have conceived this
gallery like a cellar around a property that is both a brilliant use of space
and a buffer to the world outside.

Fustel de Coulanges in *La Cité antique* tells how ancient walls were double, with a thoroughfare between, the origin of alleys and streets. Walls,
sacred to the god of boundaries Terminus (herm, garland, phallus) could
not be shared by adjoining grounds.

Uncle Jacques, the man in the wall, was spoken of if at all by the few who
remembered him as *cet boudeur au séjour mélancolique,* the bones in the
cupboard of what he called our proud and distinguished family now in a
sorry way, whose *secret fâcheux* he was.

II

Now me, Jolivet Bonnat, of a summer morning the year of the regimen of
these *brouillons,* waking with a stretch and a yawn under my model in
balsa and doped paper of L'Avro 504K (1917), fuselage checkered yellow
and black, and a poster of Delaunay's *Blériot.*

With my legs tiptoe up and my hands in the small of my back, I balanced
on nape and shoulders, crowing. Catapulted onto the floor, I approved
the progress of my tan, doffed pyjamas, and called my little brother Victor a pig for sleeping in his singlet and shorts.

Because they were new, he explained, and came to watch me pee with an erection, beginning with an arc nicely aimed, moving closer as it wilted, until a shake over the bowl, Victor adding his stream alongside while knuckling a sleepy eye, ramming my runnel with his.

To Victor and me, Uncle Jacques was The Man in the Iron Mask, the wall his prison, some abjured figure in the hidden corridors of the fateful mansions of Maurice Leblanc and E. Phillips Oppenheim. The wall was our privileged domain, our secret and refuge.

Pulling on a football jersey and minim of flowery brief that Papa brought me from England, I gave my usual cursory thought to what part of the wall Uncle Jacques paced in his musty dark while Victor and I dressed in sweet light and nipped downstairs hungry.

III

Old Postel, our gardener, concierge, and steward, would be bringing Uncle Jacques his strange breakfast and taking away his chamberpot while Victor and I ate our *croissants* with jam and butter and drank our coffee with *Le Sud-Ouest* spread all over the table.

As far as Maman was concerned, Uncle Jacques didn't exist. She flatly refused to discuss him at all. She understood the natural affinities of boys for attics and treehouses, to which family the wall belonged. Mice and recluses, she would have added to boys.

While Victor, who had begged to, was grinding the coffee and making his usual mess of it, Maman said that sleeping in one's clothes was bad for the circulation and that she hoped I was not going out to see Uncle Jacques the way I was dressed, in underpants.

Especially those underpants. Do you realize, Joli sweetheart, she said, that Jacques writes me letters, through the post would you believe, about the indecency of the way you and Victor dress. I think he wants to see you in knickerbockers, jacket, and golf cap.

Let's, said Victor, grimping his gilet into a gruff around his ribs, go out in nothing, *tiens.* I pulled my crotch at him. *Bêh! Bêh!* Maman bleated like a goat diddering its wattle. Get out, both of you little buggers. Go see your idiot Uncle in his dungeon.

IV

At the traffic light where the Judaïque crosses St.-Sernin a Fiat rammed a Renault from behind and all eight hubcaps fell off. The drivers popped out. The one called the other a Chinese, a species of moron, a Picasso. The other told him to do it with his mother.

She's used to it, he said, swishing his hands around his hips. Horns, razzes, and Schubert from a radio. Slaps with driving gloves, kicks at testicles. Whereupon through the snarl of cars came Marc Aurel in his wheelchair, pushed by Monsieur Trombone in a duster.

I ran to meet them. That Balkan, I shouted, called the bastard he rammed a Picasso. I saw them smash. What fun. We resent it, Marc Aurel said, Picasso and I. Picasso, part collie, part Bordeaux dog, sat on Marc Aurel's footrest switching his feathery tail.

He raised a paw and shook hands with me. I shook hands with Marc Aurel and Monsieur Trombone, who murmured *yes yes* in his manner, mopping his brow with his sleeve. Move on! an *agent* cried at us on his way to the fighting drivers. Picasso gave him a big grin.

We're off to the Gambetta, Marc Aurel said. Come with us, Jolivet. There are things to be told about our new linoleum and lots of new books and soupbones from the Culte Baptiste. Monsieur Trombone held his hand high as we crossed the rue du Palais Gallien.

V

Uncle Jacques' wet eyes shifted and glistened in the lamplight. That boy with no legs, he said, don't he act not bright sometimes? I thought so. I guess it would make you simple not to have legs, wouldn't you think? *Hein!* And as for that bastard who pushes him!

I see them any time of day, the scum of the earth, sometimes in the dead of the night. You'd think that as worthless a shit as that what do you call him? Trombone, I said patiently. Trombone! Mother of God, even he could do better than push a halfwit through the streets.

What gets me is that they don't care who sees them. I'd be ashamed. Anybody else but them would have some self-respect. But people don't care about anything anymore. And you hang around with them! What does your mother think of that? I don't think she cares, I said.

She wouldn't. Families mean nothing anymore. I wonder the Sassards had such a daughter as your mother, I really do. His trembling fingers shaped a gutter of cigarette paper into which he sprinkled villainous shag. Twisting the ends, he sealed the seam with a lick.

The match made a sudden spook of shadow behind him. Isn't Marc Aurel his name? Yes, I said, I've lent him my *Village aérien* and he's lent me his *Cinq Semaines en ballon*. Uncle Jacques was puzzled, angry. Books? he gasped. Verne. You'll never see your book again! he cried.

VI

Tout Bordeaux and scholars the world over, Papa says, know the outsized bull walrus moustache of the Italian 'Pataphysician and *vincianista squisito* Ugo Giangiacomo Tullio, aesthetician, iconographer, and professor of the History of Art at the University of Bordeaux.

It was not quite as pathologically copious as Nietzsche's but was rich, black, and glossy enough to hold the field against all contenders for the most Italianate moustache in southwest France. His cigars were pungent, his conversation impassioned, his prose famous.

His moustache, Papa says, is Mark Twain's translated into Italian by Leopardi, tamed by wax and scissors that snipped at it like a goldfinch working its way around a cluster of sumac berries. Any morning you could see the moustache at the Globe or the Régent.

At the Brasserie Globe if Tullio were in the mood to talk with students and friends, at the Régent further around the Place Gambetta if he wanted to be alone to write in his notebook. It is always fun to be invited to join him at his late coffee and croissant with jam.

Young Bonnat! he says. I park my bike by a boxwood *jardinière,* dance my eyes at him for the mischief of it, and straddle a chair. This pot of jam, he says, taste it. It was sent me from Taiwan. You know the lovely ginkgo, there are several in the botanical gardens.

VII

Ginkgo biloba, Tullio says, an archaic conifer with the needles spread into a notched fan, remarkable bit of morphology, gold in autumn. This is ginkgo jam. But the fruit stinks, I say. The greater the triumph of the *confiturière.* The only real alchemy is *la cuisine.*

Especially the Chinese. Nature, you know, designed the ginkgo to stand in the great Eocene washes that would in later ages sort out into lakes and rivers. The female was pollinated by a male upstream, not by bees. Are you, dear Jolivet, having a splendid summer of it?

I said I was. And you, sir? At my age everything is always the same. I am grateful for each day and what I can get done in it. We are coming to dinner with you, I believe, next week. The Bonnat household is one of the few places my wife genuinely likes being asked to.

My good wife, you know, is terrible at French and you French are so unforgiving of unskilled speakers that she prefers not to risk embarrassment. Your mother and father are perfectly understanding and both can manage a fair Italian if they are urged. What lovely manners!

Everywhere she goes people correct my wife's grammar. My God, but at the market on the Victor Hugo the peasants selling vegetables give her lessons in the subjunctive. The oyster and the flatfish man sorts out *y* and *en* for her. She says the French are a nation of pedants.

VIII

I suppose we are a nation of pedants, aren't we? In everything, dear Jolivet, in everything. The ginkgo jam from Professor Wu in Taiwan tasted like zucchini boiled in perfume and honey. Tullio had been reading Georges Dumézil's *Tarpeia,* a hundred francs for bookmark.

He also had the miniature *Massime degli Egiziani antichi* of Boris de Rachewiltz, and his notebook, in which he had written *Ignorance is a kind of knowledge, knowledge a kind of ignorance.* And *Inside custom there is a natural life.* Look here, he said, turning a notebook page.

In *The Book of Coming Forth by Day* Annu says to the sun that *the earth becomes green through thee,* the ash tree, shent and aser. The history of science, Jolivet, is the history of intuition. Over at the Department of Chemistry they will tell you Egypt was ignorant.

That they knew no more of photosynthesis than a Sicilian grandmama. Yet there it is: *Hail, great sycamore of Nut: grant me the water and air that is in thee.* Water and air! The observation is precise, the truth exact. The idea of carbohydrates in ancient Egypt! There it is.

Ah, he said, looking across the *place,* there's Signora Cavolfiore, admirable woman but what a name, and Signorina Giunchiglia, what Parisian eyes, how Mediterranean her grace. He waved a finger and gave them a merry eye. So beautiful the day! shouted La Cavolfiore.

IX

A Milesian smile from La Giunchiglia, a Bach partita, wine and bread, and a lizard hot with Aegean light ran doubtless down his spine, as if from a frieze of ruined and rampant centaurs into basil and gentian. And there was Marc Aurel, with Trombone, from the Vieille Tour.

Do not they, Tullio said, live in some desperate room in back of a garage? What an odd collection of clothing they seem to own, both of them. From the Culte Baptiste, I explained, and the priest at St.-Seurin, and one place and another. My mother sees that they don't do without.

We have, Marc Aurel said rolling up to the Régent, been by the bar of the Théâtre to see Auguste the cat, the big yellow fellow with plenty of whiskers. We only stop at the door, they don't like us inside, and Auguste comes out, pretending there's no Picasso.

And Picasso pretends there's no cat. He lets me scritch him under the chin. Then down the Bonnet Rouge and the Intendance, where we met up with Noé, and had a chase, round and round, up through the Tour into the Ramparts. They got into a sand pile and didn't they make it fly!

Noé dug to China while Picasso ran with his ears on backwards, higgledy here, piggledy there, I thought he would turn himself inside out, and then he rocketed into the sand pile and scrambled and scattered and scrummaged while Noé zipped back and around, around and back.

x
It was worth your life to get in his way, and when they were winded his tongue hung out nearbout to his toes. O what a day! We saw the morning news on TV at the Brasserie Montaigne, you can see it through the glass from the sidewalk, and a flic, *figurez ça,* set us up.

A red wine for us both, and a free cigarette for Trombone. And then we did the botanical garden, and read the names of flowers, some from Canada, some from Java, some from South Carolina, and then all the Catherine, to the Place Victoire, for the newspapers left on benches.

And Picasso married a yellow bitch in front of everybody, including a priest and a nun, and here we are back again, Monsieur Professeur Tullio and Jolivet! Trombone lifted his Beckett hat in greeting. It had in its ancestry a chimney pot, a gumboot, and a Cannibal King.

Of Marc Aurel's cap slanting dapperly on the spikelets and whorls of his rambunctious hair, Trombone remarked that it was English. It flew from the head of a rich *anglais* tooling a Jaguar toward Arcachon. A Jaguar costs the roof of the Hotel de Ville. The English are all rich.

Why should he stop for a cap that has sailed from his head when he has ten more, all different fabrics, in his armoire at home? You can smell his pomade inside, said Trombone passing it around, brandied coconut. It's a jolly cap, Marc Aurel said, don't you figure?

XI

Uncle Jacques' washstand was like the ones in the Musée des Arts Décoratifs in the rue Bouffard, as were his candlesticks, shoehorn, flywhisk, covered soapdish, hairbrush, and bronze and enamel pomade box, antiques all, presences of past authority, objects for a museum.

The Man in the Iron Mask would have had such portables in whatever ambience he was banished from. The rainy afternoon I found and read Alexandre Dumas' essay I recognized Uncle Jacques in the Man in the Iron Mask. When I ask why Uncle Jacques is there, Maman says *qui sait?*

Voltaire may have known who the Man in the Iron Mask was, but died with his secret. One of Napoleon's first orders when he was First Consul asked that the records be searched for his identity. Nothing was found. If Uncle Jacques wanted to, he could walk right out, free.

I watch the rain on the flowers and laurels. If I want to, I can go out snug in my English raincoat and walk down the Clemenceau, around the Place Tourny, through the Jardin Public, the Jardin of the Mairie, both lovely in rain. But Uncle Jacques only looks out the slits in the wall.

He walks that long, cornered corridor. Like the Man in the Iron Mask he is circumscribed by stone, resourceless, trapped. Papa says that he won't ever come out. Why, I ask? His jailer won't let him. His jailer? Himself, says Papa. He lives in mortal fear of letting himself out.

XII

The Man in the Iron Mask once wrote his history all over a newly starched shirt and threw it out his barred window, but the guards got it and burned it. The mask was not actually of iron, it was molded velvet, with eyes, nosehole, and mouth. Uncle Jacques' face is his mask.

I lie on top of the wall and look into the reticulum of leaves and branches, comfortable on old stone and moss, and inventory my hoard. *Des plaisirs.* Jules Verne's *Journey to the Center of the Earth* read in the windowseat looking out into rain, in bed, finished in the garden.

Tullio's lecture on the house Wittgenstein designed and built in Vienna, with slides, and what Papa said about it afterwards at the Régent, *genius rising to perfection in a fanatic's hands.* Tripton, plankton, nekton, seston, an old coelocanth tarnished silver and green deep down.

Blériot's Antoinette at the Musée des Arts et Métiers in Paris: Papa lifted me up to touch the wheel. Hands at Pech-Merle, dotted horses, the play of light in the cavern. Les Frères Goncourt: Victor and I with a house together, music at midnight, ice cream for breakfast.

Rain on the laurels. The old coelocanth, silverscaled, inches through the benthon. Turning the pages in the windowseat of Maillol's *P. Virgilii Maronis Eclogae et Georgica.* Tullio asks to look at it when he visits, as a treat, and he and Papa talk about its *latinité* and *éclat.*

XIII

The wall is not as inert in its weather as a cave with its still temperature and blind fish in subterranean lenses of black water, but it has a cave's quiet and sterility. A little dawn freshness gets in, and something of the hush of sunset, *l'heure exquise* hinted at, local tones.

These slight graduations of the hours must be as real to Uncle Jacques as the range of light on the Tourny, as bright as Mexico on a summer day, as grey as Paris in winter, a different tone for every day of autumn, every day of spring. I forget, outside, the strangeness of the wall.

September inside is distinct from April once you learn the difference. Some perfume of blossoms and the whistling and piping of birds come into that narrow darkness. God knows cold walks through its stone with an iron knee, and the August sun can make it a baker's oven.

Those for whom, Tullio says, the night of time has no dreams must live in the cruel suddenness of day by day. I think he lives in his mind in an old Florentine autumn of horses, bridges, and churches, and in Jarry's frolic, in the Venice of D'Annunzio, the Sicily of Virgil.

Faustroll in his sieve slides across Brittany, the mesh of his 'pataphysical skiff afloat through surface tension on the microsphere, punted around obstacles with his Bulgarian shepherd's goad, with which he also propels himself smoothly forward, backward, sideways.

XIV

On the wicker chaise longue by the oval taboret covered with blue velvet on which sat an Italian gramophone with morning glory horn and a purfled scroll of gold and green olive branches and wheat, Maman was reading a cookbook with an old woodcut artichoke on its cover.

She was also reading the novel by Italo Calvino about a boy who lived in the trees of his estate. It was open over her knees. The gramophone was a gift from the Tullios, and had cylinders of Galli-Curci and Caruso to go with it. Sweetheart, she greeted me, whatever's that?

New style, I said, for around the house, explaining why I was wearing only a white singlet. I leaned for a kiss and was gathered in for a hug. Michel never wears anything at home. It feels great. I don't care, she said, but what about other people, Jolivet, eh?

I've washed that behind thousands of times. Won't Postel, however, swallow his false teeth when he sees you? You can hear him clumping forty meters away, I replied. Postel could swallow his teeth except for the flack I'd get from Uncle Jacques. Postel is his spy.

You're getting to be a man, she said, if I may be permitted the remark. About time, I said. This is the summer, Maman, that I'm going to learn all sorts of things that have nothing to do with school: art and Tullio's 'pataphysics, and politics. I'm a Socialist like Michel.

XV

And read the books I want to read. I'm going to build a World War I Spad and keep a notebook of exact observations, to examine emotions and focus ideas, and get brown as gingerbread, and shape up my body like Michel's, and make out like crazy with Jonquille when I can.

We threw up our hands together, for the fun of it. Is, she said, seducing Jonquille, lucky girl, to be effected between the Spad and dear Ugo's discourses, or between swimming and being the new Amiel? Really, Jolivet Bonnat, you never cease to amaze. You'll be careful?

Natch. Does Jonquille, she asked, know about this? Does she like you so much? She seems to. A willing comrade, that girl, I said. Meaning that you've already begun. Mothers have X-ray minds. I don't get a lecture from Papa, do I? I wouldn't think so. He'll be envious.

But, sweetheart, she went on, lighting a Gitane, I want you to do more things with Victor, who worships you. He sulks so when he's left out. Last summer you positively ran from him. Make a friend of him, bring him out. I love the little pest, I said, and may even like him.

She told me about the boy who lived in trees and asked me to be on the lookout for other things by Calvino for her. I left to sunbathe on top of the wall, daring to sprint britchesless across the garden, shinny the elm, and go on all fours to a bright stretch hot as noon.

XVI

Victor whistling the Persons with Long Ears part of Saint-Saëns' *Carnival of the Animals* shook baffled curls from his eyes to inspect in the thin first tender light on the Dordogne his Cupid's tump for fuzz. I added The Royal March of the Lions, which he made a duet.

Swinging a straight leg in a slow arc to bump Victor's backside with my heel, I asked him what he was looking for, crabs? Any attention, even a kick, makes him shine a smile. We waded into the river together and hollered to Michel kneeling in green dapple, kindling the fire.

What's that you two are whistling? he called. It's crazy. The animals, Victor said, peeing. It's like the Poulenc and the Apollinaire *cortège*. Tullio once reeled off a list as long as your arm of troops of animals in procession, from Noah's ark and Orpheus the charmer onward.

The Saint-Saëns was one of the first records Victor and I ever had. We must have played it a million times. Don't, Michel said, let a minnow nip Victor's *queue* thinking it's a grub. O lion! Victor recited in his school voice, sitting in the river up to his chin.

> O lion, malheureuse image
> Des rois chus lamentablement,
> Tu ne nais maintenant qu'en cage
> A Hambourg, chez les Allemands.

XVII

Make room in the river, Michel shouted. I chose the moment to admire his coming four times last night. He grinned his goldenest, soaping. Your shoulders look like a boiled lobster. Who's making coffee? Sarlat by noon! *Mon pauvre coeur,* Victor intoned, *est un hibou.* Four times?

Animals are the genius of Aquitaine. Rosa Bonheur's *Horse Fair* is a continuation of the frieze of bovids and tarpans in Lascaux. There were bronze horses in the Quinconx which the Nazis pulled down and melted, to be replaced someday, Papa says, rampant Roman horses.

Tullio lectures on the cortège as symbol, all about shepherds, kings, judges, poets, Orpheus in Rilke, Cocteau, Apollinaire, Picasso, Redon. About wild and tame, civilization and savagery. Ausonius liked to have things in series, like Noah and Orpheus: rivers, professors, cities.

A cortège of fellow Bordelais: Catulle Mendès, Rosa Bonheur, Odilon Redon, François Mauriac, Montaigne, Montesquieu, Jean Quidor who thought that the eucharist was God and bread chemically bonded, not the one replacing the other. Charron, Boetie, many cats and dogs.

Goya died here. The *Bulls of Bordeaux* etchings unconsciously rhyme with the Lascaux hunter and his disemboweled bison. Picasso's *Guernica* fuses the cave paintings and Goya. A cortège is a tribe of tribes. Michel, Victor, Jonquille and I constitute a kind of tribe.

XVIII
In the leaves, green creel freckled gold, in an uncertainty of flowers and leaves, bright flowers sweet as a kiss in a dream, a faun pert and startled looks out from this embroidery of blossom and branch, two eyes, white teeth: he is eating a red flower.

In the calm of the riverbank at morning our voices lost their familiarity, were a surprise, low and resonant against so much silence. I sat in the sweet cool threading the aglets of my new white laces, bought back in Bergerac, through the grommets of my sneakers.

Maman was right as usual about the life expectancy of the old ones, though she agreed out of habit that things are not yours until they are worn to the scuffs and creases and give of possession. A string of stubborn knots, however loved, is not a shoelace up to a point.

They were sacrificed in a campfire by the Dordogne. That they had lots of wear in them yet was Michel's rotten opinion, Victor adding his copycat second all the way. Dark and winey with chewed flower, the faun's mouth opens wide with laughter among the shaken leaves.

They flutter, the leaves, after he has left, quick as a squirrel, and only a bullfinch, unseen before, remains, and brightness scattered in the wood, like a shiver after a kiss. From Sicily to Charleville to the Val Dordogne, do teachers know what they are passing on?

XIX
Three quatrains of Rimbaud to replace a pair of laces. It made Victor, who was quiddling his foreskin while sipping his coffee, look at me cross-eyed, and Michel, pulling on socks after giving them a dog's sniff and pulling a face, flashed a splendid smile.

Whether out of brimming friendliness, that bright grin, or for Rimbaud one does not ask. At home you dress from the top down, shirt first and shoes last. Camping out, you dress from the bottom up, socks first. Thus Victor, babbling, on Michel in socks only.

I reached across him grumping and hooked Michel's jockstrap from his sleeping bag, inspected it draped between my thumbs, its cup sprung, crupper twirled, cingles shirred, and standing to recite Rimbaud again, drew it on, settling the fit as neat as a shell on an egg.

Michel mugged a mope but accepted the swap by hitching all of my toggery in a swoop from the handlebars of my Peugeot. Poor me! said Victor monkeying his ribs, I'm too little to switch britches with anybody. Keep pulling your puppy's dock, Michel said. You'll get there.

Graceful child of Pan! I intoned. From under the chaplet of honeysuckle and berries around your forehead, your rich eyes stare, wine stains on your flat cheeks. Your dogteeth show white, a lyre your chest. A music on its strings flows rippling into your blond arms.

xx

Michel flexed a biceps, the faun. Victor stuck fingers through his curls for horns. Inside the flat rondure of your abdomen stands a second cock. Stride out, come night, gliding lightly that thigh, the other, and the one between. Michel jaunced his sex with a hunch.

That's a poem? Victor asked in his voice for rooting out fraud. It's beyond your years, Monkey, said Michel, hefting Victor by the armpits. Crying *catch!* he tossed him whooping to me. I caught him, turned him upside down, swung him around, and heaved him back.

Michel scooped him into a hug from his squealing flip, rolled him over his shoulder, and swivelled so that they collapsed with Victor topside in the grabble, crowing. You were jiggling it when I woke, said Michel taking hold, let's see if it works beyond make like.

It works all right, I said, hunkering beside them with a huff and whistle, overtime too. He only comes a smidgin but he's been an eager slogger at it since I showed him how. So, said Michel, let's drive him crazy. As slow as that? said Victor. As slow as this, scamp.

It's a matter of style, ask anybody, ask Jolivet. I was myself feeling like Proust's little weatherman, who popped out and removed his hat for fair. It's clear, I said, that you don't have a little brother. If I did, he said, this is what I would do to keep him happy.

XXI

Settling back with a roll buttered and bejammed, I asked Michel depraving Victor when we were setting out. Michel wanted more coffee, Victor another roll. It is not true that one pleasure precludes another. Victor will make his babies while tucking into an andouillette.

He lay spread on the grass, jutting his tongue through pursed lips to show his approval of Michel's knack, feigning sophistication with his hands under his head, looking into the early blue of the sky, with the chance casual peek at the pink bud of his glans bobbing in his foreskin.

Sleeve up quick, peel down slow, Michel said, how's that for good, Monkey? Is it ever, said Monkey. None of this was doing anything for my composure, starting a tickling in the roof of my mouth, a giddy swarming in my balls, a flutter in the tummy, a rush of affection.

And then, said Michel, there's sleeve up with a long pull, and a slow peel down. Jonquille, I offered, fiddles with my balls while she's doing it, and scrunches them about. Like this. Feels funny, was Victor's opinion. And moreover, said Michel, there's fast for awhile.

O wow, said Victor drumming his heels. And stop and grip, and a nice trotting rhythm. I'm about to come, said Victor munching his roll. No, said Michel, you're not. He nipped the glans with two fingers, pressing into the frenulum with his thumb, pulling up smartly.

XXII

We're in the capable hands of a champion, I assured Victor, who sat up to watch, puzzled of brow, round of eye. I stared, erect, learning. Let it wilt, Michel said, finish your roll and suit up for the road. We'll come back to it, build up and stop, till you're dancing randy.

I whistled my amazement, which was really admiration. Michel is always good for a surprise. Victor studied his standing cock as if seeing it for the first time. Perhaps he was. Michel made me see mine. Jonquille rarely looks, and says it's the funniest thing she's ever seen.

We struck camp, strapped rucksacks and *porte bagages,* wheeled out of the wood where we'd slept, and pedalled down the leafy road by the river, past other campers setting out, past farms and fields bright with sun. Why did I think with a sinking feeling of Uncle Jacques in the wall?

Of the stale air in the wall, his body sheathed in long underwear, heavy socks, woolen trousers, a beret pulled down to his ears. He would keel over dead if he knew how we made each other's bodies thump with pleasure. We snaked in and around each other all the way to Sarlat.

We shed our gilets as the sun rose high, reddening our tans. We hailed cows and a file of Boy Scouts and the Citram bus. What, said Michel, shall we do when we've camped this afternoon, once we've made pulp of Victor's brain, something perfectly awful but good clean fun?

XXIII

In moted, slant museum light through old panes blebbed and undular, there is a photograph on a wall of the Institute of Prehistory taken in 1912 of the little river Volp as it flows out of the cavern of the Tuc d'Audoubert, a portrait group of discoverers all.

The Comte de Bégouën, through whose estate down near Spain the river runs, wears a cloth cap and English tweeds, and has a brass lantern and a stout stick in his hands. His three sons, for whom Trois Frères is named, who discovered that cave and the Tuc, are with him.

That's Max at the left, a shock of hair pushed down to his eyes by a wide-awake hat. He resembles a pony. His sailor's turtleneck pullover and double-breasted jacket with big buttons give his clear, oval, long-nosed face a seagoing air. That's Louis on the Count's left, fourteen.

The third son, Jacques, sits rubber-booted in a bateau named *The Volp*, homemade and steadied by a lashed outrigging of casks. That's the Abbé Henri Breuil sitting on a rock, and the old professor with staff, sack, and beret, is Émile Cartailhac, all of prehistory in one picture.

We learn about it from books, I said to Jonquillle, but the feel of it is here in this photograph. The boys all seem charmingly devilish, she said. The old Count was a political firebrand, a womanizer, and a gourmet. The boys were raised without a mother, more or less freehand.

XXIV
Papa once met Breuil when he was very old, back from South Africa, from the prehistoric murals at Bulawayo. Jonquille was all ears to hear what he was like. When we asked Papa, he said that he was gracious, sweet, intelligent, lively, and impatient to get back to his study.

In the tearoom of the patisserie across from the Jardin Public on the Cours de Verdun, among nurses and their charges, ladies of family and breeding discussing the difficulty of finding a properly made pair of gloves anymore, Jonquille teased me for bringing her there.

I was under Maman's orders to. She says I need exposure to *bon ton*. Proust, Tullio says, would feel at home here. All these mirrors with frosty scrollwork, this oak panelling, the tile floor. It doesn't quite give me the creeps. Jonquille said that she loved the place.

Used to come here, she said, with my nurse or with my Aunt Eulalie, who talked about microbes, which she thought were the size of fleas. Why the authorities did not make a concerted effort to get them all was beyond her. *What can they be thinking of that they don't exterminate them?*

She suspected, did Aunt Eulalie, that doctors, all Freemasons, did not particularly care to obliterate them. She would put on her edifying voice and tell me that microbes were not even dreamed of until they were found by the good Docteur Pasteur, from Dole, did I know?

XXV

The trouble with your *bon ton,* Joli *mon vieux,* Jonquille said, is that you don't know how to tap your lips with your napkin, or how to say *Can you imagine?* like Aunt Eulalie. I don't think, I said, I could get my Uncle Jacques to believe in microbes. Your Uncle Jacques? she said.

Maman's brother. We don't mention him in public. He has ideas that Vercingetorix would consider outdated. He's our skeleton in the closet. When we get married you'll have to meet him, poor you. When we get married, she said. *Mon Dieu!* all this propriety has gone to your head.

Afterwards, in the trellised arbor in the Delahoussaye back garden, she brought out for study, with me for company, Renfrew, Gordon Childe, Maringer, Piggott, Marshack, Breuil, Lhote, Bordes, Leroi-Gourhan, Peyrony, Annette Laming, Torbrügge, lecture notes, guidebooks, maps.

Maman says that sex lives up to only part of its name, and that she'd rather Jonquille and I learn how to spend an afternoon being good company to each other than a frolicsome hour, her phrase, discovering how many different ways we can fit our bodies together, her words again.

Picasso, Papa said as his sole remark when he was told, began at fourteen. To which Maman felt obliged, I think, to say *Men!* Jonquille feels certain of her interview if she passes her exams. If only the committee could see you now, I said. Smart and beautiful carries the day.

XXVI

Palaeoethnobotany, she said, palaeoethnobotany. Tolund man, frogs and meadow weeds for his last snack. I have a feeling that they pulled and ate a handful of grass ever so often, don't you? And river clay scooped up and munched, their usual tummy filler between bullfrogs.

Salmon baked with dill on Saturday nights. Jonquille sat crossankled on the straw mat, leaning against the wicker lounge at her back, my cheek on her knee, Bordes' *Deux Grottes,* which she was marking with a felt pen, resting in the hollow between my neck and shoulder.

She wore only a batik blouse that showed her nipples the diameter of a franc where her breasts smoothed the fabric with their jut, and panties, slipped free of her hips and crotch, stretched across her thighs so that I could fiddle with her accelerator, tuft, and tump.

I untucked ruffled folds of the lips with a sialagogic finger, to probe congenially and jiggle on the signal of a compliant whistle. My unzipped jeans were parted from my jersey and my briefs slid down enough that Jonquille's idly gressorial free hand could wander and dandle.

Of course, she said, the big microscope in the lab is going to do me in for a fool, a total fool, if they get me flustered on the powers. They are so wonderfully strange, the pollens and spores and bits of plant trash that Madame Deslarbes can identify halfway across the room.

XXVII

Quit that, Jonquille said, not forever I mean, and reach me the pollen and fruit ID manual. We're just keeping things warm, *d'accord?* I gave her, along with the manual, a kiss on the mouth, ear, nipples, and navel, and a tickling one down the groin, wet and wiggly.

She found her page while circling the rim of my glans with a fingertip. Proto this, proto that. Berchemia multinervis, Acer trilobatum tricuspidatum, Heer, Daphnogene elegans, wouldn't you like to see her in a flowery smock on a fine spring day? Ficus tiliaefolia, Betula prisca.

Everybody's maiden aunt. Juglans nigella, which I have hold of I do believe, Populus oxyrhyncha, Pterospermites minor, that's Victor's real name, Viburnum perplexum erectum, who is beginning to butt and throb. And who, I added, feels great. Which made the doorbell ring.

It's Michel and Victor from the pool. They said they'd come by at five. Jonquille pulled her panties on and sprinted across the garden to the street door. *Miche? Petit frère?* Michel wore a straw hat, his eyes bright in its bucolic shadow. *Très Renoiresque,* Jonquille said.

You can wear anything with an air, Miche. It's wicked. His sailor's summer cotton middy was as thin as cheese cloth, his jeans abbreviated to the culmen of his inner thighline. What, he grinned, have we walked in on? Smooching is what, Victor said, holding his nose.

XXVIII

We're studying, Jonquille said, with some higher mammalian displays of affection. No wonder, Michel said, I can't pass the trigonometry section of my apprentice seaman's exam. I've been studying all wrong. I need a bare-bottomed girl, a patio and garden, to smarten my brains.

Trees, Victor said, you're studying old trees and leaves, and what are these? Fossil pollen. Possil follen! Jonquille plucked Michel's red *slip Hom* from the roll of his towel and whistled. Don't things, she asked, tend to get loose and poke out, the odd *verge,* the chance testicle?

I was lying as Jonquille left me, my clothes discontinuous from navel to knees, my erection, which Michel nudged with his toe, wilting. Victor's becoming a porpoise, he said, truly. He goes and goes in the pool, like a fish late for dinner. Victor beamed and tested his biceps.

Michel, having hugged Jonquille, given my foreskin a tug, mixed up Victor's hair, sat, got up, sat again. He jigged a foot, reached down his collar to scratch between his shoulder blades, lifted his shirt to roll the flat of his hand on his midriff, and inspected his navel.

He tried the hardness of his abdomen with a whack, stood to hitch and resettle his briefs, retied his sneakers, and combed his hair with his fingers. Jonquille retook her place cross-legged beside me and sleeved my glans with an upward pull, bared it in a downward, sweet girl.

XXIX

Two repeats of which, with a twirl of tongue around the eyelet, restood him stiff. I won't be responsible for myself, Michel said. You have no notion what that does to me. *Juglans nigella,* Victor read in a bantling voice. But I do, Jonquille said. You mean for you, not to you, *oui?*

You like Joli and you like to see him pleased. Pleased! Michel howled, the *bougre d'idiot* should have that grin freeze on his face and be trucked off to the asylum by the loony catchers. Quit it! In a minute, she said, when Joli begins to jibber. Don't ever, I sighed, if you love me.

Acer trilobatum, Victor read. O sacred blue, I'm got by the leg! Michel hauled him by the ankle, hopping backwards, until he had him close enough to fetch his *caleçon* off in a clean peel from hips to feet. That looks practised, Jonquille said. But absolutely, Michel said.

He turned the fissling Victor around and plumped him onto his lap, pannelled on his thighs. Last time, he said, Master Victor joggled me to coming it skeeted in his eye. And up my nose, Monster, in my hair. *Formidable,* Jonquille said. Have I unknowingly unleashed primal forces?

You must believe all this, sweet, I said, so that you will have the facts of life straight in your head for your exam. I have them in hand. I really don't think, however, the faculty knows about Bordeaux boys. *Tiens,* Ogre, Michel said, your starter fuzz is getting sort of silky.

XXX

In the right light, Victor said, it looks like something. What is this thing, Michel said, that seems to grow? Jonquille sweet, I said, beautiful soul, charming creature, I can hold off coming about three seconds. Wrong, she said. Ten more, twenty more. Think hard of other things.

Long and slow, long and slow, and then we're all going to the Intendance, our minds alive and our hearts full of love because we're fizzing at the ears and our faces will shine. Talk big, Michel said, my virile member is pulling the stitches loose in my pants. Just look.

His virile member he calls it, Victor said, laughing at his and making it jump. Stop, sweet, stop, I said. Michel set Victor on his feet, held his crotch with both hands, and drummed his heels. She stopped, put her hands behind her back, danced up, and skipped over to Victor.

Scooping up his pants on the way, she held them for him to step into, giving his peter a kiss before she drew them up and fitted them with nursemaidly plucks and smoothings. I gingerly squeezed into my underpants, sucking in, and edged with silly caution into my jeans.

Jonquille nipped away for a skirt and sandals. At the Intendance we sipped *kirs,* Victor a small *vin blanc*. Quicksilver for balls, Michel said. You too, Joli, but of my sympathy you have none. We gave the Place Gambetta a full view of our comradeship and sophistication.

XXXI

I was telling Uncle Jacques in the wall about pushing Marc Aurel around the Market of Great Men while Monsieur Trombone ran an errand in La Bastide. How did he lose his legs? he asked. In a car wreck, wasn't it? He doesn't, I said, remember it at all. A complete blank.

What do you mean, doesn't remember it? How can you not remember a thing like that? Worrying about having to go to the hospital and all. I've never forgotten anything in my life. But perhaps he's not bright. From everything I've heard, he couldn't be, not having legs like that.

He says he doesn't remember. He can say that, said Uncle Jacques to have his way, and still remember. People will tell you anything and think you're a big enough fool to believe them. How he can associate with that Trombone is more than I can understand, white trash both.

Trombone pushes him, I said patiently, looks after him. They're pals. Disgusting, he said, slapping his knees, the whole thing is disgusting. Those pants, I'm surprised your mother lets you wear them. She bought them for me, I said, and two pairs more, brown and blue.

They're not big enough for a baby and you're thirteen. Fourteen, I corrected. They show your tranklements as plain as day. One man can say that to another, out of a woman's hearing. There's no modesty anywhere anymore. She don't allow you to wear them downtown, does she?

XXXII

Marc Aurel and Trombone live in a room in the back of the garage in the bend of the rue de la Vieille Tour, a dogleg street that zigzags from the Intendance to the Porte Dijeaux. Originally part of the garage, it's zoned off by a wall of rough lumber fitted with a door.

It has a sink and is ceilinged with plywood, cardboard, odd lengths of planking and corrugated tin. Light comes in at two small windows high up on the stone outside wall. There are two cots, one at each end of the room, a triangular table bearing a radio and kerosene lamp.

There's a stove also fueled by kerosene, an upholstered chair, once yellow, for Trombone, and when it's there Marc Aurel's wheelchair with its tall wickerwork back, walnut armrests, solid-tired wheels with rims for the hands, gripper brake, steering handle, and klaxon horn.

The chair has an umbrella socket, useless footboard where Marc Aurel stores a haversack for his flashlight, blanket, thermos, comic books, comb, water jug and dish for Picasso, and the bottle he urinates in with the aid of a funnel and hose. An American flag for the umbrella socket.

The floor was so dirty when I first saw it that I thought it was the ground. Some scraping proved it to be of admirably thick planks half a meter wide. Someday, Marc Aurel said, we will have a linoleum, a beautiful linoleum. Maman bought a linoleum when I told her about it.

XXXIII

Marc Aurel chose the linoleum in an ecstasy, one with platters of red and purple flowers on a latticed pattern of mustard hue, and all on a ground of greenish orange. Trombone and I washed the floor four times with detergent and sand before we got the automobile drippings off.

Maman commanded me to bring her a list of things Marc Aurel needed, first, to make life bearable, secondly, to make life comfortable. A parrot in a golden cage, the list began, followed by a color television, wallpaper of a floral design, richer and busier than the linoleum.

A manicure set, an espresso coffee machine, a refrigerator, a bowl of goldfish, a lamp with a fringed shade, a leather collar for Picasso, with his name and address on it, a telephone, a mirror, a toothbrush, carpet slippers for Trombone, and a suit of clothes for Sunday wear.

A dictionary, a telescope, a map of the world, a set of reflectors for the wheelchair at night, an insecticide for roaches and fleas, a fly swatter, a picture of Jesus suffering the little children to come unto Him, a ballpoint pen, the complete works of Shakespeare and John F. Kennedy.

A box of crayons, a stamp album like mine and Victor's, an ice bucket with silver tongs, a framed picture of Franklin Roosevelt in his wheelchair, a vacuum cleaner, a bottle of Sloan's Liniment for Trombone, a dozen rolls of toilet paper, birdseed for the parrot and a piggy bank.

XXXIV

Uncle Jacques, you know, Victor said from his bed, is a troglodyte, isn't he, Joli? Rain and a thundery wind batting the windows made us the snugger. As near, I said, as makes no difference. What did it feel like, he asked, to be socketed in Jonquille, warm and wet?

I can't bear to think of Uncle Jacques out there. He's as cozy as we are, I said, in his long underwear under six édredons, nightcap, socks that smell like a Spanish outhouse, farting and snoring, bats with locked ears flying from his brain. What a wonderful wild night!

Victor, reading as he calls it the Danish sex manual, jogging his pizzle, making a moue, his eye a bird's on a junebug, bargained among subjects to make my Maigret flicker like an old movie. Why did Hitler have a moustache? Why do we say cyclone and anticyclone?

Jonquille looks like the watermark in a hundred francs, didn't I think? How long does a fuck last? Why is Uncle Jacques in the wall? What does Papa mean when he goes on over the typography of a book? Does Michel come that much every time? Will Merckx win the Tour again?

Were Marc Aurel and Trombone as cozy as we? Jonquille? O, she's in her third year of reading Proust, and is somewhere in the fourth volume, playing Poulenc on her *allumage*. A skeet and a drop and a drip, he reported with a whiffle and whew. I like his saucy ribs.

XXXV

Sequence is the grammar of tone. A run in the park with Michel, a visit to Uncle Jacques in the wall, Simenon's *Novembre* which promises to be a good read, from the bookshop on the Clemenceau, a quick jabber with Jonquille, a nip through Papa's drafting rooms.

Rolled Marc Aurel through the botanical gardens, where we fed the ducks and talked silly and saluted the statue of the man who conquered mildew. Lunch at home. Transferred Bulgarian stamps from the Jugoslavian where Victor had mounted them, the little nerd.

Called Jonquille for a conversation in code. Asked and got permission for Michel to spend the night, as Maman and Papa will be at an architectural congress in Marseilles. Then, hats off for fair weather, began a terrific mind movie in richest tone and fine fettle.

A paratrooper colonel built like Jean-Claude Killy and hung like Michel, athletic, *chic,* unflappable, I made love five times to a mistress in a Parisian hotel room, riding through her orgasms like a dolphin butting waves, coming like champagne popping its cork.

Roared away in a British racing car to a second mistress in the suburbs so devoted to sex that she had been coming all afternoon with an equally devoted girl in her teens and with her gardener's strapping lout of a son who does it till his tongue hangs out.

XXXVI

Décor George Barbier, gruff satyr and tender nymph, I came five more times, a litre of sperm the gusher, a swamp of glutinous froth the bed, she half passed out from so many and such awesome orgasms but whimpering for more, tongue rolling around tongue.

Whereupon Maman asked from the hall if I were home and what was I doing. I was so close to coming that I said as conversationally as I could that I was playing with myself, and then more boldly, I'm jacking off. Oh dear, well yes, she said. I won't come in.

In moderation, Joli, she added. Wilted, my film blank, I knew better than to let the moment escape. Trotted into her room, my erection sagging but on view according to the hang of my shirt. You gave us, I said, the book that says that we can and should.

The book with all the drooly pictures and scary anatomical diagrams. Didn't you read it? I glanced through it, sweetheart, she said. It was Papa's idea. He thought there might be something, at a chance, two boys nowadays could still learn from a glossy book.

Well, I said, the book says to, and that it feels great, as it does. Has Victor begun? she asked. Sure. Your door wasn't closed? I don't have to hide, do I? She opened her arms for a big hug and said I was marvellous and shooed me out, a whack on my behind.

XXXVII

Victor once, I remember, came into the sitting room with his fly open, his hair a mess, his knees black. Very Henry de Montherlant, Papa said. Now he is more Gide, little Caloub perhaps, expert all at once at infuriating Uncle Jacques, impressing and charming Papa.

A captain for Fourier's puppy pack, says Tullio. And of Marc Aurel Fourier would make a minister of grand affairs who would recivilize the world along lines beyond even the imagination of Fourier, the real France implicit in the imperfect France awaiting epiphany.

Tullio says that he loves France, loves Bordeaux for its ironic caution, everybody on guard against everybody else, and all so polite, so formal, gracious, courtly. There's no irony in Italy, no caution. The French, he says, are a razor, the Italians a spoon.

Your door wasn't closed? No. We don't have to hide, do we? I suppose not, she said. Did you invite Michel for dinner as well as to spend the night? May I please? There are plenty of cold cuts, yes. We're off in a bit. Michel doesn't know about poor Jacques, does he, Joli?

No, thank goodness. I'll warn Postel, she said, to be extra crafty. Give me a kiss. We should be home day after tomorrow. Back to your piggery. How long do you do it, may I ask? Like an hour, I said, giving optimum for fact, if it really goes good. My God, she said.

XXXVIII

At the Gare Autobus Citram, rue Fondaudège, I mounted the bus to Bourg-sur-Gironde with Marc Aurel in my arms, followed by Michel and Victor with knapsacks. Trombone, anxious and morose but smiling, stood by the empty wheelchair, Picasso distraught beside him.

It was Victor who saw that Picasso must go too. The motor was running when we shouted to the driver and to Trombone. Picasso leapt and bounced by the door. He slipped on the metal steps, frantic. *Ici, bon bougre, ici!* Marc Aurel and I shared a seat with Picasso between us.

Victor and Michel sat behind us with our gear. Commentary on the appropriateness of taking along one's dog who wants to go a journey buzzed among the passengers. Picasso was so happy that he licked my face, Marc Aurel's, and attempted a woman's in the seat in front of us.

In among the deliria crowding Marc Aurel's heart, going by bus to see Pair-non-Pair with us vied in the blur of all the rest with being outfitted, by Maman herself with my help, in one of my *slips très sportif,* a *caleçon cycliste sans braguette,* and a rugger shirt striped red and blue.

And all after a luxurious hot and soapy bath with Victor. Our bus crossed the Pont de Pierre, went through Bastide, out through vineyards and towns into the countryside which Marc Aurel says he has never seen. Picasso shivered from time to time to adjust his dignity.

XXXIX

Down a path through trees, in a dazzle of summersun flaught and spatterdash of leafshadow shuffled by a sweet flaw in the dip of a hollow, we filed behind the guide, who was about Michel's age, spinktrim in an unsprung red-brown pullover and snug jeans, to the mouth of the cave.

His jeans were perficiently his by dint of pliant fit and accidence of bleachscores in seams and creases and in the weathering wash of the scotched edging of fly and pockets. I carried Marc Aurel on my back. Picasso, round-eyed from having seen the scamper of a shrew, kept close.

Why the name Pair-non-Pair? I asked. The name of the farm, said the guide, won way back, maybe a hundred years ago, in a game of pairnon-pair, a thing they do out here in the country. You show your hand with so many fingers from behind your back, matching or not another's.

This cave was discovered by François Daleau, from Bourg, in 1883. He didn't notice the drawings until 1896 when the animal designs in La Mouthe were announced. The cave was completely filled with deposits. He saw the drawings at first, but not what they were of until later.

You have to learn how to see them, I'll show you. He unlocked a wooden door, took an electric lantern from its back and lit the way for us inside. The cave is a tholos with a round extension at the back and another to the left. The guide found the lines of a mammoth for us.

XL

The tusks, he said, using a pointer, the eye, the head, the line of the back, the tail, hind foot, fore foot, snout. I see it! Marc Aurel said. It's an elephant. No no, the guide said, the extinct ancestor of the elephant, the mammoth. It grazed here in the Gironde long ago.

Thirty thousand years ago. Victor didn't see it and the guide traced the outline again, naming the parts. His recitation was as polished as a poem. Victor thought he saw it, and saw something else above it. Three ibexes. In a line going up. The middle one is a head only.

And facing them, two more ibexes, here over the bison, which he fixed in raked light and showed us its lines. It is, he said, challenging that bison, here over these horses and ibex, to a fight. These marks are signs of some sort, perhaps writing, perhaps the sun and the moon.

Or a house, or some magic object. You've had all this in school, haven't you? Not me, said Marc Aurel, I'm learning it now. I explained that my girl was going into prehistory, and was in a special *lycée* course to qualify as assistant in palaeoethnobotany on a field team.

He nodded politely to my professional connections, nothing like *his* I was to understand. We saw the kingly, grandly antlered Celtic elk, the overlapping horse and ibex, the aurochs looking up expectantly, the second mammoth. It's a puzzle, Marc Aurel said. Find the picture.

XLI

They were painted, you know, the guide said, and as distinct as a church window, as at Lascaux. See how the contours of the surface gets worked into the figures. This protuberance becomes this horse's shoulder, and very like. The mammoths are drawn on the bumpiest parts.

Because, he said especially to Marc Aurel, they were shaggy, big, lumpy fellows. We had a lovely day of it, and the guide condescended to eat lunch with us, at the edge of the vineyard by his office, a single-roomed shack with maps and shards and his spiffy bike in it.

When we got back to Bordeaux, late, I had to report in to Uncle Jacques, as we'd set out so early that I had not yet done my daily duty by him. Cave? he said, what kind of cave? He smelled of stale sweat, tobacco, and rotten socks, mingled with the damp, kerosene, fusty furniture.

How big was this cave you say you've been to? Pair-non-Pair, I said, is about the size of a small house divided into three rooms. Three domed ceilings, so to speak, inside. Most of the animals are on the right, at the front, with more to the back, a few over to the left.

And, said Uncle Jacques, you think these scratched animals are from the olden time? Do they teach you this muck in school? Come *on*, Uncle Jacques, I said. It's in books. I've showed you. The geological deposits inside could be dated just like any other strata, don't you see?

XLII
This cave, Pair-non-Pair, was discovered in 1883 by Daleau. What kind of family, said Uncle Jacques, did he come from? How should I know? I said. Don't lose your temper with me, he said. I'm only discussing the point you raise. How old, again, do they claim this cave to be?

The engraved animals are Aurignacian: thirty thousand years back. Fiddlefaddle, Uncle Jacques said. Some farmers put them there, nothing better to do with their time I suppose, or some no-account boys, maybe in my grandpapa's time, maybe a little before, and lied about it.

But, I sputtered, they're art, Uncle Jacques, art! The very beginnings of art. I almost said he should go see for himself, if only to the Aquitanian Museum, but to mention going out put him in a sulk for up to a week. I'll bring you the books again, I said. Read them and see.

What I can't get over is that you took that boy with no legs. I guess he understood nothing, didn't know where he was, even? But he did! He said it's the greatest thing that's ever happened to him. He loved every minute. That lout Trombone, he said, he didn't go too, did he?

He stayed here. He said he was glad of the chance to visit a crony. Who? Uncle Jacques asked. I don't know, I didn't ask him. God knows you wouldn't think to. The dog Picasso went. He liked it all as much as Marc Aurel. Whatever in God's name, said Uncle Jacques, will people think.

XLIII

The guide to the cave, I said to fill out my time, was a boy not much older than Michel or I, and he knows his stuff. I suppose, said Uncle Jacques, his mother's not bright, that she would let him do such a thing. I suppose he acted as if he was better than you? They do nowadays.

But, I said, I'd love to be a museum guide at a prehistoric cave! No uniform, just neat jeans and a pullover. Folks from all over, all day long. You can't make out the animals until the light is right and the lines are traced with a pointer. Some Dutch were driving up when we left.

And there you were, said Uncle Jacques, more alarmed than ever, disgraced with that trash with no legs, for all the world to see. But foreigners, did you say? I can't think that they matter. And how did this Marcel or whatever he calls himself get about? Swing on his hands?

I carried him on my back, I said. Michel carried him some, too. Does your mother know about this? he asked. Why not? I challenged. Victor would have carried him, too, if he could. Uncle Jacques looked ill, and said he needed to lie down awhile and rest, if I would excuse him.

In my room I took off every stitch and joined Maman and Papa at their *apéritifs*. If you had a horse to lead, Papa said, you would be a Picasso. I have, I replied, a little brother to carry on my back. *Eh!* he said, you're developing an eye. Half an hour in the wall, I explained.

XLIV

Eros, la chevelure en accroche coeur, tout nu, charmait mes rêves. When I woke, dawn latent in the thin dark of the room, a delectable elation lingered from a dream, residual in the pliant helve of my sex, a euphoria of images, Jonquille, Deus Amor, *quelles fossettes*!

Jonquille's crotch dark under sheer cotton panties from Prisunic printed with an American roadsign, *Slippery When Wet*, my mouth cupped to hers, tongues frolicking, her nipples stiff, the crinkled matted damp lure of her underhair warm, suffusing benevolence through my sleep.

The fine reality beguiled me of her slick fluttered flaplets with their marine taste of iodine and oysters, her neb of high-spirited flesh under its pellicule, which when thrummed, wiggled, twitched, quivered, licked, bobbled, joggled, launched her into a rapture.

Not into a built-up and spent one like mine, but one enviably perdurable, spasm after spasm, until, as she bragged as a secret traded in our huggermugger of sensual exploring, convulsions set in, her eyes bubbling, just short of fainting, the brain sodden in one dense feeling.

Until every smidgen of her, flesh and spirit together, is all cunt, quintessential girl, vibrant voluptuous chiming succulent delirious driveling convivial girl. *Vive la nature!* I melted back into sleep as I tried to recapture a darb of an eye, Jonquille's, a long kiss.

XLV

Enticing eyes had invited me to some delight in a dream, and shifting between waking and dreaming I felt glans and intent shaft snoove richly into sliddery labia, a wellbeing like wine, like prancing music swarming through me, and slept again. It was full day when I woke for good.

Victor was trampolining on his bed, imitating a chimpanzee. My ruttish encounter in my dream was still somewhere boisterous in me, partly in the idle imagination, partly in my scrotum. Had I really dreamed about Eros, as lean a gossoon as Victor, silver of ankle, hyacinth curls?

Slim, with a bubble of cod and a curtal puppy's tail of a peter, he was accoutred properly with bow and quiver. *Une bêtise vraie!* As soon as I had coffee I telephoned Jonquille: she was in Bayonne visiting her Aunt Eulalie. I ate my croissant at the door to the parterre.

Jeans unbuttoned and unzipped fly ajar, I cosseted the snook of my cock in the pod of my briefs, *un akène gros de chêne, enchâssé dans une cupule charnue.* What's that you're doing, Victor said, missing nothing. *Demandant la vigne sans ivresse et le champ sans ivraie.*

Is that a poem? Hey, you're hard. It woke up feeling good, I said, I'm just being cordial. Let's go out to see Uncle Jacques. Can't, Victor said. Postel hasn't dumped the chamberpot. We're not supposed to turn up until he has. Because there is no chamberpot, anywhere, ever.

XLVI

Show us your peter. *Balkan!* Maman's not home. There's a note: Good morning monsters I'm at the market and the hairdresser see you at lunch your devoted Maman. I cambered my *queue* over the waistband of my briefs. Gross, Victor said, clucking. I polished the glans with a thumb.

A serious fit of adolescence, I said. I hear Postel, said Victor with cocked ear. Dressed, I said, cramming in and zipping up, and in my right mind. Uncle Jacques was having his coffee, unshaven yet, and had drawn his trousers on over the long underwear we knew he slept in.

Postel had removed all traces of the night. An ornately fringed counterpane covered the bed further down the wall. With the paper open, he was eating grilled whiting, a slice of sousemeat, fried potatoes, and some camembert. He took his coffee from a bowl like country people.

I see your father's name in the paper, he said. It would embarrass me to have my name in the paper, for anybody to see, but I know that nowadays it's considered respectable to be in business. It was about the contracts for the new buildings. Papa will make a stack of money.

Will we be rich? Victor asked. *Guillaume Bonnat, l'architecte.* Neat! Jolivet's name was in the paper when he won the prize at school and mine was in the list of kids going to summer camp. Can I have the comics? Then the ritual. Uncle Jacques asked for news of the house.

XLVII

I supplied information in the frank style I knew Uncle Jacques disapproved of. He preferred hints and indirection. My candor seemed a reproach to the subtlety of his questions. *Picking the boys' brains,* Maman called it. We had thus and so for supper with Tullio and his wife.

Talks funny, don't he? He tends, yes, I said, to add syllables to words, as most Italians do, as if all his words were poetry. And him a professor at the university! They're both fat, I've seen them. The daughter, I've heard she's not bright. From whom? Never you mind. A little bird.

Postel thinks he knows so much! He says she looks afflicted. I'd be ashamed to bring her into society. There's nothing, I said, wrong with Marcellina as far as I know. She's real dumb, Victor said over the comics. When Papa says anything to her, she jumps. So she's awkward.

There was so much we couldn't tell Uncle Jacques. The swimming pool was a suppressed subject, as he was shocked by bathing suits and considered swimming dangerous and unhealthy. We edited all accounts of Maman. It was her he was not speaking to, perhaps why he was in the wall.

The reason he was there, Maman has said, was so complex that a committee of psychiatrists and monkeys together could not figure it out. Uncle Jacques' ideas of school, forty years out of date, had to be played to, as well as his notions of decency, piety, honor, respect, and manners.

XLVIII

I hear Postel coming, Uncle Jacques said. Is my pension early in the mail this month? It's that boy named Michel, your friend, Jolivet, Postel said in a whisper. I didn't say where you were. I said I'd look for you. Did you invite him? Uncle Jacques asked, scandalized.

What does he mean, coming without an invitation? There was more of this Sassard squawk, which Victor and I, ducking out the door, through our tunneled path in the laurels, running across the yard, did not wait to hear. Who's for a swim? Michel said. Look what I've bought.

He tossed over a small narrow flat box. *Hé!* I said, Bordeaux has them! At the Sportif, he said, on the Clemenceau, forty fucking francs. Come up, I've got to see. Show me, Victor said. What is it? Bathing suit: the new *mode minimum,* the littlest ever. They're wearing them at Arcachon.

It's just a *cache-sexe* like a jockstrap with a cincture and a thong from the cod to the middle in back that goes up the crack of your butt. Weighs 112 grams, neat as a cricket's knee, elastic groins to keep your nuts from popping out. Just wait till I hit the *piscine* in it.

Stripped, Michel unkinked the wad of white polyester and tricolor webbing, stepped into and drew its stringent scantiness up his brown thighs, fitting it onto his genitals, and stood symmetrical, trim, Olympic, and wonderful. With your behind bare? Victor asked. *Cela fait rire.*

XLIX

With a rump that *poilu,* you don't look quite as snake-naked as I'm going to look in one, I said. Michel has a nice thicket of hair at the *fourchet,* and he'd tanned his bathing suit mark away in the Dordogne and at Arcachon. He could strut and crow. I had to have one too.

We left a note: *At the piscine on the Judaïque with Michel who has new ultra mode maillot de bain ce n'est qu'une braguette scandaleuse avec ceinture I must have one embraces J. Me too more embraces V.* Applause, satire, and looks askance at the piscine. Bordeaux is not St.-Tropez.

I heard that *la mode* is *la mode,* that Michel is a conceited ass, *un vrai Narcisse,* too much the *gamin* to be *chic,* that we are young but once, that this *outrecuidance* follows logically from the monokini, and that all things logical are correct, that he would be less obscene naked.

A decidedly plain girl said that Michel's smiling glance made shivers run under her skin. I was not supposed to overhear that he was Henriette Bonnat's lover, or that he would be, if Henriette fancied changing his diapers and feeding him with a spoon. Will these *jours anticyclonals* last?

At lunch Maman said I could buy a *cache-sexe* like Michel's, *immodeste* as it was. She would make Victor one on the sewing machine. But they won't have a size for you, *mon cher.* You'll look a *cupidon,* Victor stomped and said he didn't want to be a *cupidon,* or anything like.

L

So be ugly, Maman said. People run from you screaming, stopping only to barf in the gutter. Suits me fine, Victor said. At the *piscine* all the girls went all smoochy over a lunk like Michel. People are crazy. The word *cupidon* summoned back my congenial dream, so strangely lovely.

After lunch I climbed the hornbeam, Victor following, and lay in cool shade on the wall. Uncle Jacques, Victor said, is down there looking out the slits at the street. He could be right beneath us. Probably, I said, slide back so I can unzip. Something new, said Victor, on the wall.

It is the tone of the lines from Virgil Montaigne meditates on in *Sur des vers de Virgile* (which Tullio likes to call *Divers sûrs de la verge*) that puzzles me. Venus is defrigerated from the cold of classical stone, yet the color of her arms is the white of snow.

And when Aeneas, stuffy soul, catches her intent, the fire in his marrow is compared to lightning in a cloudy sky. There is no salt in the lines, no detail. *Optatus dedit amplexus!* It is like algebra, or the fat women in Rubens singing Rossini with dockhands in leather gilets.

The rest of the essay is consummately lascivious, as good, if you get your imagination going, as the magazines Michel gets from the Sex Shop in the Great Men. Virgil is as infuriating as Corneille and Racine, rounding everything into a blurred, depilated generalization.

LI

Romance, Jonquille says, is a bore. Love, passion, all that rhetoric, hot air. Of course we love each other, she says, but I'd rather know that I can trust you than float on pink clouds when you call on the phone. The nervous system in nice anatomy is lovely with local attention.

Ignea rima micans. You were supposed to know, Jonquille says of my fretting at the cold Latin lines, that Aeneas was hung like a horse, that Venus brought a pillow to put under her butt, that she thrashed her head from side to side and groaned, and came like a tilted cement mixer.

Nor did she have to keep an ear cocked for the unexpected footstep, the phone, or Victor caroming in and pretending to cat while walking in a circle. *Cunctantem amplexu molli fovet.* Beginnings, said the Greeks, are gods. *Pour lui à quinze ans la sensualité devenait érudite.*

For a book of essays as chiselled as Barthes, as epigrammatic as Cocteau, and as frank as Montaigne I will begin with that sentence, third person for objectivity, fifteen less vulnerable than fourteen. To record with precision beginnings, progressions, clarities, discoveries.

To record with precision the plenary surge spang in my midriff when, by eye, by comradely intuition, I took Michel's intent the first time we conspired to jack off together. It was, he said, a thing he was good at, getting better, and that if we were to be friends, I must too.

LII

Montaigne in middle age could not recall when first he pushed his pizzle into womankind, whether as a mop-polled, snub-nosed dabster given a treat by the ostler's daughter or as a moony adolescent, with a cockstand straining his codpiece, who had flustered the scullery maid's eye.

Jonquille wore a floppy straw hat with meadow flowers that memorable day, daisies, pinks, dandelions, tucked into the blue ribbon around the crown, the ribbons' streamers hanging down her slender naked brown back to the maker's tab, *Printemps Fantaisie,* of her underpants.

The lettering was Peignot, and the tab scutted out over her downy holy-bone from the rump of her gentian and leafdazzle underpants, *style micro,* above the hind crease between the cheeks of her butt that ticked from side to side as she stepped barefoot, daintily, me right behind her.

We'd had coffee on the terrace, where she put the flowers she'd already been out for in her hat. A daisy in her teeth, a daisy smile for me, girls doing hats or their hair put their toes together, and hold their hips as if they are balancing on a narrow height, knees folded well in.

Her hard breasts were rosy tan, firepink violet the nipples. My sex nudged circumflex and petulant in the constriction of bobbed jeans. She, prodding this kilter with her toe, said she saw *natura naturans*. Only the shy made brave are truly bold. Girls are weatherly creatures.

LIII

When, graceless in the fever of desire, I encountered the wet reality of so many imaginings, she was as fluent as a weasel in the hips. There was a rimple in the neb of her nose, a spritely squinch of dimples at the corners of her mouth, when I lifted the elastic of her panties.

And travelled fingertips back and forth along the silky edge of her pubic tangle. She wiggled her tongue, first in my ear, then across my upper lip, then against my tongue. With her guidance I found the fleshy tip under its pellicle and spent a lovely while learning it.

When, after much purring and urging me on, she gave a silurid and lyric flip from haunch to heel, the hair crawled above my ears. For days thereafter I could scarcely believe I had done it, I, Jolivet Bonnat, all the precautionless way with a willing and demanding girl.

Gauche, we decided later, but unmarred for all that. Montaigne forgot. Perhaps, like Proust, he would have remembered. One self forgets another in the same body. From the house to the wall I might start out as a *pilote de chasse* in a rustling blue flight overall and silk scarf.

Sunglasses mask my eyes that run with swift attention over a hundred dials. I reply curtly to voices from control towers, map rooms. *Migs at three o'clock*. In the wall, listening to Uncle Jacques deplore the passing of manners, my flight boots become sandals laced to the knee.

LIV

A round shield with a dolphin painted on it swings from my left arm. An ash spear rides in my right hand. An unbleached tunic belted with a thong scarcely covers my ungirded pizzle and balls. A tumpline holds my Dorian hair, bright with olive oil flavored with dill, out of my eyes.

Leaving the wall, I straighten my cavalier's lace cuff, and make sure that the message to the king from The Man in the Iron Mask is secure in my boot. My glossy horse champs and neighs to see me. My sword clinks, my spurs chink as I swing up into the saddle and dash away.

Running with Michel in the park at dawn I am an Australian lifeguard, gladiatorial of physique, girded in Olympic swimming trunks made of a handkerchief's worth of weightless cloth, a yellow canvas cap strapped under my handsome chin. I read like Tullio, eat like Papa.

Going to my tree to mount to the top of the wall in the leafy shadows of August, cobwebs across the garden paths, I dip under a single silverpoint line from a laurel to a dusty boxwood, let spiders be none the worse for me, let me tear down nothing that I cannot put back together.

Slipping on the mica snail track over brickwalk moss, I watch white butterflies, a bike of fat black bumblebees deepening the quiet. Silent motion, swallow swoop, a curtain billowing, the frantic scurry on resplendent water of shadow and shine, a leaf spinning down, enchants.

LV

Affinities I do not understand link secret with secret, Uncle Jacques doomed to the inside of the wall, The Man in the Iron Mask, legless Marc Aurel and the peculiar Monsieur Trombone in their garage room, reckless couplings with Jonquille, Michel's stoutly cordial sexiness.

I am a different person with everyone I know. I would never have met the Jolivet I am with Jonquille had she not created him. This is strange. I have had to find it out for myself. No one has ever explained so clear and obvious a truth about people and identity to me.

Jonquille's Jolivet was a surprise to me, Michel's Jolivet a delight. I like Michel's Jolivet as much as Jonquille's Jolivet. I like Victor's Jolivet, a splendid person I could not otherwise have been, Maman's Jolivet, an uncertain but confident son, and Papa's affectionate Jolivet.

Marc Aurel's Jolivet is an imaginary and improbable character I have never met, called into intermittent being by Marc Aurel. In Trombone's presence I do not exist. With Tullio I have the feeling that I represent somebody Tullio mistakenly thinks is there by happy error.

Liking, then, is not only of the person liked, but of the unique and otherwise absent person the other develops in us, releases in us, creates of us. A friend is an engendering. We love those who make us lovable. A friend is the friend a friend finds and brings out in another.

LVI

The Gambetta was sodden with swivelling rain, the stiff wind chill. Picasso wore a sweater, his forelegs through the sleeves. It hung udderish from his trim waist. His laugh said, however, that the sweater gave universal satisfaction. The Globe was made for bad weather.

Marc Aurel wore an aviator's cap with flaps and goggles, a yellow mackintosh, plaid mittens. Trombone carried an umbrella that advertised Pernod. His nose was blue. What a life! Marc Aurel said, rolling into the comfort and warmth of the Globe. I do love a nasty day.

Picasso's sweater is a gift from M. Zamora. Noé has one too. Ain't he the cat's whiskers in it! They could take his picture for *The Southwest*. Wind from the Atlantic shirred the Garonne and dashed rain against the windows. An agitation of *footballeurs* jiggled on the TV.

Picasso put his front paws on the bar so that everybody could see his sweater. Jolivet! They settled with me by the glass wall, having a hot rum and chocolate, dripping disastrously, reading a newspaper they assembled from several tables. Trombone donned Prisunic specs.

These, he said, focussed the type but made it jump. Marc Aurel knew as well as I that he was only pretending to read and honored his acting. I was waiting for Jonquille, who was late. It is a grand thing, Marc Aurel said, to sit in a brasserie and read the newspaper.

LVII

Blue dusk, a knoll over the Vézère, our bicycles hung with doffed clothes, bedrolls laid out, we sprawled and sipped red wine we'd bought at a grocery after dinner in Sarlat. We'd had to tell the *patron* to serve us what our money would buy, which put him in a snit.

We are three boys from Bordeaux, I recited again to Victor and Miche, on a cycling trip to Les Eyzies, with only so much money for every meal, as our mother came up with the dumb idea that we'd spend all our money the first day out, and starve thereafter, and die in a ditch.

I'm full, Michel said. I'm stuffed, Victor said, and getting drunk on this wine. Yours is half water, dummy. I've got a little extra money, Michel said, like for this rotgut. Drink up, Victor, total depravity is your fate today. Cigarettes and girls and we'd be sailors on leave.

Still for it, *petit*? But absolutely, Victor said with a catch in his throat. The depraving of Victor had continued midmorning when we halted for a wade in a creek, during our rest just inside a wood after lunch, late afternoon in an *abri* where we stopped to put our feet up.

It was here that I succumbed to the wild embrangling lickerousness that Michel's skipjack gamut of delight and interval was charming into an abandoned Victor, spoiled rotten, and cravingly added my hand after Michel's. Victor wasn't the only one with balls like a woundup spring.

LVIII

Lie back, Michel said, his left hand straying to his own categorical scrotum, we're going to make it feel like a million francs in the bank. If Tullio could see us now! He does blush, doesn't he, and edge the subject around to some *bizarrerie sexuelle* or another, bless him.

It's his Renaissance mind. Italian, you mean. I don't know whether he comes to the house so much to see Maman as Victor running around with nothing on. Why? Victor said. Never mind. *Merde.* You think I'm too little to know anything at all. That's super, Miche, a real buzz.

There's a cabin boy on the *Jean Parmentier*, pretty as a peach, who has jacked himself cross-eyed and on one occasion, when the crew laid bets on how many times he could come, raised a blister on his dick. It's that smarmy Antoine with his talk about Gide who should see us.

He'd drool himself dry. *Sensible* he says everybody should be. I'm sure he never farts. A jog, an easy jaunt, throttle. Victor tucked his nether lip under his buckhare's incisors, rimpled his nose, and pummeled the ground with his fists. Michel ungrasped and wet his thumb.

Engaging frenum and pollex in a sweet slide, he took up his grip. Victor bared in surprise the whole blue discs of his eyes, skeeted high, throbbed, skeeted, throbbed, skeeted. Something like, Michel said with approval. Goodness gracious! Lots and lots, some in my eye.

LVIX

It's still not real sperm, I said inpoliticly. Sticky, but clear as water, with no population. But Victor, Michel said, is a real boy. In about half an hour, no less, Michel said, you will see a liter of the real article in a spectacular geyser, with or without cooperation.

I'm your man, I said. I want to! Victor crowed. Let me, please. I've never even done it for Jolivet. Ring some rocks instead, little comrade, so's we can have a fire by nightfall, and gather some wood. You can take over in good time. I've got to see you start, Victor said.

I uncowled Michels' pert stand, twenty centimeters of veined rib's curve and stout underridge, its drupelobed slant damson head welled with beading sap. Slick all that mucilage about for slide. Michel grunted with pleasure, and squeezed my cock to promise favors returned.

Since age ten? I remembered. Well before that. My mother, *qui exerce,* as she once told the old nanny goat next door, *la profession de prostituée,* used to fiddle with it to keep me quiet, probably from my first howl onwards, until I found it for myself and took over.

I must have toddled about with my hand in my diapers and a silly grin on my face for years and years. Papa thought it disgusting, I can barely remember. There was a nice sailor, friend of Maman's, who showed me, at nine or ten, what diligence and single-mindedness can do.

LX

Out one window the uncombed crown of a slatted and slit-leaved palm, out the other a perspective of roofs and houses yellow, pink, and grey. Michel's Peugeot tenspeed hung from a ceiling hook by its handlebars, its chrome spokes and pedals bright against a map of France on the wall.

And against the prancing tarpan of Lascaux and a tall poster of a girl as fresh and healthy as a horse, naked on a pebble beach. I'd pulled on my jersey when he snapped a towel and popped me on the butt. I tackled him around the waist and we whomped the bed in our fall.

He hasped me under the ribs in an armlock. A scramble of grunts and elbow digs, heel jabs, and body arching, and we had each other in a knot of arms and legs that slowly came apart, exploded, and sprung. We circled poised on our toes, open-mouthed, feinting with forearms.

Quick as fish we closed, grappled, tripped, and went down with a thump. A knee nudged into my groin and a shoulder into my thropple stilled me and I cried quarter. *Pouf! Con!* You win. Michel gravely inspected his balls, off guard trice enough for me to flick the nib of his cock.

Pig! Camel! Shitabed! Balkan! I broke his throttle with a heave, hooking a heel, pounced howling, and pinned him. *D'accord? D'accord.* What are you two doing up there? his mother called from below. We're getting in shape for the Revolution, Michel shouted, when it comes.

LXI

Manfredo Tafuri's *Progetto e Utopia* open on a *Sud-Ouest* among cups of chocolate on our table at the Régent, Papa, Tullio, and I were talking about the Bordeaux Board of Renovation, the lost bronze horses of the Quinconces, football, and Corbusier's sugar cubes at Pessac.

There gathered on the traffic island opposite us a group of plainly dressed folk among whom Tullio noticed even as they were crossing from the Intendance Marc Aurel and Trombone wheeling him. Who in the world, he said, are those people our young friend is with, Jolivet?

The Culte Baptiste, I answered. They arranged themselves, the Culte Baptiste, along the traffic island, facing the Régent, and at a signal on a pitchpipe from their pastor, began to sing, their voices carrying fitfully across the line of passing cars and gabble of the tables.

I waved to Marc Aurel, who waved back gaily with both arms. He is a Baptiste, this poor boy? Papa asked. He is not Catholic? O yes, I enjoyed saying, both. Goes to mass every morning, and to the Baptistes on Sundays and Wednesdays. They're good to him with clothes and food.

They are cautioning us, Papa asked, against this fleshpot, the Régent? O yes, I said, holding up my cup to show Marc Aurel that it was chocolate we were drinking. He nodded in understanding. Monsieur Trombone raised his hat respectfully. Uncle Jacques would be scandalized.

LXII

Up at six to begin our regimen for the summer of running daily in the Parc Bordelais, I trotted in the bright dawn past St.-Seurin to the rue Ormière and whistled under the window, once, twice. Michel in a white *gilet* only, vented at the hips, let me in, a finger to his lips.

We tiptoed up to his mansarde. I imitated his sprack step, toes in, back straight, knees jaunty. By the crumpled sheets of his severe cot, shelf of soccer balls, hockey sticks, records, rocks, Michel stretched and yawned, kneading his prosperous balls, waggling his big noddle.

I stink like a billy, he laughed, sniffing his armpits and fingers. The thing about putting yourself to sleep every night with your hand is that you smell like lobster and garlic in the morning. Do you stay raunchy all the time, Miche? Since age ten, never a moment's peace.

Through the park we ran in little white pants and sneakers, hair scrumpled, past deer and swans, chittering squirrels and long-haired shambling sheep, along paths dark with shade, bright walks lined with roses and laurel. At 7:30 we jogged to the rue Roquelaure, sweetly unwinded.

A gasped greeting to Maman and Papa having coffee on the terrace, up to my room to scoop Victor out of bed squawking, and stripped to shower. You didn't take me! We will when you can run for an hour. I can now. Your legs aren't long enough. Fuck, said Victor. We want our butt beat.

LXIII

Joli? Yes, love? Victor whispered through cupped hands that we couldn't go see Uncle Jacques with Michel here. I whispered back, rolling his pudgy scrotum with the flat of my hand, that I didn't give a damn. Now who wants his butt beat? he said aloud. A brotherly exchange of whacks.

I asked Maman from the window if we could come down and have breakfast with them in our underpants. No. Come on down, Papa called up. Make your beds, straighten your room, Maman said, and I'll bring your coffee up there. *Les durs!* Victor set to, smoothing sheets.

Michel plumped bolsters, I hung up towels, hid socks, chucked magazines and books onto shelves. Maman wanted a word with me in private when she came with rolls, butter, jam, and coffee. I went into my act about not having a cat or dog because Uncle Jacques was terrified of them.

I have to lie about everything to him or he'll throw a fit. And now I have to sneak out to him when I have Michel to breakfast. Don't you want me to run and be healthy? Jolivet sweet, she said, I haven't said any of that. Jacques doesn't deserve having you visit every morning.

What I meant, she said, is that if you go, don't let Michel know. I couldn't bear it. We're having breakfast, Victor sang, like in the Dordogne, naked and piggy. I'm off to Suzanne's, Maman said. One crumb on that rug! Who, Michel asked, is Uncle Jacques? Victor drank the cream.

LXIV

I sit here, Uncle Jacques said, the better part of the night sometimes, thinking. There was the war, the Germans, the Jews, the communists, and who's to say who was right? I personally saw nothing wrong with the Germans. They are an orderly self-respecting people.

They took no backtalk from Jews and communists. Every war the government in Paris has to come here to Bordeaux. Do you know why? I can tell you why. Because the Bordelais are somebody. Down through history. Ask your teachers if I'm not right. To Bordeaux they come.

Our old families are of the best stock in France. People look up to us. We are quality. Your mother has never understood that. She married well enough. I'm not going to knock your father to your face. Honor thy father and thy mother, it says in Scripture, that thy days be long.

The Bonnats are somebody, Toulouse people, it's true, but they've been in Bordeaux for several generations now. They are not, however, Sassards. Never forget that. I can see Sassard in your face. Victor, now, looks more like a Bonnat. But damned if you act like a Sassard.

I'm told, don't deny it, you have a sweetheart, young as you are, that Delahoussaye girl. Who are the Delahoussayes? School teachers! What does education do for anybody except make them think they're somebody when everybody knows good and well that they're nobody?

LXV

That wop Tullio who's always coming here, I wouldn't be surprised that he thinks he's better than I am. What the world is coming to: that's what I turn over in my mind here by my lamp the better part of the night. That Michel, your buddy, what's he trying to get out of you?

His father left him and his mother to starve for all he cared. She works, I think you said. I imagine she would have to, or take to the streets. Both, for all I know. He has a bicycle like yours. Where, I'd like to know, did he get the money for that? If, of course, it's bought.

He presumes to be your equal. He would. That's the way the world is now. That's what I brood about, worry about, can't understand. The world is filling up with trash. People have no respect for anything anymore, none for family, for name, for manners, or for decency.

Postel had gone to an early sale, in search of bargains, and Uncle Jacques was still unshaved. He looked terrible, like the derelicts in the Jardin of the Hôtel de Ville. Nor had his chamberpot been taken away. I could smell it, but of course had to pretend that I didn't.

In order for me to take it out and empty it, which I would gladly have done, wash it and air it, discreetly behind which bush I've known all my life, Uncle Jacques would have had to admit that it exists, and this he was never going to do. Never step on his pride, Papa says.

LXVI

I have my good days and my bad. Pray, Jolivet, that you never have a weak back. With a strong back I could have been a different man. I nodded sympathetically, knowing that Maman says there's nothing whatever wrong with Uncle Jacques. You will never have to work.

You will be a true Sassard in that respect. You tell me that you are good at your lessons, but I worry about this English. Tell me again what they mean by English. Nothing could convince Uncle Jacques that there are languages other than French. I had failed in every attempt.

He used to hear Greeks and Spaniards at the docks. They had different words for certain things, but they still talked, like everybody else. Talked funny, but talked French. But, I said, if you speak to an American who doesn't know French, he won't understand a word you say.

He would have to, unless he's deaf or an idiot. They like to act hateful, these foreigners. They know better. They think it's something fine to be different. I began a poem, by Keats, in English, but he wouldn't let me finish. It throws him into a rage to hear another tongue.

Have you not had your breakfast, Uncle Jacques? Postel, he said, will be here soon. I'll get you some coffee and croissants, I said. No, no! You are not a menial. But, I protested, I'm your nephew, I like doing things for you. No, no, he said, it wouldn't be right, not right at all.

LXVII

On the Eyre in the Landes. The *Modulor* of Le Corbusier, notebook, ballpoint, Papa's flat English cap, towel, *slip Hom micro,* sun glasses, extra underpants and shirt, toothbrush and paste, comb, an outing kit without fuzz, and all neatly in one nylon haversack.

Victor half the room until Maman and I scaled it down, removing two stamp albums, his microscope, bathrobe, calico monkey, soccer ball and boots, skateboard. Jonquille, a big sack of stuff, Michel nothing at all except what he's wearing, making me feel overloaded.

Thus we Robinson, featherlight except for a hamper of eats, lotions, and antimosquito gunk. In responsible freedom within the bounds, good old bounds, of taste and decency. We will follow Victor, Michel says, whose taste and decency are purest Early Magdalenian.

So you stood there, says Jonquille, gulping like a guppy, Madame Bonnat being her cool modern self. Joli, you're wonderful, a prize calf. I asked what promises she made, if any, fingers crossed or uncrossed, to be asked, what news, citizen, do you have from Africa?

Pine forest in all directions, the shining river, the cabin, the two rooms of which face a screened porch half the whole area. We've claimed territories, made all shipshape. Our playhouse, says Victor. An elate brave holiday feeling, voices strange in the quiet.

LXVIII

Camp without the hassle, says Michel, or the wimps. There's nobody within a kilometre. Let's hit the river. Do we go savage beginning now? Victor asked, remembering Maman's phrase at home for sunbathing in the altogether. And Jonquille too? Jonquille especially!

Jolivet loves Jonquille, says Victor gravely. Victor loves Michel, says Michel. I don't, he pipes, I love Jolivet. Everybody loves his brother. But I love Victor, says Michel, hoisting him onto his lap and running his hand into his pants to make him squeal.

This, says Jonquille, is where the chaperon faints the first time. Let's stash the billygoat curtain raiser and make for the landing. I begin to strip and remark that we are ridiculously asymmetrical for the life of the heart and its warm expression in affection.

Michel drummed his heels when Jonquille peeled down her panties and Victor blinkered himself with his hands, turning in stomping circles until Michel caught him and pulled off his pants and briefs while he squirmed and boxed and laughed, happy as a grig, hooting.

Victor, countering, tugging at Michel seated, cried, Stand up, *cochon!* Hunching his hips for Victor to slide off his *caleçon*, leaning forward for him to haul off his jersey, Michel hale, brown and trim, in briefs of cordial fit, humped in the pod, went limp.

LXIX

A game, this. Jonquille and I, towels around our necks, watched and waited. How, said Victor, can I take off your underpants if you don't stand up, silly? Snatch 'em off, Victor, says Jonquille, I want to drool. Eyes dancing with mischief, Michel crossed his ankles.

He bunched his chest until his nipples were as tucked as his navel. Victor walked up his legs on all fours, had reached to pluck when he was lifted, held kicking, and ended upside down behind Michel's chair, held by the waist, saying words I didn't know he knew.

Something rather sweet is happening, Jonquille said, sitting and pulling me down beside her. The crop of Michel's *slip* prodded out. He lifted Victor onto his chest, who reached backward, got his thumbs under the waistband and shoved. *Foutre!* You're up!

C'est gentillette, Jonquille said. Michel pulled his briefs back on, blushing. Victor tugged them off again, this time all the way. Michel crossed his hands in his lap and gave his erection a disgusted look. Stubbornly it throbbed, arched, uncovering its head.

Nature has her own ideas about these things, Jonquille said, nuzzling her cheek to mine. It's just us here, Miche. Victor leaned shyly against the door, looking out from under his jumbled shock of hair over his forehead. The river, said Jonquille getting up.

LXX

The river, the shining river. Mud and turpentine it smelled of, and whirls of gnats met us at the landing, Victor riding on Michel's shoulders, Jonquille and I with a hand on each other's outer hip, and the sky, radiantly blue, had the daytime moon in it.

Jonquille had given Michel's cock a congenial squeeze as we set out from the cabin, and Victor's an upward flip—*hey!*—and mine a pull and we were all feeling deliciously friendly by the time we swam, glistening in a river so rich in trash and mud.

We sat on the jetty, swatting mosquitoes, silvery brown in our summer tans, wet eyelashes crimped into serrations of fine brushpoints, soaked hair drying into thickets, knocking ears that had shipped riverwater. Cézanne, Jonquille said, these pines, the river.

She sat on her towel, legs spread, propped on arms straight behind her, pert breasts tilted out. I lay with my head on her thigh. Michel sat cross-legged beside us. Victor was afoot, inspecting things about the landing. I'm hungry, he said. I'm horny, I said.

The vulgarity of it would not dissolve into the air, and Michel said that if we two wanted to make out, not to mind him. Jonquille said she minded, and included me in my minding, and I added that Victor would describe it all graphically at the next meal at home.

LXXI

Don't make me feel like an outsider, Jonquille said. What are you talking about? Victor called. Look at this snail shell, the fine grey line that goes around with the spiral, and these rocks as smooth as glass. Taste this rosin. It comes off the tree in beads.

Michel, Jonquille said, is giving Jolivet and me permission to be pigs. Fine by me, Victor said. Like you do in the sunroom, kissing and monkeying around? O God, Jonquille said, holding her head. I suggested that we make everything up as we go along.

With, as Jonquille describes it, my smiling frown. You don't know what I can make up, she said. Let's eat, Victor said. Let's confuse Michel some more, said Michel. On the porch, the sun level, we sat in a circle around cold cuts, salad, bread, wine, strawberries.

So, Jonquille said, everybody hug, and let's see what happens, embracing Victor, who gleefully closed his arms around her neck but took her kiss on the mouth as an awkward surprise about which he had his doubts. Pass it around, said Jonquille with a big smile.

Victor pivoted on his butt and hugged and was hugged by me. I ventured a kiss on his forehead, lost in a duck to the top of his head. I turned to Michel, who rose to his knees, rubbing crumbs from his lips with the back of his hand, giving me time to rise.

LXXII

We forwarded the spirit of the game by locking arms around each other's backs, squeezing close, and mashing our noses together. Victor's eyes widened but Jonquille ran her hand up his back and ruffled her fingers in his hair, charming him as easily as a puppy.

Michel turned to Jonquille, who met him with parted lips, so that they kissed with flirting tongues, hip to hip, Jonquille's hands smoothing down his flanks to press his buttocks. Victor gave me a brother's look. *Voilà!* First invention, she said. It works.

Strawberries then, in the last of the sun, and sugar to roll them in, followed by a tot of brandy which Victor announced instantly had made him drunk. Michel pointed out that the number of relations among things is half the remainder of the number squared minus the number.

That's, he said, sixteen less four, twelve halved, that's six. Jolivet has still to hug Jonquille and Victor me. Your circle shortchanges. Long live math! I said, stepping over plates to lift Jonquille to a standing long hip-tight double-tongued lovely kiss.

Michel remarked of my cantered sex and tight scrotum that interest mounts, and crawled over to a dubious Victor to roll him into an arm-clasp, snuggle his chin, navel, and pizzle, each with a wiggly nudge of his nose and a gruntle, laughing and making a nasty face.

LXXIII

Victor chirped and gruffed at Michel, who pretended helplessness, and rolled him on his back to waggle noses, fluff a kiss onto his midriff, and scamper loose, having scandalized himself. How far do we go? I asked. That's our affair, Jonquille said with authority.

Shove the strawberries closer, she added. What pleases us, that's what we'll do. How lovely the evening comes on. We are us, Victor said, sucking a strawberry. It's your turn, Victor *cheri*. Tell us what we do next. Aw heck, he said, surmising with pursed lips.

God knows, Michel said, what might sound sexy to my friend Victor. We might end up playing piggy on our toes. Victor whispered in my ear, begging advice. I whispered back. I guess, he said bravely, I want my weewee pulled some. A lots, I think I mean.

I'm good at that, Jonquille said, as you'll see. Victor abided her hand with closed eyes and gritted teeth. He was hard by the third stroke and convinced of her skill and good intentions by the tenth. Something else you didn't know girls were good for, Michel said.

I watched Victor studying with his first unfurtive gaze the rimpled flesh that seamed Jonquille's crotch, wondering if that's what gaped and how it did it. His face was flushed, sweet fellow, and he clearly tingled from the crown of his head to his feet.

LXXIV

Give in and ride with it, old soldier, said Michel to Victor, who protested *but I am, Miche,* and clutched again when Jonquille bobbed down with a cupping kiss. *My O my!* Precisely, Michel said. A twirl of tongue to the hilt and she sat up, smacking her lips, a rakish grin for all.

Pass it on, she said, through the mathematical permutations, I dare you. I didn't come, Victor said. Not yet, I said, fitting his grasp. I was feeling great, bone hard, and ready with yips and moos of bliss. You two, she said, seem right at home. Old hands, I said. Hey, drool!

Squish it around, brother. What do we do, Victor asked, when it's Jonquille's turn? You'll see. *Woof!* Add some spit with your thumb, friend. You've got to stop soon, but not just yet, lovely sweet generous Victor, not just yet. Jonquille was tickling her button. The world sang.

Michel, abandoning patience, anticipated my tendance, so that when I took over, his foreskin's slide was on a slick that smacked on the down-pull and brimmed on the up. Put your heart into it, Joli. *Ai!* And Jonquille coddled his balls with her free hand, making him whuffle.

The glissade richened to a viscid slip, with lather. He spurted. A blob spattered my nose, cheek, forearm. Such a shower! said Jonquille, admiring. It's in the hair on your chest, in your pubic hair, on your tummy. It's on Jolivet. Enough to make triplets. You're a bull.

LXXV

If all that gushed into me while I was coming I'd turn inside out, Jonquille said, making me a touch queasy with a surge of jealousy. This she saw and squeezed my shoulder. I'm coming, Victor said. I'm playing with myself by myself until somebody gets around to me again.

Michel to Jonquille, I said, by the rules. Show me, he said in a small voice, and all my jealousy drained away. She placed his finger, showing him how to keep on the fold above and rotate. Also, she said, catch it between two fingers and jigger. Victor watched, eyes narrowed.

I crawled around, so that she was between me and Michel. I held her breasts, as hot as loaves from the oven, and kissed her nape and behind her ears. Am I, Michel said, getting through? The top of my head, Jonquille said, is going to blow off any minute now, for starts.

By midnight the top of her head had blown off around twenty times, some by my practised fingers, long kisses and accurate caresses, and by my tongue, some to Michel's rather frantic hand, some to her own lavished skill while she watched me and Michel reciprocate lecheries.

She charged our erotic decorum with bourgeois prudishness, which caused Michel to stick out his tongue at her. She came once by Victor's inept but eager fingers, tutored by her, as at some antique Roman orgy. She bolted my sperm thrice, viscid, alkaline, and sappish, her appraisal.

LXXVI

Her cap, all our caps, well over the windmill, we wallowed and clung and ventured by lamplight. Jonquille managed twice to take Michel's big fellow in a sheathing kiss until he came, awed and open mouthed, milty, saline, and abundant, and gulped Victor's scant mucous spurt once.

Jonquille remarked, gasping, that we made a can of worms seem shy, and Victor said that if shyness could kill he'd have been dead an hour ago, and Michel said that he was spoiled for life. I missed privacy, but in animal pride of pack liked the four of us all tangled together.

Spent and sleepy, we put our two beds together on the cabin porch and by lamplight consulted each other's opinion of the modishness and universality of our extravagances, deciding that they were mild by some standards, glorious by others, and giggled, and praised ourselves.

We fell asleep to the sound of frogs and crickets, Jonquille and I in each other's arms, Victor nestled with Michel, warm in the gurry odors of sex, the grassy sweet of hair, the fodderish smell of crotches, and the winey buckreek of armpits, the night must of pine and river.

Jonquille's kiss tasted of boy as mine of girl. We breathed together close under the sheet, chastely hip to hip, all lust swamped in a surfeit, leaving us bound by an affection unruffled by any demand, warm against the chill that seeped down from the high cold of the stars.

LXXVII

Victor, naked to the nackers, walked on his toes and looked sideways out of the corners of his eyes. The stipe of his peniculus poked out like that of Eros on Corinthian painted jugs from a mist of foxred pubic frizz. Sine twangs pulsed a manting dazzle on the Eyre.

With a leggy rush he splashed in, a frog, a tadpole. Bobbing, his gape and round eyes asked how water could be so cold. He scrambled out at the landing, hopped and cantered and danced over to help himself to my coffee. *Cochon*. It is, he sang, the summer, the summer.

No more horrible Latin, no more old arithmetic. Everybody, Jonquille said, was in critical need of a bath. I can't believe how utterly abandoned we were last night. The teenaged Messalina. I was egged on and inspired, God knows. I said she smelled lovely, sniffing her cheek.

Perfume, she said, holding the bottle up from the flight bag of toiletries she'd brought down to the river. A dab on each teat. Smell. Mamans teach daughters such wiles. Let me too, Victor said. Soon I will have done everything there is. There's always more, Michel said.

We sat in the greenish morning light of the Landes, having coffee on the landing, cool from a dip in the river. There are things never mentioned, Jonquille said. After yesterday's homemade orgy, I'm bold. Look at the acorn of Michel's *verge*. He obligingly made it jump.

LXXVIII

Adsum! See how it's a kind of warped mushroom, squat and plump. I know what it is by way of style: it's Olmec. Exactly! Whereas Jolivet's is long and like an egg: Cycladic. The difference is that between an apple in contour from the front and a celt. Do you see?

Tullio, I said, says the French are pedantic about everything. This he should hear. For which she kicked me with her heel. Michel, she continued, is square-faced, the Bonnat face is longish, *dolikhos*. There's a consistency of design. Victor's glans is long, too.

I didn't think girls looked at us that way, I said. Generalize about women and I'll bat you one, she said. Who gets to see lots of cocks together, anyway? We French taught everybody that the *grivoiserie* of the *slip masculin* is more fetching than the bare facts hanging out.

Which is simply our vestiary sensuality in a specialized mode. What decides, by the way, whether you wear your cock up like the baculum of a dog or down over your balls? Varies, Michel said, interested. Some years it's up, some down. If I wore mine up, the head would show.

He then explained, with native pedantry, that he and I have started keeping our foreskins back in a collet behind the acorn, and for that you want to be downward in the pod. Why? Feels sexier, and gives you an excuse to guddle in the ullage to trice it up when it rolls down.

LXXIX

Marc Aurel, as I rolled him past the tricolors of the Hôtel de Ville, saluted them and the gendarme in his box, whom Picasso, wearing a rakish red bandana, gave a polite sniff. We turned right, by the public notice board with proclamations, contracts, and stamped affidavits.

We entered the park between the art museum and the museum of Aquitanian antiquities, prehistoric, Gaulish, Roman, Frankish, and stopped under a row of chestnuts, Picasso taking a turn through the flower beds to look pop-eyed at a brace of thrushes and to pee a trash basket.

He scattered some gravel and did a canine dance of several twirls and some fine flourishes of his feathery tail. Here, Marc Aurel said, we are sure to see our friends, l'Abbé Perrier or Pastor Séjac, your pretty girl-friend Jonquille or your friend Michel who's to be a sailor.

Monsieur Zamora and Noé come this way to take their *repos*. Would Monsieur Ramuntcho ever come into the park? Never! Sister Joseph-Marie and Sister Louise-Vincent-de-Paul take their constitution through here, *l'agent* Maurice and *l'agent* Gaston. Those people are English.

Look, Jolivet, you can tell by their BOA *sac* and flat shoes and having no dog. In England the busses are two storeys high, the *brasseries* are open only a few hours a day. The queen of England lives in seven palaces. What beautiful linoleums she must have on all her floors!

LXXX

In the cave on Donkey Hill, or Pech de l'Azé as they say in Périgord, between Sarlat and the Dordogne, near the train tracks where the road forks to Souillac and Gourdon, the archeologist François Bordes found in 1968 an ox rib engraved by an Acheulean hunter 230,000 years ago.

Bordes, director of the Institute of Prehistory at the University of Bordeaux, was digging in stratum Riss I, third of the classical glacial periods, when the Val Dordogne was a grassy steppe with stands of pine, birch, and hazel roamed by black-maned red horses in herds.

The archaic cave bear, Merck's rhinoceros, the great Irish deer, rabbits, wolves, elephants, cows, tarpans, and men unknown to us in any way except for their hand axes, flint scrapers, and quartz cleavers, and this proximal section of an ox rib and its strange lines.

An ostrich? A river, mountains? Is it a map of hunting territories? A deed? Notation perhaps (Marshack) of the changes of the moon. The attributes of some horned and stalking god to whom one owes an owl when he shakes stars from the night, else he will freeze the world?

The top of the wall, achieved by shinnying up the hornbeam, handwalking a limb, and dropping down. I come here for my sulks, long thoughts, and secret pictures in my mind. I locate myself as soon as I get here, under leaves slashed by light, or bare branches in winter.

LXXXI

Three cows tread in a line, muzzle to hindquarters, between deer above, horses below. A delaunay of tricolors and footballeurs, a dufy of race horses. Brancusi's *Fish* is the shape a fish makes in water, the hollow. It has the polish of a river pebble. Streaming bubble of stone.

Victor, having gone through the personae of Astérix, Robinson Crusoe, Jean-Claude Killy, Captain Nemo, and Graham Hill, is piloting a space module to the surface of Mars, a red desert with jibbering humanoid celery. He speaks to them in mouse's French, they reply in chipmunk.

He monitors his descent on screens marked off in grids and revolving radii and intermittent algebraic sprays of numbers that come and go with beeps and tings. We daydream in duet. Roman trumpets, tabrets, sifting tinkling sistra. The fleet stands on the Garumna at Burdigala.

Decimus Magnus Ausonius, disciple of Arborius and Minervius Alcimus and rhetorician at law, takes a cup of wine at the Taverna Bellenus on the Plateia Aemilia with the elderly Attius Patera Junior, a descendant of the Druids of Baiocassi. Students, tabellions crowd on benches.

Tullio and I achieve the Globe through milling students and resolute boulevardiers, take our favorite table, and over coffee talk of silver and pepper. For two centuries western silver from German mines and the new world changed places with the pepper of the east, silver ever eastward.

LXXXII

Victor, in from football, is mounting stamps in the wrong places in the albums, Papa's in his drafting room, Maman's out shopping or having tea with Eulalie on the Clemenceau, Marc Aurel and Trombone are watching television at the Globe, Jonquille's reading Proust.

Tullio's talking the afternoon away at the Régent, Michel is working out at the apprentice mariner's gymn. Below, inside the wall, Uncle Jacques is rolling his cigarettes of shredded horse manure and gun powder, darkening his grievances, listening to his staticky radio.

I stride up the Catherine, rounds in wild mynah birdcalls singing into Dien Bien Phu. I run with Jonquille naked down the great dune at Arcachon, watch a finch fly in and out of the entrance to Les Combarelles, recite, giddy with mischief, Uncle Jacques' ailments.

Catarrh, hemorrhoids, a weak back, ingrowing toenails, flat feet, arthritic knees, dandruff, a hernia, smoker's hack, a bad liver, inflamed kidneys, a ringing in his ears, a heart flutter, chronic indigestion: to Papa's merriment, Maman's feigned annoyance, Victor's stare.

He's below, pacing, cracking his knuckles, sucking the sweet from his misery. With me to admire: a thirty para bice and magenta Jugoslavia: a spray of *Salvia officinalis*. A twenty para autumn crocus. *Erythraea,* the ten para. Hectic traffic on one side, quiet garden on the other.

LXXXIII

Tullio in a generously cut suit the color of tobacco, his cravat lavender, lecture room sunlight from tall windows finding as he moved the elusive gold of his watchchain and rings, eyes rich with sincerity, shaped with his hands in the air an antique cylinder of stone.

Soon after the young Cicéron, he said, came to Syracuse around 72 before Christ to take up his post there as quaestor, he set out like the philosophical Roman he was to visit the grave of Archimède, who had been murdered in 212 by a centurion who mistook him for a wizard.

To Cicéron's stoic mind the turbulence of Sicilian history contained one man of genius and sober virtue. But whereas the memory of the tyrant Dion, whom Cicéron thought the most despicable of men, was still green, no one at all remembered the great geometrician Archimède.

If the name recalled anything, it was the work of his left hand during a siege years and years ago. Time was flat and perspectiveless to the classical mind. Myth grew around every fact like a vine. Old campaigners talked of the man who burnt a fleet with a sorcery of mirrors.

A pale rose Sicilia on an oilcloth map in the frailest blue of the Siculum Mare lay poised to be punted by the toe of Italia. As Tullio moved left and right, I could read Messana, Syracusae, Heraclea Minoa, Drepanum, Henna. Italian colors have a grammar all their own.

LXXXIV

The tomb of Archimède, as he specified in his will, depicted a cylinder and sphere of equal diameter and height, the one inside the other, with an inscription saying that their relation is as two is to three. Nothing of Greek fire, or of specific gravity, or of fulcra inscribed.

This elegant proportion alone appeared on the austere column at his grave, and his immortal name. He lived long ago, the Syracusans explained. He was anyway but *humilem homuncionem,* a little nobody of a man. But where was he buried? Nobody seemed to know or to care.

So Cicéron looked and asked, asked and looked. Like his emulator and disciple Pétrarque centuries later, and like our own Montaigne here in Bordeaux, his piety ran to the tactile, the actual presence, the Chinese sense of standing in the very place, touching the thing itself.

Cicéron in Sicilian light with a legation of secretaries and patient sergeants major, Plutarque on a Boiotian porch with scrolls in jars around him, Montaigne in his chateau looking out over acres of vineyards, such attention has educated our own ever since, fixing our focus.

And then one day outside the gate opening onto the road to Agrigentum he found an abandoned cemetery, its tombs overgrown with thorns and brambles. There are no spikier weeds than the Sicilian, nor any rustier in color. And, I can assure you, they have a bite like fire.

LXXXV

Among these yellow and vermilion thickets the tombs were red with lichen and alive with lizards. When after a briary hour he saw the cylinder and sphere and cried *Heureka!* his cultivated Roman company appreciated the perfect allusion perhaps more than the discovery.

They slashed the bramble away, scraped off the lichen. The name was indistinct. Cicéron writes that if he had not come to Sicily as its first Roman administrator, Syracuse might never have known where it had misplaced its finest citizen, *ita nobilissima Greceiae civitas.*

A judiciously dressed crisp green salad, Tullio's Latin. *Quondam vero etiam doctissima, sui civis unius acutissimi monumentum ignorasset, nisi ad homine Arpinate didicisset.* That *quondam,* that *once upon a time,* will lead Pétrarque to Paestum and D'Annunzio to Mycenae.

It will take Schliemann to Hissarlik and Arthur Evans to Cnossos. It is for years and years still the spirit of romance, and in time will become true archeology, Bordes digging with watercolor brushes at Combe-Grenal, Breuil clicking on his flashlight that day in Lascaux.

In the seventeenth century the Englishman John Locke, shown the ashes of Cicéron, remarked with British phlegm that *aye God they seem to have interred Tully in a very urinal.* With what awe, by contrast, do we all hear about the bone Professor Bordes found in his Sarlat cave.

LXXXVI

It is, he conjectures, 230,000 years old! Hallam Movius, at Harvard, the disciple of Breuil, thinks it is only 100,000 years old, but the American paleontologist Alexander Marshack puts it at 135,000. It is written all over with lines incised by three separate flint burins.

It is by far the oldest writing or drawing that we have discovered. To Cicéron's attention it would have meant nothing at all. History has its own history, which is the history of attention. Tullio ended with an anecdote that has survived of Archimède's love of geometry.

Like the one about the displacement of a body's weight in water, it finds the master in his bath. His servants, having to dress him for a dinner party, would pull him away from his tablets. As they oiled him, he would grab the strigil and draw geometric figures on his body.

Tullio says that Plutarque and Montaigne were the same man, 1500 years between the two parts of his life. An *emulatio* of genius so close that this can be said. Papa proposed Cicéron as a third incarnation. No, Tullio says, he did not have the wit, the fun, the passion.

Knowledge is not to be tested by the question of practicality. Papa says that in architecture school he had to learn every stone in the Parthenon, every dimension, every volume, knowledge that has been perfectly useless to him in his career, but also infinitely useful.

LXXXVII

Maman was translating Tullio's *La geografia 'patafisica dell' idee inno-cue nello rinascimento 1910* with many a *pouf!* and *qu'est-ce que* and *que diable!* She was into the essay on the body as exoskeleton, as insect, as puppet, as mute presence. Cartesian robot run by thought.

Ensor's masks, the Noh masks of Yeats' and Pound's translations from the Japanese, Picasso's African masks in *Les Demoiselles d'Avignon*. The puppet gestures of *Ubu roi* and the mechanization of the body in *Le Sur-mâle*. Marinetti's body as animal in *Il re Baldoria* and *Mafarka*.

Hat blocks, tailor's dummies, and humanoid constructs in Carrà, de Chirico, and Morandi. Scarecrow and doll in Yeats, Guy Fawkes stuffed in Eliot, Rilke's puppet and doll, Pound's dry husks and insectification of flesh, Wyndham Lewis' wild body and Bergson's machine.

Pathetic gesture and erotic surface in Picasso progressing from languor to melancholy paralysis to violence to comedy. I've followed the translation all along. And now, from her desk, Jolivet *mon cher!* Where are you? My tongue was in Jonquille's mouth, my hand in her panties.

Oui, Maman? We're in the sunroom, Jonquille and I. Come here, she said, what in the world is this quotation from Wittgenstein? Be down in half a minute, I said. What are you doing, anyway? Don't mean to curtail your camaraderie or whatever, something disgraceful to be sure.

LXXXVIII

I trotted down in the raw except for little white pants which I complacently did not check for the seep of probable goo, my hair mussed. Does this, she said, thumping the page, make the least sense to you? I laughed. *You can't catch the measles over the telephone,* it says.

That's the translation? What does the poor fool mean? It's one of Tullio's favorites from Wittgenstein, I said. It means that you can know something without feeling it, and that there are experiences you can be exposed to without contagion, that machines intervene, and.

Maman sighed and relocated a strand of hair swinging across her face. What a beautiful child you are! Your hair is getting to be quite savage, Joli. While you're down, is there a good reproduction somewhere about of Duchamp's *Large Glass?* There's an awful lot about it coming up.

I'd better have it before me. The one here in the Italian text seems to have been engraved on burnt toast. There's a clear one, I said, in Paz and one in the Skira. I nipped off to fetch them. Jonquille, sweet! Maman called. Bare girl footsteps padded to the head of the stairs.

Yes, Madame Bonnat? Sorry to take Jolivet away from you, Maman said. Is he behaving himself? I think so, Jonquille said. Well, have fun but don't be an idiot. Maman! I shouted, please, please, eh? Just bring me the Duchamp, sweetheart, and back upstairs with you now.

LXXXIX

Michel and I prone under the covert of elm branches that thatch the wall near the gate lay shoulder to shoulder, bumping sneakers to josh and sign. Uncle Jacques was not beneath, for this was a part of the wall stacked with junk rich in spiders and silverfish.

Bumble of traffic on one side, green quiet of the bushiest part of the garden on the other, the top of the wall is as private as a roof, and Michel turned over, slid his jeans zipper down, deposed his briefs, and lay bareballed for the sweet broadmindedness of it.

Below us, I knew later, Uncle Jacques crouched like a baboon on a folded rug atop a trunk, his ear to stone, hearing us, with garbled intervals, at our talk, my voice and a voice unknown to him, which for a man who liked his gossip exact must have hurt.

Miche was telling me about the chippy in the Place St.-Projet who invited him in for free because she thought him a *beau garçon* with serious business in his britches. She does a big turnover with the apprentice seamen at the maritime barracks, Miche explained.

Her left eye's wall but she's a good old girl ready for fun. But, comrade Jolivet, this able-fisted Socialist was as red as his flag. This steadfast buddy went into a sulk, afraid of a dose I think. He absolutely would not stand up. Might have been the wobble eye.

XC

I was equally intrigued and appalled. What did he do? What did she do? Lay there like a frog on her back. Later, when Uncle Jacques said *you are as nasty as he is,* what he'd half heard was my opinions about what a competent chippy might have done to help matters.

What trash your hopeless mother lets you run with! Uncle Jacques, even if he'd heard well, couldn't have understood a great deal. In copulation he thinks that a testicle is ejected through the *verge* into some unspeakable opening, so Papa says, both of them for twins.

Personally, he'd told Papa, *I don't think I could have stood the pain.* Maman, freely admitting the pity of it, laughed until she was weak. It was after this that Victor and I were presented with a sex manual photographed in Denmark, with nothing to imagine.

Michel's member, shy at St.-Project, was impudent on the wall. An enviably rippled rootage of myoid sinuosities ran its length and the peduncle suspending his brace of eggs was stout with the bulbous tubulature inside. The Danish sex manual had nothing like it.

Uncle Jacques, listening below in deviltry and anguish, would have heard me explaining fine points of foreplay, boasting, talk about ships, trigonometry, airplanes. And heard scuffled leaves, chuckling, flopping about. What are they doing up there, O God, what are they doing?

XCI

Tullio turned up fanning himself with his panama, followed in by Postel, aproned and with a towel, waiting for an opening to ask Monsieur le Professeur if he could serve him a cooling drink, a mineral water gaseous or natural, or spirits with ice introduced.

He chose coffee, calling Postel *my good fellow.* Never too hot for coffee, he said. *Ah!* Jolivet, dear soul, it's your mother I've come to see, to consult. My paper on the metaphysicals has taken an unexpected turn, and is now to be the text for a Mondadori album.

All the discussions of individual paintings were to be made more particular. He explained it all as if I were Maman herself. She was at Merignac with Papa, inspecting a building site. My luck, said Tullio, asking to stay anyway to have the coffee offered.

Do I interrupt you? How wonderfully brown you are. Victor and I, I said, were only mucking around with our stamp collection, partly true but useful. Victor came around from the parterre in his minim of white underpants, saying that Michel was here, just coming in.

Hello, Professor Tullio. Enchanted, I'm sure, dear Victor. And explained again that he had dropped by on the off chance of finding Maman at home, but didn't quarrel with having two naked boys for his hosts, handsome as the young Castor and Pollux, not in the least.

XCII

We aren't naked, Victor said gravely, we're wearing *slips*. As nearly as makes no difference, said Tullio. Thank you kindly, Postel. And here's Michel: an afternoon of pleasant encounters indeed, indeed. Tullio's manners, Papa had said, were to be studied for style.

Michel gave me a wink over Tullio's shoulder, patting the pout of his *caleçon*. The ruck of his worked pectorals tried his *maillot* and made its hem ride above the thick thirl of hair around his navel. He said *sir* to Tullio, *camerade* to me and *bougre* to Victor.

Mon bon bougre d'idiot, giving Victor's tummy a poke with his middle finger, asking Postel if there were any Cocas. He sat across from Tullio, a charming smile for all. That he wore nothing under his short pants was evident from the neb of his cock poking out.

And an eggy testicle protruded from the other side of his crotch. Victor gave me a look out of the tail of his eye. I nipped behind Tullio and mimed to Michel that he was indecent. He looked innocent, a hint of shrug in his shoulders. It was one of his teases.

Tullio, sipping his coffee, was not to be raddled, and explained again that he had looked in on Madame Bonnat who was helping him prepare an article on the Italian metaphysical painters, but she is out, and hospitality was thrust upon me before I could retreat.

XCIII

Caruso in full aria, Tullio at his best. He is the Napoleon of conversation. I was just saying, he addressed Michel as if he were his oldest friend, how fetching Jolivet and Victor are in their merest *cache-sexes,* wholly Mediterranean, *soavemente seducente.*

Postel, bringing three Cocas on a tray, showing off for Tullio, gave me a signalling eye to come into the house, Victor shaking his Coca to gobble the exploding froth. To Michel Tullio was saying that he saw that he had developed his body to a perfection.

How I envied the fine bodies of my agemates, he said with a trill of fingers, when I was a student in Torino so many years ago. I was a bookworm, corpulent even then. And there were bodies to which no care was given at all that were naturally well proportioned.

Just as there were skinny or otherwise amorphous boys, who half killed themselves on the parallel bars and the track, for whom no amount of exertion was of the least help. The body is an expression of fate, a sign and the content of the sign all in one, I think.

Miche! I had to say, returning from Postel, your peter is sticking out of your pants and Postel says that he has never been so mortified in his life. Tullio boomed with laughter, and Victor joined him with a bray. Sorry, Michel said, shifting the set of his crotch.

XCIV

Apologies, Michel said. It's not Victor's *revolver joujou*. But we're all male here, Tullio said. I was commenting on the athletic finish Michel has given his physique. It's a privilege to see more of it than is afforded by the figleaves in the Italian museums.

They take them off on Thursdays, did you know? If, said Michel full of himself and at his most brattish, you want to see me in the altogether, nothing easier. He drew his jersey over his head with one hand, unzipped his pants with the other, and stood snake naked.

And then and there was Maman saying, Whatever's going on out here? Postel tried to keep me from coming through my own house. Michel! You're beautiful. What have I walked in on? Miche scooped up his jersey and held it against his sex, his face blank with confusion.

Don't dare blush so, Michel! Maman said with her kindest authority. As the mother of two boys, there's nothing left for me to see, and I grew up with two elder brothers, though they scarcely prepared me for the fun of having New Guinea underfoot day in, day out.

It's my fault entirely, dear Henriette, Tullio said. I was admiring Michel's body in a philosophical way and he volunteered to display it in a full state of nature. So quit looking miserable, Michel, Maman said. Life is one surprise after another. Let us see you.

XCV

Along the stone *abri* at Mouthiers, la Chaire à Calvin, Charente, carved thirty thousand years ago in fine, low relief, once painted, you can see a bison, the dorsal and ventral lines of a bovid, three horses, and a stallion mounting a mare, a frieze discovered in 1927.

Pierre David, a nineteen-year-old shepherd, discovered these images. Jonquille, like Maman and Papa, has been in Lascaux. Michel, Victor, and I only saw slides of it when we were there, though the man who showed the slides was Jacques Marsal, who discovered it as a boy.

Someday, Jonquille says, we'll know what these caves are, and what their images mean. Of course, Tullio agrees. Some genius will find out. If anybody can, Jonquille will. And I will find out why Uncle Jacques is in the wall. Images are more meaningful than words to me.

Their power is of a different order. Marc Aurel looks like a Luca della Robbia choirboy and Trombone like Montaigne's teacher at the Collège de Guyenne George Buchanan, poet and heretic, with the long face of a pensive horse. I fancy that I look like Rimbaud with a sun tan.

Michel looks like St. John in Masaccio's *The Tribute Money* and an athlete by Despiau. Jonquille is Marie Laurencin in clothes and skinny Balthus in disarray for hugging. Tullio looks like Rossini in disguise. Maman and Papa look like France, Victor like a freckled rabbit in a wig.

XCVI

At the top of the stairs to Michel's mansarde I swung Marc Aurel around from the fireman's carry by which I'd brought him up, slung him over my shoulder like a duffel, and set him laughing and bouncing on the cot. And this is Michel's home! Look at all the things!

He wore the pair of my blue cotton short pants that Maman had sewn the legs of closed and a tacky nylon blouse with Eiffel Towers and champagne glasses emitting bubbles all over it. The bicycle hangs from the ceiling! Naked girls on the walls! LP records, maps, ships.

Gymnasium things. Look at that lamp: show me how it changes around. Picasso took in the room with a comprehensive sniff, noting that a jockstrap and socks over the arm of a chair were part of Michel, as were various shoes, record sleeves, books, weights, caps, pullovers.

Allons-y! said Michel, loosing the tongue of his belt from its buckle and unzipping his fly. I signalled *no!* from across the room and he asked *why not?* with his eyes. I've never been up so high except at the hospital, Marc Aurel said. A room of your own, like Jolivet.

Like Victor. Your mother has the rest of the apartment? I'll bet she has lovely things, too, a bright linoleum and knicknacks on whatnots and paintings of mountain lakes and funny clowns so sad. I pulled Victor off of pretending to ride Picasso and hugged him.

XCVII

If you're going to be a pest and stay, I said in the kind of whisper brothers use among friends, to be overheard but not noticed, you must remember none of this happened, understand? Otherwise you're a *crapaud* and a snitch and you'll have to live by your rotten self.

You won't have a friend in the world. Are we, Victor asked, going to jack off? Has Marc Aurel got a peter? Of course he has, rabbitbrain. What do you think he pees through? Oh yes, Victor said with maddening vagueness, I saw it in the bathtub. The day we all went to Prignac.

And now, Marc Aurel said, we're talking about the bathroom. *Tiens,* Michel said, giving me a puzzled look. I'm confused, Victor said. Giddyap, Picasso old boy. The rustlers are after the sheep and the redskins have massacred Chicago. Want to take your pants off? I asked.

No, Marc Aurel said, I'd be ashamed. Of what? My question, but Victor asked it. Of taking my pants off. It isn't nice, is it? Among friends it's done. We do it all the time, Miche and Victor and I. But only if you want to. We won't embarrass you. What's embarrass? Victor asked.

You wouldn't know, I said. Uncle Jacques, Victor said, I mean somebody we know, way off in Toulouse, is always saying he's embarrassed by this and that. He doesn't know about sex from a rat's ass. He told Joli that if he plays with himself he'll go crazy and his wizzle will drop off.

XCVIII

Marc Aurel stopped his ears but was grinning tremendously and turning pink. Naughty! Naughty! Naughty! he sang. Michel looked disgusted, Victor amused, Picasso interested, and I hacked. Uncle Jacques, Michel said, is an imaginary recluse the Bonnats think they live with.

They all believe in him, including old Postel. Where do you keep him, in the attic? I used to have a playmate, Marc Aurel said, a dear friend, I can just remember, back before I lost my legs. He was that word, imaginary, though I remember him as real, as real as you are.

He never came to the hospital and he has never come afterwards. *He* did things in the bathroom like what I think you're talking about. Michel's mouth fell open. You don't, eh? he asked. Marc Aurel blushed redder and looked lost and confused. I was miserable. I was stumped.

We thought, I said, we'd give you a treat, because we're all friends to-gether. You're a friend, too, you know. Yes, Victor said, you and Picasso are our friends. Joli does everything. He and Jonquille lie on the floor with their heads between each other's legs hugging hard.

They hug so hard they grunt, and it makes them wiggle their toes. It looks real funny. Jonquille sucks his *verge,* Jolivet says it feels real good, and then they switch around and Jolivet gets on top and makes zigzig. They say *oh!* a lot and say mushy things about love.

XCIX

That sounds beautiful, Marc Aurel said. I remarked that we might as well do it in the Gambetta, for all the privacy at home. And on our weekend in the Landes, Victor went on, the family historian. That will do, little brother, I said. What, Marc Aurel said, is my treat?

We were just going to mess around and get to feeling good. It's a thing we do. Will I like it? Marc Aurel asked. I think I'll like it. Things in the books Michel has, photographed in true living color. On our cycling trip, Victor said, we had our britches off more than on.

Michel was out of his jeans and had his briefs off in time to catch Victor who, trying to hop out of his pants around his ankles, made the comic most of tripping and sprawling. I untrousered and gave my dick a lively pull or two, for courage. I'd never felt less sexy.

I swallowed hard, feeling my forehead burn, and helped Marc Aurel bare the stumps, radially scored with starfish of mauve and pink scar tissue, between which dangled a puckery scrotum and slim spout tipped with a waxy calyx of foreskin, which Picasso poked his cold nose to.

Victor and Michel set to on each other like deprived and long parted buddies, hot as monkeys, showing off. With what emotion Marc Aurel watched them, consternation or delight or unrelenting surprise, I could not tell, but watch he did, hard, and his munchkin stood up.

C

I pushed the bell and waited, knuckles on hips, feet defiantly apart, head cocked, a leaf for luck in the corner of my mouth, my stance of confidence evolved over the years. Madame Tullio answered the door, surprised. Ugo you want? she said. He read. I mean, he glad to see you.

Please to enter. I tell him you come. Tullio was in the midst of a spill of books, linguistic, structuralist, phenomenological, encyclopedic, iconographic. He wore a bandana knotted at the corners on his head, a collarless shirt, two pairs of glasses, one on his forehead.

His old-fashioned pantaloons were a kind rarely seen outside Italy and the remoter marches of Scandinavia, as were his carpet slippers (Ibsen, Croce), and the mask over his moustache held on by loops around his ears. Bonnat, he said uncertainly, and switching glasses, Jolivet!

Caro Jolivet! You find me very much at home, I'm afraid, in the mire of research. This frightful thing under my nose holds my moustache in place after I've dyed and waxed it, no sight for the public eye. Let me excavate myself and we will go to the parlor and be comfortable.

Madame Tullio was opening windows, dashing at tables and chairs with a duster when we entered. Tullio shooed her out with a torrent of Italian. She curtsied at the door before she departed altogether. Apologies, Tullio said, for the disorder, not what you're used to.

CI

You live in a well-run, beautifully appointed home. I'm the one, I said, who has come to apologize, startled by my own courage. Whatever for? he said. *Angelina!* bring us coffee, light of my life, and the bottle of *alcool framboise.* Guillaume Bonnat's son come to visit!

To apologize? For the way, I said, Michel Coudray acted yesterday afternoon. I'm afraid you thought his display disrespectful, perhaps insulting. He was showing off. Maman says we must make allowances for his upbringing. Even so, it was a breach of good manners, I know.

It was not, he said, as if trying to recall the matter, the most well-bred behavior, was it? I took it to be a prank for its own sake, a bit of surrealism, more to make an entertaining joke for you and Victor than anything to do with me. I'd forgotten all about it.

Madame Tullio brought coffee in a porcelain jug, filled our cups, pointed to sugar, spoons, and napkins, threw up her hands and fled, returning immediately with a tall bottle of *alcool* and glasses. I said that I didn't think I was allowed to drink the *alcool framboise.*

Just so. Nor my Marcellina. I never know what the French take or at what age. And you came to apologize for your friend? That is a handsome thing for you to do. I hope he wasn't remorseful? Not Michel, I shouldn't think. Tell me, said Tullio, have you read the *Salammbô*?

CII
Campari and Perrier water. Tullio puts his Risorgimento fedora on the table after a *coup de chapeau* to the brasserie at large. Sardou *maman* Trilby. And in its dent his Gauloises and matches. I, chin on knuckles, strike an aspect Guynemer, practised at the mirror.

It is a handsome frown of intelligence that gets a young man through straits Tullio negotiates while stirring his Campari and milking an ear lobe. There are things that can be measured but not observed, like time and intelligence, observed but not measured, like space and stupidity.

But animal faith knows nothing of measure. It knows only the congenial and the alien. He dusted Gauloise ash from his vest, viewed the Gambetta, lifted his glass to me with a wish for my continued good health. And yours, I replied. What I really want to write is this.

I want, he said, to write a history of the imagination in our time. Oh, never mind the history of the imagination from Bordes' ox thigh to Picasso and Ernst, which will be written several times over, but some understanding of Jules Verne, Boullée, Jarry, Rimbaud, Balzac.

All these need to be reseen. The new modifies everything before, and even finds a tradition for the first time. Imagine what Proust looks like to Simenon, Simenon the Utrillo of writing, and what Maigret would think of Swann, Rimbaud of de Gaulle. Here Marc Aurel rolled up.

CIII
And welcome, Tullio said. When we have sight of the angels they will look like this child. So high-backed a wheelchair, I surmised, must survive from the age of carriages and top hats. Marc Aurel's smile was as sweet and silly as Picasso's grin beside him, room for them both.

You're talking books, he said, books about science and people in Paris and faraway places. We have looked up Maupassant, first name Guy, you were talking about the other day, in our dictionary. He is a noted French author whose endings surprise. And we looked up Balzac.

He wrote the bestseller *Human Comedy*. Wouldn't I like to read that! Trombone touched two fingers to his hat. A poem about the Moselle river is by Ausone. He was a schoolteacher right here in Bordeaux. In the period of the Romans. What an erudite fellow you are, said Tullio.

Do you read a lot? Yes sir, I do. I've read my Sunday School book all the way through, and five or six Tintins, and Jolivet's books by Jules Verne and Victor's book about the kings of France. Mademoiselle Delahoussaye has presented me with a book about caveman paintings.

I have visited these myself, by bus, as the guest of my friends. I get to see many books at Jolivet's house, they have as many as the library on the Mably, some in foreign languages, English and Italian, which the Bonnats read without batting an eyelash, all the time.

CIV

And I have, Marc Aurel went on, looked through books belonging to Michel Coudray that he lent Jolivet and Victor which have pictures in color of nice young people without a stitch of clothes on making love to each other, which I wouldn't dare mention to Pastor Séjac.

I don't think Abbé Perrier would be shocked, provided these people are married, of course, though I don't see how some of them could be, so young, God moves in wondrous ways, and I read all the news in *The Southwest* every day here at the Globe, there's always a copy.

Il tribunale dei angeli e dominazione, Tullio said. Marc Aurel went on about books. A great book author of the *Anglais* was Soeur Voltaire Scut. He held out his hand. Made of cells, he explained. Thousands and thousands. *Ah!* Tullio sighed. School. Go back to Sister Walter Scott.

That's, I said, not *soeur* but *sire*. Say *milord,* he was a baron. Marc Aurel listened with cocked head, eyes wide. She was a man? The last gentleman of Europe, Tullio said. Waiter! A *rouge* and a Coca. O decidedly a gentleman. He suffered as terribly as Montaigne with the stone.

I was about to add that he was also lame but stopped the words in my throat. Picasso licked Coca Cola from Marc Aurel's hand. Trombone remarked that Protestants are surprisingly decent people, and touched two fingers to his hat in acknowledgment of his glass of wine.

CV

Michel carried the great beach umbrella over his shoulder like a javelin. Marc Aurel, a hamper on his lap, rolled behind, propelled by Monsieur Trombone. Victor followed with Picasso and Tullio, Jonquille and I, each with an arm across the other's shoulder sweetly.

It would look something like Duchamp's *Glider with Water Mill,* Tullio was saying, walking in the Neapolitan manner as we passed a window in which a canary seemed to be singing Charpentier, that descends of course from Leonardo da Vinci by way of Otto Lilienthal.

The ocean! Marc Aurel shouted, I can see the ocean! It is the Atlantic. It's *everywhere*! Space, Tullio went on as we staked the umbrella's punch into the sand and made its dome of paisley bloom, is a solid, time a liquid. In space time saturates every moment.

He had been talking about Jarry's time machine all the way to the beach. We had driven from Bordeaux to Arcachon in Tullio's rattling Renault, Marc Aurel's wheelchair tied on top. Wouldn't Fellini like this! Tullio had said, tooting the horn for fun as we set out.

Trombone rode in front with Tullio and Picasso, Marc Aurel on his lap. In the backseat Jonquille sat on me, Victor on Michel, and we trifled with them both in an intimate and Polynesian way. Jonquille managed with successive plucks to transfer her panties to her ankles.

CVI

Michel by a similar furtive *perirepsis* of Victor's *caleçon,* discussing time machines all the while, no one in front the wiser, made him, as I Jonquille, hold a rounded tongue in his teeth and shoot his eyebrows straight up, Jonquille and Victor trading merry looks.

About here, sir? Michel asked of Tullio, spreading an old travelling rug on the sand. *Ah oui! Mon toc!* And indeed it had a sphinx at each end, was four greens, and had a border of Empire devices flourishing at the corners. Very Boudin, Tullio exclaimed, this beach.

A silvery sea, golden light, a sweet air. Trombone parked Marc Aurel at the edge of the umbrella's shade and knotted the corners of a bandana that was to be his concession to our outing, protection, he explained, against sunstroke, which can fell you without warning.

He took off his redingote that had seen Jena and sat on its skirts. Tullio unfolded two beach chairs, insisting that Trombone take one until with huddled shyness he did, and settled himself in the other, rolling his shirt sleeves above his jovial elbows in pedantic folds.

He took off his tie, shoes and socks, donning sandals of arts-and-craftshop origin. His toenails were curiously warped and discolored, some black, some purple. There were cruel pink bunions on the balls of both feet and radicular veins, like tattooed cobweb, on his ankles.

CVII

Victor, Michel, Jonquille, and I nipped to the other side of the umbrella's tilt to change into bathing togs all frugal of cut but at Maman's insistence a bikini with top for Jonquille rather than the monokini she wore to the *piscine, slips* rather than *cache-sexes* for us.

Victor too, who still went naked on beaches, sported a *slip.* We held towels for each other to change behind, and sprinted to the waves, shoving each other all the way. I could see Tullio saying something about us to Trombone, but Trombone was pointedly looking the other way.

When, salt and cold, I went back to the umbrella, leaving Victor to flip backwards from Michel's stirruped hands and Jonquille to make cheeky remarks from beyond the breakers, I found Tullio trying to get Marc Aurel to take off his heavy pink satin shirt.

He will take cold, Trombone protested. He's susceptible. Nonsense, Tullio said. For a little bit? Marc Aurel asked. You don't think it would be a liberty? Trombone asked Tullio in confusion. With all these people about? Never, said Tullio, pointing to naked children.

Marc Aurel took off his shirt. Picasso, who had followed Victor to the waves and into them until their unpredictableness had discouraged him, returned with me, spraying water in rainbowed shakes. I had my eye on you, Picasso! Marc Aurel sang. Oof! Love you too, big dog!

CVIII

There are, Tullio said, refreshments, and was naming them on his fingers when Jonquille, Victor, and Michel came running, dazzling wet, giving our signal. I lifted Picasso away from painting Marc Aurel with his tongue and whispered what we were ready to do.

Tactic, go! Michel said. Trombone sat up in confusion. I picked Marc Aurel up in a hug and carried him behind the umbrella. God and all the saints! Trombone shouted. Relax, Jonquille said. We're taking Marc Aurel into the ocean. Trombone covered his face with his hands.

Victor can go bare assed, I said. But it's perfectly all right, my good fellow! Tullio was saying. He will be in no danger whatsoever. They're all splendidly athletic, look at them. It will do him good, the sea water, I assure you, and the fellowship of it too, you know.

I held Marc Aurel in my arms while Michel stripped him of undershirt, wool trousers with the legs sewn closed, and drawers grey with age and lye soap. Fine fit! he said as Michel seated Victor's blue *slip* on him. We carried him between us, his arms around our necks.

Naked Victor pranced monkeyshines before us, Jonquille raced around us into the tumbling waves, Picasso barked alongside, braving the water with eager eyes. I managed a breaststroke with Marc Aurel on my back. They're drowning him! I could hear Trombone groaning.

CIX

The sun, a red disc, snicking the green meadow at sunflush before set, red point, green point in granular vibration, gleamed upon us mealy gold, frecking snarl-curled hair, our bare bodies acorn brown, glossy silver at rondures and pilosities, a solid quiet around us.

We were, Michel and I, outside our Danish blue tent pegged to a tautness, trig and snug on its aluminum frame at the top of a slant field under the edge of a wood between Montignac and Brive the end of a long fine day of cycling radiantly naked except for briefs and sneakers.

And the shine of sweat. The briefs now hung lining outward on the handlebars of our Peugeots, vestments and machines of irreducible spareness. Bathed in the creek down the slope, fed on cold chicken, bread, wine, and cheese, we were easy with fatigue, and happy.

Michel, grinning superbly, fondled his scrotum. I, proleptic, mirrored both grin and caress, adding a pendular flip of my cock for punctuation. Friends? he said. Friends, I said. Precision of emotion. With Michel's transparent honesty one's imagination can unfold in light.

Corydon and Alexis, Cézanne and Zola, shepherds in the cricketshrill, noonbright, gnatstippled, sultry swelter of an Aixois summer, eyes as I imagined for a Cézanne never achieved, a thumbsmudge of umber in lush biconvexities of lashes, a nubbinnostrilled highshinned nose.

CX

A plenary upper lip finely corbelled under a philtron deeply notched, the nether rimpled and thrust, rounding quadrature of chin, shoulders bolled and bossed, chest burly and briskly hairy, strait flanked, narrow haunched, heftily quadricepsed, and the knees cunningly geared.

Long hummocked calves, ballpeen-huckled ankles, gracious feet smelling of trod sage, wild mint, wool, and all pungent, from hair to toes, with the vinegary odor of axial, the doggish odor of inguinal sweat. *Iam resonant frondes, iam cantibus obstrepit arbos: i procul o Corydon.*

Michel ducked into the tent, with the gnats and grasshoppers, crickets and midges, and sprawled with his shoulders against the packroll. Flaps reefed, inside was outside, the cool of the meadow rising fresh around us. He lit a Gauloise and called me in with the thermos.

Where else, I came asking, except away from everywhere, can you pee while pouring coffee? I put the cup on the flat of his midriff, nudged a knuckle along his mesial villosity, and begged a drag. We both drank from the thermos cap and shared the cigarette.

The light went green, fireflies blinked, the crickets chirred shriller. I skimmed Michel's brush with the flat of my hand and prowled fingers around his scrotum, perineum, the hollow of his hip. Being bold, I said. *Agréable au goût?* He crossed his eyes and wrinkled his nose.

CXI

Precise, he asked, in your emotions? Don't josh me about that, I said, I'm serious. I want to know exactly what I feel, the exact essence of things. I geared my fingers between his toes and rocked his foot, slid my hand up his shin, and batted his knee with my fist.

Trailed spread fingers inside his thighs, cupped his testicles and lightly squeezed. Michel sipped our coffee, smoked his Gauloise, and looked prosperous. If, he said, you want to know what that feels like precisely, it tickles, is friendly, and tells me you're horny.

You want to come all spatterdash on me, the tent, and all these insects who think we're such nice company. I leaned and nudged a nipple with my nose, the other, his navel, mumping. He sat up with a questioning look. Go ahead, he said, whatever the fuck you're doing.

I cheerfully said that I didn't know. He pulled me down beside him, we rubbed noses, and rolled into a hug. He switched around, shoulder to hip, and skinned my foreskin down, and I his, cockering erections in three feat trices, pulling and sliding with correlative stresses.

No complaint, Michel grunted. None here. Agreeable, is it? Like butt high in clover, Joli. Crickets, the fresh summer evening, fugal, congruent deliciousness obstinately worked to a plenary brimming richness the sumptuous sweet of honey. Good? Good. Friendlier, friendliest.

CXII

Want to slow down, Michel said, and space it out? We've got all night. So we left off at the pitch, shared another Gauloise, watched the fireflies, planned the morrow, kittled touchinesses for curiosity's sake, and went back at intervals to our double and sporting piggery.

Once we'd spurted, with practical wantonness and sound technique, we flumped flat, laughing into the heavy silence that a moment before was ruckled only by boys' yips of pleasure and the nittering about of bugs. We sat up, whacked each other's shoulders, and whoofed like zanies.

There was light enough to see the splat across Michel's nose, his cheek, on his chin. He wiped viscid fingers on my knee. He smeared together the dollops on his tummy and tasted his fingers, milked a residual gout from me, dipped, and flicked it off with his tongue tip.

He pedantically tried it on his palate and fastidiously pronounced it alkaline. We lay shoulder to shoulder looking out on the darkening meadow, the stars, the risen moon. Michel asked tactless questions about Jonquille and me, revealing an unsuspected ignorance.

Rings of trees, giving their age, is first mentioned as a fact by Montaigne, though suspected by Leonardo. Tullio says Montaigne learned about them from a goldsmith in Italy who, it has been recently discovered, was an apprentice in Leonardo's studio.

CXIII

Jonquille and I at the Porte Dijeaux, glum. A whippet in a red coat with brass buttons sniffs us, tightens the coil of its tail, and prisses off. Michel, eh? I said, *tiens*. I'm afraid so, she said. Sort of like being fucked by a puppy, or in the operative detail, by a horse.

I had, she said, this intuition that you wanted us to. Oh sure, I said, what else? Try not to feel it that way, Joli. It won't happen again, word of honor. Besides thinking maybe you wanted me to, my only excuse is that I'd been enjoying myself rather well and raving for it.

You know how loose I am when I have the house to myself of an afternoon, and was beginning to popple and squeeze in on some really juicy ones. So help me, *Joli bébé*, I phoned you. You were taking a roll of linoleum, of all things, to Marc Aurel, sweet of you and good-natured.

And there was Michel, who thought you were with me. Right there at the door, with that body. I did everything, my fault from beginning to end. He was all for galloping away and blushed like a crossing signal. I told him he was acting as your stand-in, what women won't do, eh Joli?

How many times? What a vulgar question: twice. He didn't calm down enough to pay attention to what he was doing until the second time. His first two times, I said. *Joli!* He tried it with a chippy over at St.-Projet and nothing happened. I feel awful. So do I. Good old Miche.

CXIV

Demanding my football jersey, jeans, underwear, and socks for the wash, Maman had to learn that she couldn't have them and sat down with the back of her hand to her forehead. You've worn them since Monday. I can smell you over here. Since last Monday, I said. *Mon Dieu, Joli.*

Talk about crazy, Victor said, who had given up all to the laundry and was finishing his breakfast as naked as a lizard. The basket heaped with clothes and sheets sat in the middle of the kitchen. Jolivet Bonnat! What is this, existentialism, a bet, something from the cinema?

From the Bible, I said. I'm losing my mind! Maman can do her mother number to perfection. You know Jonathan and David? I said. Everybody, she said patiently, knows Jonathan and David. They wore each other's clothes, because they were friends, the best friends ever in the world.

I didn't know about the clothes bit, but Marc Aurel was swatting it up for the Culte Baptiste, and was telling about it at the Globe. Miche and I have had the same idea, but not only to wear each other's clothes, clean clothes, girls are always doing that, but dirty clothes, to swap.

Horse Jolivet, horse Michel, reaching his wry scantling briefs snugger and nestling the hitch of the pod, having hefted a fifty kilo barbell a hundred times in four sets of presses, Michel of the precisely synclined philtrum, leavened chest, suavely bunched calves, and long trunk.

CXV

We prance, skittish in the scarrow, shy of thunder, candid neck rubbing fellows galloping bellydeep in flowers, proud inwardly beasts snorting at shifts of the wind, watched by dark, hidden, concerned human eyes. We nicker and neigh and stomp. Les Eyzies a flowery prairie.

In the Grotte de la Mairie, Teyjat, discovered in 1903 by Denis Peyrony, its drawings deciphered and copied by Henri Breuil, the animals were painted late in the twenty thousand years when horse and his kin revolved around an axis, opposing and complementing bison and her kin.

Horse kin were ibex and stag, bison kin were ox and mammoth. The one was phallus, the other vulva, one was spear, the other wound, one was mortar, the other pestle, one was light, the other dark, one was hunter ranging the savannas, the other weaver at the hearth, circle and center.

Bison pairs with horse, horse with reindeer. Horses stand inside the contours of larger horses. Horses upside down share the same space with horses rightside up. Bear is suspended on a surface already occupied by ponies, tilted as the creatures descried in the stars are tilted.

Bison shambles through a clockwhirl of tarpans and ibexes. Three reindeer, one on its back, one raising his lordly head, one lowering his to graze, pace in montage across a horse of the steppes, wild ass grey, its mane running from its tousled foreshock the length of its chine.

CXVI

So we're wearing everything for two weeks and will swap on Saturday. Everything, Maman said faintly, fanning herself with the morning paper. Actually, I said, testing an armpit for aroma, we're going the Bible one better. David got Jonathan's clothes, not Jonathan David's.

A pair of thumbslot dimples flank his sacral bight, his well-hung engenderer froggishly nubbly and clinched by runner veins when it's standing spritraked, steep flare to the glans rim, plumply snooted. I am slenderer, tan, trim, and everywhere on the sprout, very leggy.

David, who was *a ruddy and comely youth,* was a shepherd, and he'd just conked the giant Goliath with his slingshot, bap between the eyes, and I suppose for clothes he had some kind of goatskin or Old Testament sugarsack with a rope for a belt, hair a mess, brown as a nut.

Jonathan was the king's son and would have been *the dernier cri* of Bible times fashion. I suppressed the phrase *because their souls were knit*. Mothers deserve being spared. Michel's are going to be wonderfully rotten. He's worked out all week on the river with the boat crews.

Maman stared at the ceiling. Is your father to be told this, assuming he doesn't ask first why you smell like a locker room? Oh sure, I said. He'll understand. *Men!* we said together. Horse Jolivet, horse Michel, we canter in the sedge of the Val Dordogne, long and red.

CXVII

The gift of apples, the beautiful gift of apples. Tullio shaped apples in the air with his pudgy hands. The shepherds in the *Eclogues* gave the shepherdesses apples to signify their love. We were around a table outside the Globe, Jonquille, Michel, Marc Aurel, Tullio, and I.

The schoolboy Cézanne in Aix, shy and awkward, made friends with the younger Zola, the pariah of their class, at the bottom of the pecking order. Boys tolerate nothing. I gave Jonquille a glance, she slid her hand into mine. They ganged up against Paul, kicked him, bloodied his nose.

He held his own nevertheless, and refused to join them in not speaking to Émile, the torture they'd chosen. To seal their camaraderie Émile brought Paul a basket of apples. *Bravissimo!* A basket of apples. I got a smiling glance, bemused, from Michel. Jonquille squeezed my hand.

They walked the countryside together, those two. The idle ramble was the vehicle of their friendship, that and Latin poetry, especially Virgil's *Georgics* and *Bucolica,* which they recited to each other. Paul was too shy ever to show Émile his translation of the Corydon and Alexis.

The second eclogue. What charm to the irony of withholding a text from Zola because of its indelicacy. What did it say? Marc Aurel asked. And from Virgil, Tullio went on, unheeding, Cézanne conceived the ambition to paint one perfect landscape with pastoral figures, an eclogue.

CXVIII

How they crouch, kneel, reach in these paintings, as if he could not imagine anything for them to do. And then the still lifes with apples, Zola's gift, painted over and over. Did anyone think to send Zola a basket of apples when he wrote *J'Accuse*? Jonquille gave me a lovely look.

Horse Jolivet and Jonquille deer, we lie kissing on the sunroom couch, brown on flowery chintz, in a disarray of parted clothes, my dactylion twiddling her thrilled nubble to a pitch, her chummy fingers coddling a dipping crawl along my scrotum seam, tongue around tongue.

Horse king of the grass, thunder and rain, kin of acorn, prong of the *griot,* lion of the fat testicles, speckled salmon of all cunning. Deer, queen of flowers, kin of apple, round-hipped moon, jucking quail cousin, mistress of basketry, randing, scallom, and willow fitching.

Sister to her slim daughters in elktooth bracelets and sons shoulder-girt with bows, nipples circled with ochre, dotted lozenges of white clay on their cheeks. A nuchal kiss, daddled foreskin, tongue and whisper into an ear together. Klitoris is a town in Arcadia, I mumbled.

Scrumptious, she murmured. I found it on a map in Larousse. Loud horse, silent deer. You are, I began. Stop there. You are. La Tène. Reindeer drinking. Pizzle slant in a tufted sheath along his belly. Delicate steps in moss. Grave eye, flicked tail, tall antlers, wolf light.

CXIX

Saturday afternoon, Michel's mansarde with its two windows, situp board and weights on a raffia mat, a tall narrow cheap mirror from Prisunic, cot, shipcabin spareness bright with posters, maps, sports gear, and all in the pitch of summer's hot western light, the afternoon.

Do we close the shutters? I asked, and he replied, shit no. Maman's off with some bum, for the night if I know her. The place is ours. And if Mademoiselle Rat Whiskers across the way wants to watch two healthy boys get each other off, it will be good for her constipation.

He pulled the dirty white jersey he'd worn for two weeks, its sleeves underarm sodden with fresh sweat soaking into old, over his head and knuckled his nostrils with droll disgust. Yours, he said. And yours, I said, dipping my head out of my striped jersey for him to wear.

How, he said, did you talk a skunk into peeing on this? It was two of them, I said. We unlaced our sneakers, drew off fetid socks, and passed them to each other. Do I read the apples right? Michel asked, unzipping his jeans. I think so, I said. It doesn't in any case matter.

After our run in the park that morning, we'd had breakfast at my house, banished by Maman to a walk in the garden, the fun of which Victor relished, holding his nose. He brought us a sack which Postel found left at the gate, addressed to Michel in lipstick. Two apples.

CXX

And with the two apples in a sack, a perfumed *billet doux*: All yours, it read, but may I have him, bathed or unbathed, tomorrow? About time. Jonquille, with kisses of various sorts for the both of you, which please pass on. Studying for exams and the interview anyway.

The punch of Michel's briefs, yellowed in the pod, pushed the shirring at the groin smooth. Looks promising, I said, stepping out of mine and handing them over in the swap. I asked if, as it seemed, he had come in his. Just after dribble, he said smiling. I slept in them for you.

We sniffed, made faces, and dressed ourselves, eye-locked, wry smiles identical, in each other's clothes. The apples, I said, mean what they say. His lashpent eyes were solving the same qualms as mine, his lips parted in surmise. Sex as a sport can confuse the heart.

Michel unlatched his belt, slid his zipper down, and spancelled his thighs with his briefs, which were mine, pissburnt and musty. He rolled his elbows shoulder high, enjoyed a roguish grin, and hunkered to unzip me and unseat my underpants. The cot. Take off our sneakers?

Everything on, however undone, else we're not in each other's clothes. Other way around, Miche? *D'accord,* he said as if I'd surprised him. A billygoat wouldn't stay in the room with us! He would if he were as horny as I am, and intend to get hornier as we go along, *joli Joli.*

CXXI

The *You're sure?* we may have each needed to ask the other our stubborn and goatish bodies bypassed, not our stiff ramping squalid cocks in their rabid willfulness alone, but all of us, legs, hands, eyes, chests, hair, shoulders, in a maniac sexiness that pitched into us harumscarum.

My heart kicked, my testicles knotted tight, the back of my neck flushed hot. Interjoined, arms locked around each other's butts, we gave as we took, with deep breaths, hugging closer as we made headway, resolutely ungagging, grunting, thrashing heels, emboldened by doing.

Up, Michel gasped, for air. And I, panting. And with sporting retches rejoined our double juncture. Late afternoon levelled the light and stretched the shadows in the mansarde. We wiggled free of jeans and briefs, which were hobbling our knees, and padded to the WC to pee.

Do we ever stink, I said, and, with awe, it gets better and better, Miche. Three times, can you believe? Four coming up, he said. Want to take off these rotten shirts? Not me. Nor me, but I'll go along with unsneakering. Socks, anyway, are smellier with sneakers off.

The armpits of this shirt of yours, I said, are so rancid foul that I don't know whether I'm me or you. Sex, he said, is what we smell like most. Isn't that why we're here, loving each other up, to be all mixed together, like? That, I said, a bit uncertain, is why we're here.

CXXII

At dusk we ran, still in each other's clothes, to the rue Roquelaure, achieved my room, Victor right behind us, without encountering parents or Postel. Stripped, we showered, brushed our teeth, gargled mouthwash, dabbed on cologne, and dressed in clean clothes, mine.

We appeared for dinner new minted. Jolivet, Victor said, promised me that if I wouldn't pester him this afternoon, not that anybody wanted to get near him, he'd mount stamps with me tonight, take me swimming all of next week, and to the movies on his allowance whenever.

I blushed, Michel beamed. Is all this foolishness over, you two? Maman asked. Yes, ma'am, I said, in a much smaller voice than I had intended. It was, Papa said, damned imaginative of you. Saves on the laundry bill, as well. May I tell Tullio? He will find it charming.

I suppose he would, instigator, among others, as he was. *Testiculus,* he had said, *et oculus.* Darwin thought the evolution of the eye the miracle of nature. There's the stomach, which knows how not to digest itself, and the cooperation of voice and ear, all the natural systems.

No system is ever quite independent of all the others. Who has studied the relation of foot to logic, shoulder to skepticism, our bodily organization into front and back, left and right, to geography, grammar, mathematics? And then consider that subtle affinity *testiculus et oculus*.

CXXIII

The great meditations on it are Shakespeare's sonnets and his *Love's Labor's Lost*, a play set next to us here in the Basses Pyrénées, and Montaigne's *Sur des vers de Virgile*, and the Greek poets of Alexandria. The Sicilian masters of pastoral, too, and Virgil himself.

But beside Darwin's wonder at the eye put Pasteur's remark that we will not understand the order of things until we understand the asymmetry of things. These two observations belong together, but how? Look. Here is an Alexandrian poem that takes its imagery from honey and wine.

And contrasts sweet and sharp, taking elements in the sexual processes of insects and plants, but each a peripheral phenomenon to those processes, both gifts, so to speak, that nature can afford to give us without in the least stinting her voluptuous onwardness. The poem.

A sharp longing and a sweet response are like honey and wine, as when Alexis, who is young and handsome, loves thick-haired Kleoboulos, who is as young and handsome as he, the two together, narrow hip to narrow hip, rubbing noses, are as sweet as honey, as sharp as wine to see.

In Alexandria Greek and Roman eroticism of the classical period, apt to serve practically any end, political, satiric, comic, except the purely erotic, became refined and charming. The poet, let us surmise, is concocting a fiction: for the eye and for the testicle, a brace of pairs.

CXXIV

His picture is asymmetrical. Boys do not think each other pretty, but admire each other for strength, skill, daring, cleverness, and so on. These are not real boys in the poem, but porcelain figurines in a neoclassical tradition, like Virgil's and Theokritos' shepherds and girls.

They are imaginary. The wine, however, and honey are there. How deep do we go? To the pseudocopulation of the bee with its blossom, the amorphous sexuality of the yeast in the grape must? What's the structural affinity of honey and love? *Pubens* and *florescens* are molecular.

At every period in history we find the body as a term in a larger metaphor. Greek physiology was a matter of liquids suffusing muscles and organs. Disease came from an improper wetness in an organ that ought for its own good to be drier. A matter of temperature of the liquids.

Michel says his stomach wants him to be a Socialist, his *verge* a sailor, his eye my friend. He says Postel letting me in when I pull the bell at the gate gives the impression of being a peasant who has been called away from getting in the harvest to tie my shoe.

The speed of gravity is a fly's weight over that of radiance, else the earth and moon and all the stars would boil away and wander in space as random dust. France, Tullio says, is perfectly poised between *julvernerie* and the sense to keep her vinestocks well tended.

CXXV

Tullio lay dead on the sidewalk of the Cours Clemenceau when Marc Aurel and Trombone found him, two blocks away from the Gambetta to which he was walking. He seemed, they said, to be a fat man asleep on his back. Just the day before he had been talking to me about Trombone.

Of Trombone's vestiary *bouvardisme* he remarked that it is more *vieux grognard* than *clochard,* a corporal on the powderwagons at Waterloo preserved by excitement until Napoleon's second coming, an observation thoroughly Tullio, as Papa agreed when I told him these last words.

He was, I suppose, riffling through the essences of his mind, perhaps (and comfort myself to suppose) Mezzani the organ grinder in Padova turning the overture to *I Vespri Siciliani,* his monkey patting her crissum under her tutu (a memory that appeared in a conversation).

He had, we know, waved to Marc Aurel earlier on the Place Tourny. What revery could follow from that? Was he, moments before the pain jolted into his neck above the left shoulder, thinking of the day before at our house, of Victor chinning himself on a bar across a door?

Quello sfacciatello Ganimede! he had said happily as two slender legs swung toward him, no break in the up and down of chinning, and as the pain beat on his heart, did he beg for mercy, or did his wonderful imagination see that *anche colui che era in Arcadia* was with him?

Guy Davenport
The Geography of the Imagination £3.50

Forty essays in criticism, each a tour of the history of ideas and imagination in philosophy, art and literature, witty, wide-ranging and erudite. Subjects include Greek culture, Whitman, Spinoza, Tolkien, Pound, Olson, Moore, Ives and Wittgenstein.

'Anyone who cares for order and for grace in the exposed life of American letters is abundantly in Davenport's debt' GEORGE STEINER, NEW YORKER

'The best explicator of the arts alive, because he assumes that the artists — painters, poets, describers of natural wonders — have the sort of mind he has: quick, unpredictable, alert for gaps to traverse toward the unexpected terminus' HUGH KENNER

Umberto Eco
Name of the Rose £2.95

'Imagine a medieval castle run by the Benedictines, with cellarists, herbalists, gardeners, novices. One after another, half a dozen monks are found murdered in bizarre ways. A learned Franciscan who is sent to solve the mystery finds himself involved in the frightening events. . .a sleuth's pursuit of the truth behind the mystery also involves the pursuit of meaning — in words, symbols, ideas, every conceivable sign' NEW YORK TIMES BOOK REVIEW

'The most intelligent — and at the same time the most amusing — book in years' DER SPIEGEL

'Intellectual delight and all the excitement of a tremendous climax enough for any thriller' BOOKS AND BOOKMEN

'Belongs with Voltaire's philosophical tales. . .an erudite fiction story, it is also a vibrant plea for freedom, moderation and wisdom' L'EXPRESS

Norman Mailer
Ancient Evenings £2.95

'*Ancient Evenings* is about reincarnation. Menenhetet, a courtier in the twentieth-dynasty kingdom of Rameses and Nefititi, is reborn three times: charioteer, general, high priest, general again. In seven books Mailer explores the seven stages or components of the Egyptian soul – Name, Power, Angel, Heart, Double, Shadow and Remains – as they range across vast tracts of time and yet are contained within one person. The book is violent, sexual, scatological. . .and is one of the most profound modern statements about the nature and destiny of mankind' THE TIMES EDUCATIONAL SUPPLEMENT

'There is spiritual power in Mailer's fantasy and there is a relevance to current reality in America that actually surpasses that of Mailer's largest previous achievement, *The Executioner's Song*. . . another warning that Mailer is at home on Emerson's stairway of surprise' NEW YORK REVIEW OF BOOKS

'Mailer conveys the exquisite sophistication of the court and the beautiful, if morbid, preoccupation of the ancient Egyptians with the afterlife. This great work concludes with an awe-inspiring account of a journey through the Land of the Dead' PUBLISHERS WEEKLY

Jamaica Kincaid
At the Bottom of the River £1.95

'Wash the white clothes on Monday and put them on the clothes heap; wash the colour clothes on Tuesday; don't walk bareheaded in the hot sun; cook pumpkin fritters in very hot sweet oil; on Sundays try to walk like a lady and not like the slut you are so bent on becoming' – Jamaica Kincaid's memories are of a childhood in the Caribbean, of family, manners, landscape and folk tales, of the ties between mother and daughter, the beauty and destructiveness of nature, the gulf between masculine and feminine. Her writing, with its West Indian rhythm, mirrors the vibrant life, brilliant colours, secret feelings and tropical landscape of the Caribbean.

'An unaffectedly sumptuous, irresistible writer' SUSAN SONTAG

'The language, which is often beautifully simple, also often adopts a gospel-like seriousness, reverberating with biblical echoes' NEW YORK TIMES BOOK REVIEW

Italo Calvino
Adam, One Afternoon £2.50

'Confirms the part he has played in revitalizing the fiction of our time. . .
Calvino's special gift is to link the physical and immediate with an allegorical
timelessness. . . All the characters and creatures in these stories conspire to
convey a feeling of wonder, mystery and terror of life' GUARDIAN

'Back in the 1940s, Calvino was writing fables and stories of comparative
simplicity and considerable gaiety. These have at last been published here. . .a
collection of animals and men, their sombre implications faintly visible below
the surface of laughter' BOOKS AND BOOKMEN

'The best of his allegorical fantasies have the power of the Brothers Grimm,
rollicking stories on the surface, with an underlying savagery' LISTENER

Mario Vargas Llosa
Aunt Julia and the Scriptwriter £2.95

'Mario, 18-year-old law student and radio news-editor, falls scandalously for his
Aunt Julia, the 32-year-old divorced wife of a cousin, and the progressively
lunatic story of this affair is interwoven with episodes from a series of radio
soap-operas written by his friend Pedro Comacho, a scriptwriter of prodigious
output and hysterical imagination. . . Llosa's huge energy and inventiveness
are extravagant and fabulously funny' NEW STATESMAN

'Pulls off that South American rope-trick with unprecedented power and skill'
SUNDAY TIMES

'A high comedy of great warmth and masterly control of form. . .tough, tender,
funny, tactfully erotic, with moments of bitterness, despair and farce' THE
TIMES

'Will confirm the opinion of all those who think that the Latin American novel is
the most vigorous contemporary form at present' LITERARY REVIEW

Michael Ondaatje
Coming through Slaughter £2.50

'The downtown world of bars, whores, street life bursting with music is evoked so vividly, so pungently you seem to breathe in the atmosphere' TIME OUT

'Based on the life of cornet player Buddy Bolden, one of the legendary jazz pioneers of turn-of-the-century New Orleans. . . The result is an often brilliantly wrought, cinematic series of short scenes, jagged, dislocated, that approximate the quality of the music that stuttered or flowed out of Bolden's cornet' TORONTO STAR

'We understand the slow ceremonial sense of time. . .we see the leaking colours of the houses and streets, and we feel the brilliant pressures of the music' NEW YORKER

'Not only the best jazz novel ever written, but one of the best novels of any kind published in English in the last ten years. Ondaatje builds up his portrait of Bolden's black New Orleans by an accumulation of small, sometimes infinitesimal details. From the handful of known facts about Bolden's life, Ondaatje spins a story that moves in the direction of myth' MUSICIAN

Running in the Family £2.95

'Michael Ondaatje has depicted his extraordinary family, who delighted in masks and costumes and love affairs that "rainbowed over marriages" in the kind of language that makes glory of their lives. He has gone on a poet's journey to Sri Lanka and the reader who travels with him enters a truly magical world' MAXINE HONG KINGSTON

'Sheer reading pleasure' WASHINGTON POST

'An outstandingly evocative, semi-autobiographical account of a journey back to the beginning, to Ceylon where Ondaatje was born into a privileged group of mixed Dutch, Tamil and Sinhalese origins. Created from asides, snapshots, poems, glimpses, in every way unorthodox and incomplete, it falls magically on to the page with all the grace of a billowing, seamless dress. Like all classic writing the motion of this book lingers on, like the movement of a boat, long after the last pages' NEW STATESMAN

Graham Swift
Waterland £2.50

'At once a history of England, a Fenland documentary, and a fictional autobiography. . .a beautiful, serious and intelligent novel' OBSERVER

'Swift spins a tale of empire-building, land reclamation, brewers and sluice minders, bewhiskered Victorian patriarchs, insane and visionary relics. . .a startling cast of characters going about their business as though it were utterly normal and preparing the way, down the centuries, for a trio of deaths' BOOKS AND BOOKMEN

'Positively Faulknerian in its concentration of murder, incest, guilt and insanity' TIME OUT

'One of the most important talents to emerge in English fiction' GLASGOW HERALD

Clive James
Brilliant Creatures £2.50

'The brilliant creatures of the title live in a world of lost innocence and vast incomes; publishers, writers, media men and consultants, they belong to a charmed circle where everyone knows everyone else's business. . .
Clive James doesn't miss a trick' THE TIMES

'Nearer to Wodehouse than to Waugh. He is not setting out merely to raise laughs. He takes vigorous swipes at most of the unacceptable faces of society' LISTENER

'Romping satire of London literary life. . .the writing sizzles off the page with a rare merriment' ILLUSTRATED LONDON NEWS

'The wittiest novel of the year' BOOKSELLER

'Clive James writes one-liners the way John McEnroe wears headbands' FRANK DELANEY

Edmund White
Forgetting Elena and **Nocturnes for the King of Naples** £2.95

'Edmund White is one of the outstanding writers of prose in America today. . .
From the brilliant hard-edge fantasy of *Forgetting Elena* to the diffuse delirious
consciousness of *Nocturnes for the King of Naples* to the fully realized world of
his third novel is a remarkable trajectory' SUSAN SONTAG

'*Forgetting Elena* is a masterful piece of work' NEW YORK TIMES

'White possesses the rare combination of a poetic sense of language and an
ironic sense of humour' NEWSWEEK

'*Nocturnes for the King of Naples* is a baroque invention of quite startling
brilliance and intensity' GORE VIDAL

'Edmund White has re-invented devotional literature' MARY GORDON

Russell Hoban
Pilgermann £2.95

'The world according to Pilgermann is a brutish place where bodies are boiled
and devoured and human heads used as cannonballs. . . Pilgermann borrows
from Hieronymus Bosch's grotesque depictions of hell and from a number of
literary traditions – pilgrimage narrative, allegory, the historical novel' NEW
YORK TIMES BOOK REVIEW

'His writing is flexible enough to handle the most weighty thoughts and deal
with the most ordinary parts of human behaviour. The dialogue is superb. . .
History, metaphysics, a tangle of mysteries, profound and simple' GUARDIAN

'Go out and get hold of it forthwith' SUNDAY TELEGRAPH

Picador

☐	**Burning Leaves**	Don Bannister	£2.50p
☐	**Making Love: The Picador Book of Erotic Verse**	edited by Alan Bold	£1.95p
☐	**The Tokyo-Montana Express**	Richard Brautigan	£2.50p
☐	**Bury My Heart at Wounded Knee**	Dee Brown	£3.95p
☐	**Cities of the Red Night**	William Burroughs	£2.50p
☐	**The Road to Oxiana**	Robert Byron	£2.50p
☐	**If on a Winter's Night a Traveller**	Italo Calvino	£2.50p
☐	**Auto Da Fé**	Elias Canetti	£3.95p
☐	**Exotic Pleasures**	Peter Carey	£1.95p
☐	**Chandler Collection Vol. 1**	Raymond Chandler	£2.95p
☐	**In Patagonia**	Bruce Chatwin	£2.50p
☐	**Sweet Freedom**	Anna Coote and Beatrix Campbell	£1.95p
☐	**Crown Jewel**	Ralph de Boissiere	£2.75p
☐	**Letters from Africa**	Isak Dinesen (Karen Blixen)	£3.95p
☐	**The Book of Daniel**	E. L. Doctorow	£2.50p
☐	**Debts of Honour**	Michael Foot	£2.50p
☐	**One Hundred Years of Solitude**	Gabriel García Márquez	£2.95p
☐	**Nothing, Doting, Blindness**	Henry Green	£2.95p
☐	**The Obstacle Race**	Germaine Greer	£5.95p
☐	**Meetings with Remarkable Men**	Gurdjieff	£2.95p
☐	**Roots**	Alex Haley	£3.50p
☐	**The Four Great Novels**	Dashiell Hammett	£3.95p
☐	**Growth of the Soil**	Knut Hamsun	£2.95p
☐	**When the Tree Sings**	Stratis Haviaras	£1.95p
☐	**Dispatches**	Michael Herr	£2.50p
☐	**Riddley Walker**	Russell Hoban	£2.50p
☐	**Stories**	Desmond Hogan	£2.50p
☐	**Three Trapped Tigers**	C. Cabrera Infante	£2.95p
☐	**Unreliable Memoirs**	Clive James	£1.95p
☐	**Man and His Symbols**	Carl Jung	£3.95p
☐	**China Men**	Maxine Hong Kingston	£2.50p
☐	**Janus: A Summing Up**	Arthur Koestler	£3.50p
☐	**Memoirs of a Survivor**	Doris Lessing	£2.50p
☐	**Albert Camus**	Herbert Lottman	£3.95p
☐	**The Road to Xanadu**	John Livingston Lowes	£1.95p
☐	**Zany Afternoons**	Bruce McCall	£4.95p
☐	**The Cement Garden**	Ian McEwan	£1.95p
☐	**The Serial**	Cyra McFadden	£1.75p
☐	**McCarthy's List**	Mary Mackey	£1.95p
☐	**Psychoanalysis: The Impossible Profession**	Janet Malcolm	£1.95p
☐	**Daddyji/Mamaji**	Ved Mehta	£2.95p
☐	**Slowly Down the Ganges**	Eric Newby	£2.95p
☐	**The Snow Leopard**	Peter Matthiessen	£2.95p

☐	**History of Rock and Roll**	ed. Jim Miller	£4.95p
☐	**Lectures on Literature**	Vladimir Nabokov	£3.95p
☐	**The Best of Myles**	Flann O' Brien	£2.95p
☐	**Autobiography**	John Cowper Powys	£3.50p
☐	**Hadrian the Seventh**	Fr. Rolfe (Baron Corvo)	£1.25p
☐	**On Broadway**	Damon Runyon	£3.50p
☐	**Midnight's Children**	Salman Rushdie	£3.50p
☐	**Snowblind**	Robert Sabbag	£1.95p
☐	**Awakenings**	Oliver Sacks	£3.95p
☐	**The Fate of the Earth**	Jonathan Schell	£1.95p
☐	**Street of Crocodiles**	Bruno Schultz	£1.25p
☐	**Poets in their Youth**	Eileen Simpson	£2.95p
☐	**Miss Silver's Past**	Josef Skvorecky	£2.50p
☐	**A Flag for Sunrise**	Robert Stone	£2.50p
☐	**Visitants**	Randolph Stow	£2.50p
☐	**Alice Fell**	Emma Tennant	£1.95p
☐	**The Flute-Player**	D. M. Thomas	£2.25p
☐	**The Great Shark Hunt**	Hunter S. Thompson	£3.50p
☐	**The Longest War**	Jacob Timerman	£2.50p
☐	**Aunt Julia and the Scriptwriter**	Mario Vargas Llosa	£2.95p
☐	**Female Friends**	Fay Weldon	£2.50p
☐	**No Particular Place To Go**	Hugo Williams	£1.95p
☐	**The Outsider**	Colin Wilson	£2.50p
☐	**Kandy-Kolored Tangerine-Flake Streamline Baby**	Tom Wolfe	£2.25p
☐	**Mars**	Fritz Zorn	£1.95p

All these books are available at your local bookshop or newsagent, or can be ordered direct from the publisher. Indicate the number of copies required and fill in the form below

11

....

Name_____
(Block letters please)

Address_____

_____

Send to CS Department, Pan Books Ltd, PO Box 40, Basingstoke, Hants
Please enclose remittance to the value of the cover price plus:
35p for the first book plus 15p per copy for each additional book ordered
to a maximum charge of £1.25 to cover postage and packing
Applicable only in the UK

While every effort is made to keep prices low, it is sometimes
necessary to increase prices at short notice. Pan Books reserve
the right to show on covers and charge new retail prices which
may differ from those advertised in the text or elsewhere